HELLBENT

VOLUME 1

KYLE ALEXANDER ROMINES

THOMAS M. MALAFARINA

CATHERINE JORDAN

JOHN KACHUBA

MICHAEL L. HAWLEY

BRIAN KOSCIENSKI & CHRIS PISANO

J B TONER

WIL FALCONER

TRAVIS LEIBERT

AMBROSE BIERCE

H. P. LOVECRAFT

EDGAR ALLAN POE

HELLBENDER BOOKS

an imprint of Sunbury Press, Inc.
Mechanicsburg, PA USA

HELLBENDER BOOKS

an imprint of Sunbury Press, Inc.
Mechanicsburg, PA USA

For information about special discounts for bulk purchases, please contact Sunbury Press Orders Dept. at (855) 338-8359 or orders@sunburypress.com.

To request one of our authors for speaking engagements or book signings, please contact Sunbury Press Publicity Dept. at publicity@sunburypress.com.

FIRST HELLBENDER BOOKS EDITION: June 2020

Set in Adobe Garamond | Interior design by Crystal Devine | Cover design by Lawrence Knorr | Edited by Jennifer Cappello.

Publisher's Cataloging-in-Publication Data
Authors: Romines, Kyle Alexander | Malafarina, Thomas M. | Jordan, Catherine | Kachuba, John | Hawley, Michael L. | Koscienski, Brian | Pisano, Chris | Toner, J B | Falconer, Wil | Leibert, Travis | Bierce, Ambrose | Lovecraft, H. P. | Poe, Edgar Allan.
Title: Hellbent.
Description: Trade paperback edition. | Mechanicsburg, PA : Hellbender Books, 2020.
Summary: The talented authors at Hellbender Books contributed spine-tingling tales of horror and psychological suspense.
Identifiers: ISBN 978-1-620062-45-6 (softcover).
Subjects: FICTION / Anthologies | FICTION / Horror | FICTION / Thrillers / Psychological.

Product of the United States of America
0 1 1 2 3 5 8 13 21 34 55

Continue the Enlightenment!

CONTENTS

FOREWORD

In late January of 2019, my publisher, Lawrence Knorr of Hellbender Books, charged me with curating an anthology. Hellbender author Catherine Jordan volunteered to serve as editor for the collection as well, something for which I am eternally grateful.

This anthology aims to feature and promote Hellbender Books authors, alongside public domain classics. The idea is to exhibit horror short stories and how they have evolved since the days of Edgar Allan Poe, H. P. Lovecraft, and others. From a self-serving standpoint, this project also showcases Sunbury Press's horror imprint, Hellbender Books.

I previously acted as curator in 2013 for the Sunbury Press collection *Undead Living*. Little has changed with my busy schedule, and as such the anthology provided a great opportunity to read other writers' work.

Author biographies are at the back of this anthology, listed in alphabetical order, including the famous, less famous, and infamous.

I trust you will enjoy this collection of horror tales and wish you many unpleasant nightmares ahead. By all means, check out the other works by these fine Hellbender authors.

Thank you,

Thomas M. Malafarina

July 2019

INTRODUCTION

A friend recently debated with me over the difference between horror and thrillers. Well, there's a fine line between certain genres. Take erotica and romance, for example. Romance uses a feather; erotica uses the whole chicken. Thrillers send a shiver down your spine. Horror opens your back and twists that spine into something sinister (like Zelda in Stephen King's *Pet Sematary*).

I'm often asked why I write horror since I look more like a Hallmark romance writer. Well, I do have five kids. Haha. No, really I think it's because I was raised Catholic, and Catholicism is filled with the supernatural. There are many cautionary tales about how to deal with helplessness and horror and fear. Confront it and embrace hope. Hope is the key word. Be forever hopeful.

Fearful situations teach focus when deciding whether to fight. And know that there's another F-word—flight! You see, some people are afraid of change. In my opinion, change brings opportunity, and opportunity leads to success. You can't soar like an eagle if you let the turkeys keep you grounded. So, challenge yourself to spread your wings and fly.

It's okay to be afraid. Everyone has fears. Fear builds character. Hey—isn't that what we writers do for a living—build characters?

On that note, I'd like to appeal to you horror lovers: If you like our anthology, tell the world. If you don't, tell the writer.

Thank you,

Catherine Jordan

editor, author, and a nice person

PARALLELISM

by Thomas M. Malafarina

Imagination is the parallel universe of a writer. If he is not responding to you in the world, he is probably responding to someone in the imaginary world.
—*Heenashree Khandelwal*

I feel like I am diagonally parked in a parallel universe.
—*Unknown*

The ceiling fan turned slowly above Emmett's head while he stood patiently waiting for it to stop. He had turned off the wall switch a few moments earlier, and the fan's momentum wound down in lazy circles. He was tempted to reach up and grab one of the five blades, stopping it immediately. But the fan was too hard to reach.

Emmett had volunteered to help his wife, Carla, clean the house that weekend, and he had just finished dusting the entire bedroom, save for the wooden blades of their ceiling fan.

He once considered buying one of those fancy dusting thingies with a big fluffy oval brush on the end of a long telescopic handle, but the problem wasn't so much height as location. The fan wasn't mounted on a vaulted ceiling but was located directly over his and his wife's queen-size bed. Their small bedroom size allowed no room for repositioning the bed, and therefore he couldn't use a step stool to reach the blades. So Emmett planned on doing what he'd done many times before; stand on the bed to reach the fan blades.

It wasn't the safest thing in the world nor the most dangerous. In fact, Emmett suspected Carla had used a similar technique to dust the blades, though she might not admit it. And regardless of what method she happened to choose, if he were to fall and hurt himself she would nevertheless chew him a new one. He wasn't getting any younger, sixty-five at his last birthday, and his balance wasn't quite what it used to be, if he were being perfectly honest with himself. As his late father used to say, "It ain't what it usedta was."

Emmett Parker was a part-time science fiction writer with several dozen novels and over two hundred short stories to his credit. He had retired from his full-time engineer position six months earlier and supposed he could now call himself a full-time author. However, the title might be a bit grandiose since the little money from his publications scarcely supplemented his savings, meager pension, and social security income.

Emmett watched the fan blade make its final revolution, then come to a complete stop. He walked to the bedroom doorway and listened for Carla's soft footsteps, hoping she wasn't on her way upstairs. He stood on the bed as gently as possible so Carla wouldn't hear him floundering about on the mattress. Dust rag in hand, he walked his free hand up the wall behind the headboard, ready to begin his task.

Emmett slowly approached the fan like a kid making his way into a bouncy house and appreciated why children enjoyed them so much. He'd mastered his technique of holding onto one blade to maintain his balance while dusting. Soon all five blades were dust-free, and Emmett was ready to work his way off the bed.

He was suddenly hit with a strange bout of vertigo, surely brought on by the uneven motion of the mattress. He had experienced such dizziness before, and it always passed quickly. But not this time. Emmett's knees buckled; his head slammed against the side wall as he fell off the bed toward the floor.

As he lay there on the floor somewhere between reality and unreality, his mind flooded with dreamlike scenarios of what had just happened to him. Some were identical, some were slightly different, but many showed completely dissimilar and often tragic results. In one scenario, he almost fell, then regained his balance and stepped down safely from the bed—as he had done in the past. In another scenario, he grabbed the ceiling fan to stop his fall, pulling it down with him in a shower of plaster-dust. In yet another, he lay on the ground with his arm broken in a twisted compound fracture, a white bone jutting from torn skin. And in another, he saw himself lying dead on the floor with his head cocked at an impossible angle, his neck snapped.

Scenarios continued to play in his head, thousands streaming like high-speed videos through his mind, and he thought he might go insane trying to follow along.

Emmett heard a familiar voice call his name as he floated in and out of consciousness. "Emmett? Emmett, honey? Speak to me."

Then a man's voice said, "Please stand back, ma'am. We'll take it from here."

A moment later, Emmett snapped alert to the pungent scent of capsulated ammonia under his nose.

"What the hell?" Emmett mumbled, still disoriented. "What's going on?"

"It's okay Mr. Parker," the man said. "You had a nasty fall and hit your head. You were out for a while, but you're gonna be all right."

Emmett focused on two young faces, one male and one female. They wore the familiar blue emergency medical technician uniforms and were apparently taking care of him. Behind them, Carla stood watching with utter terror on her face. He knew there was going to be hell to pay for his cleaning stunt, but for now, it looked like he might be able to ride the pity train for at least a little while.

"Carla? Sweetie? What going on?" he asked in the most pathetic voice he could muster. After all, the back of his head throbbed, and a couple of EMTs were kneeling over him.

"You fell, Emmett, and hit your head," Carla said sympathetically. "Don't talk. Just do what the nice boy and girl tell you to do." The EMTs, probably in their thirties, exchanged glances. To Carla, everyone under forty was either a boy or a girl.

The male EMT placed a cold stethoscope on Emmett's chest. "Mr. Parker, do you remember what happened? Do you know how you fell?"

Emmett wasn't about to admit to standing on the bed to clean the fan, so he simply said, "I don't know for sure. I was standing by the side of the bed and must have turned too quickly, lost my balance, and fell."

Carla glared knowingly at her husband; she wasn't buying his story. "From downstairs it sounded like someone dropped a bomb on the house!" She looked to the dust cloth on the floor, then upward at the ceiling fan. Then to the wrinkles on the bedspread. She didn't have to say a word. Emmett knew she knew. It was that unspoken language passing between partners who've been together for many years.

The female EMT sighed heavily. "Well, here's what we're going to do, sir. We're going to take you to the hospital for an MRI to make sure there's no internal bleeding or other such injury. They'll want to examine you to figure out how you lost your equilibrium."

Emmett sat up. "I don't want to go to any damned hospital. Look at me. I'm fine. Just give me a few pain pills. After a good night's sleep I'll be as good as new."

Carla wagged a pointed finger. "Don't you dare tell these fine people how to do their jobs, Emmett Stephen Parker!"

Emmett went silent. By invoking his full name, Carla had passed out of the pity stage and was now loaded for bear. Emmett reluctantly conceded. "Fine. But I'm telling you there's nothing wrong with me that a shot or two of whiskey and a good night's sleep won't fix."

The EMTs exchanged glances again. The girl rolled her eyes.

* * *

As it turned out, Emmett had been quite lucky. He didn't have any damage to his skull or brain, and even the concern of concussion was minimal. Carla sat by his side the entire time. She didn't mention his accident or question how it had happened. As he waited to be released, a strange feeling washed over Emmett; he had experienced something unusual while unconscious, but he couldn't recall what. Yet the feeling wouldn't go away.

The ER finally sent them home after grueling hours of tests.

Carla drove home, since the doctor had put Emmett on bed rest and recommended no driving for several days. She glanced over and said, "How you feeling, Emmett?"

"Fine, babe. Just a little bit off. I still have a bit of a headache and my thoughts are a bit foggy."

"Too bad. I was hoping you'd remember being up on the bed, dusting the fan before you fell."

"I . . . I . . ."

Carla smirked. "Relax, Emmett. I knew what happened as soon as I heard you fall. Seeing the clean fan blades and your footprints on the bed just confirmed it for me."

"So you're not mad at me?"

"Oh yes, I most certainly am. I'm mad because I could have lost you today. Mad because you know better than to do something so stupid. But I'll get over it now that you're okay." There was a catch in her voice. "It's just that it scared me so much."

"Ah, jeez, Carla. I'm really sorry. I'll try to be more careful."

"No, Emmett, you won't. And that's the problem. It's the way you are. And I've to come to terms with the fact that one of these days you're going to do something really stupid, and I'm going to lose you. I don't know what I'll do when that happens. I don't know if I'm strong enough to go through something like that again." Her eyes began to pool, and Emmett realized she was fighting back tears. He knew why.

He had no reply in his defense. He understood exactly what she was talking about. They had both survived that unspeakable event together twenty-five years ago and had moved on as best as they could. For a while it looked like they might not make it, but they had found a way. Since that time they often spoke of Stevie, but never about what had happened. It was just too painful. They both knew it was not the best way to deal with things, but it was their way. Now Carla and Emmett were reliving the tragedy. And it was his fault for being such a klutz.

Truth was, Emmett was careless and tended to be accident prone. Carla was right about that. But still, he had never come so close to seriously injuring himself. Maybe it was time to accept his age and stop taking such risks. A psychiatrist might suggest Emmett was unconsciously punishing himself. But for what? He had known tragedy; they both had shared one of the worst. It wasn't his fault. Why should he punish himself? Then Emmett noticed the street sign. "You're taking Oak Street?" He was going to ask Carla why she didn't continue down Main but decided not to question her since he was already in hot water. Either road would get them home.

"Yeah." She sighed. "I don't know, I just thought I'd try a different route today."

He looked out the front window in time to see a car speeding toward their intersection. He shouted "Carla!" at the exact time she slammed on the brakes.

Tires squealed as their car skidded into the intersection. The other car sped past, narrowly avoiding their Prius. When they came to a stop at the far side of the intersection, Emmett saw the offending car zoom away, apparently oblivious to the potential disaster it nearly caused.

Carla sat trembling for several seconds. "Emmett, you all right?"

But Emmett didn't reply. He sat staring into space. To Carla, he probably appeared to be looking at nothing. What he saw in his mind's eye was a far cry from nothing. He was watching thousands, perhaps hundreds of thousands, of scenarios simultaneously playing out in his mind. He could barely comprehend them all. In one version their car collided with the other and both he and Carla were severely injured. In others, one or both of them were killed. Or the car missed them but collided into another vehicle, or into a building, bursting into flames. In other scenarios, they hadn't turned onto Oak Street, so either the accident didn't happen, or it happened to another car.

"Emmett!" she shouted.

Emmett turned as if waking from a dream. He stared at Carla, not recognizing her, and that frightened him. The look on her face said the same about her. "Emmett, are you all right? Were you hurt?"

Still dazed, Emmett said, "I was killed," in a strange, detached voice. "We both were killed. Then we weren't. We were safe. Then we weren't. Thousands and thousands of times over. Again and again."

"Honey, what are you saying? You're not making sense."

The trance had passed over him and then began to disappear. Emmett's eyes became clear and focused. He said, "I'm okay now. Yeah, I think I'm fine."

"You sure, Emmett? You were talking strangely. Maybe we should go back to the hospital. Maybe they need to check you out better."

Slowly Emmett replied, "No. Honestly, honey, I'm fine. Let's just go home now."

* * *

For the remainder of the trip, Emmett sat quietly in his seat, contemplating. For whatever reason, he chose not to share his thoughts with his wife. When they got in the front door, Carla helped Emmett to the sofa, then sat next to him, placing her hand gently on his leg.

"Emmett. Tell me what happened back there. It was like you went away for a time or something. It was frightening."

After a moment, Emmett raised his head and met his wife's eyes. "I suppose in a sense I did go away. I saw things."

"What kind of things?"

"I saw the accident, our near accident, played out in my mind with different endings. Some of the results were the same as ours, but most were different, more catastrophic . . . some were even fatal."

Carla gasped, then looked down and folded her hands in her lap. "I don't know what to say. Then again, I haven't suffered a potentially serious head trauma. Maybe it was just because the accident was such a close call. You know, maybe coming on the heels of your fall. I'm sure you're very susceptible to such things at this stage."

Emmett asked, "When we almost hit that car, did anything like that happen to you?"

"No, but to be honest, I think I did pee my pants a little. In fact, I'm going right upstairs to clean up and get changed."

"I suppose I got off lucky then." He chuckled. "I also just recalled something else. I had a similar experience after my fall, when I was regaining consciousness. I had forgotten about it until now. I saw my accident played out in different ways. "

"Oh my God, Emmett. Maybe we should go back to the hospital."

"No. I don't think we need to, honey. I'm feeling fine. I think you were right. I think the stress of the day may have been too much for me. You know I have an overactive imagination. Maybe the stress of the accidents just triggered something and put my brain into high gear. Let's wait a bit. I think if I just rest for a time, everything will be fine."

"Well . . ." She gave a sigh of relent. "I suppose, if you say so."

Unknown to his wife, Emmett had a very strong suspicion of what had happened to him. His science fiction writer's mind understood what it was he was seeing. He needed time to rest and to contemplate.

"I'm going to sit and watch TV for a bit and maybe nap," Emmett said. "The doctors did clear me to sleep, right? I know sometimes with head injuries they frown on that."

"Yes," Carla assured him. "They said it should be okay. I just have to keep my eye on you and check on you from time to time. You're not feeling nauseated or anything, are you?"

"No, not at all. A bit exhausted from everything is all." Emmett plopped into his chair and squirmed, getting comfortable and situated in his recliner.

"All right then. Maybe you should rest like the doctor ordered."

"Very well, Nurse Carla. Say, maybe we should get you one of those sexy nurse's outfits. You know what I mean?" He wiggled his eyebrows, Groucho Marx style.

Carla rolled her eyes and said, "Easy there, tiger. I think you've had enough excitement for one day."

* * *

Emmett slept for several hours; however, it was anything but restful. His slumber was bombarded with images of alternate versions of his fall as well as their near-miss on the way home from the hospital. The problem was, the dreams seemed to be much more than just dreams. They seemed to be alternate versions of the same reality.

He awoke with a start in his recliner. A cool dampness trickled down the center of his back. He lowered the recliner's footrest and attempted to stand, only to realize his body was not happy with what he had done during his fall. He had been so focused on his head injury that he hadn't taken into account how much the rest of his body might have been affected.

Every single muscle in his body screamed with pain. His back and neck tightened in a mass of knots. Arms and legs felt like charley horses were waiting in the wings to spasm when he least expected it. Even his fingers and toes ached. Emmett had been dealing with growing arthritis in those joints for the past several years, and his fall had done nothing to help relieve that discomfort.

He flopped back down into his recliner, sweat streaming from every pore. After a few minutes of panting in pain, shock, and realization, he was about ready to make another attempt to stand when Carla entered the room.

"Thought I heard you moving around down here. How are you doing?"

Not wanting her to know the extent of his pain, Emmett gritted his teeth and managed to push out the words, "I'm fine . . . stiff is all."

"I'm not at all surprised. That was quite a fall you had. I suspect it might be a long time before you'll try a stunt like that again. Are you sure you're okay, Emmett? You're sweating, and you look pale."

"Yeah, I think I just need another of those pain pills the doctor gave us."

"I'll get you one right away," Carla said as she headed out of the room.

9

With his wife safely out of earshot, Emmett once again began what he knew would be the arduous task of trying to get out of the chair. After several agonizing minutes of suppressed curses and gritted teeth, Emmett got himself standing in front of his recliner, sweating, panting, but alive and able to move.

Carla met him with pills and water as he was shuffling out of the room. "Here, Emmett. Take these. You'll feel better."

"I certainly hope so."

"Maybe you should sit down again for a while; you're white as a sheet."

"Honestly, honey, sitting down is the last thing I need. All it does is stiffen me up. I would actually love a soak in a hot bath, but you'd probably have to call in a tow truck to get me out. So, a shower will have to do."

Carla cocked her head, then said, "I suppose that'll be okay as long as you feel up to it. Are you sure you're all right?"

"Yes, I'm sure. I think this hot shower is exactly what I need."

"Well then, I'd better let you get to it. Leave the bathroom door ajar and I'll stop up and check on you periodically. Okay?"

"Of course. In fact, you're welcome to join me if you'd like." Emmett gave her his Groucho eyebrows again.

"Steady on your feet, tiger. You're not ready for that level of exhaustion yet; hopefully soon, but not yet."

Emmett breathed a sigh of relief. Romance was the last thing he was ready to tackle. "Well, in that case, I'd better get my butt into the shower."

Hot water coursed over Emmett's aching body. He doubted if he had ever felt anything so good in his life. He wondered if the hot temperature was causing his heart to beat faster and pump his blood more quickly through his bloodstream. Since he just took a pain pill, he imagined the tiny particles of medicine racing through his veins like kids zooming down the tubes of a water slide. Just the idea of that seemed to make his pain subside. He assumed it might just be the placebo effect, but if so, then so be it. Whatever the reason, he was feeling much better.

As he stood under the refreshing water, his mind cleared and he was able to recall what he had seen both after his fall from the bed and their near collision. Emmett was more convinced than ever that he had somehow gained the ability—maybe through hitting his head—to see beyond what he thought of as the normal world.

Although he had read dozens of stories about the concept of parallel universes, he had never given the idea any credence before; until now. And if he was right, and if he could find a way to focus this newfound sight, he might be able to see someone he never imagined he would ever see again. Even if just for a moment; it would be worth any price. If only he could see his Stevie again.

* * *

Steven Ellis Parker had been an inquisitive and intelligent little boy who had grown to be a wonderful young man. Carla had always hoped her only child might attend one of the best colleges in the country. Unfortunately, that was never to be.

Harlan Edgewood was a local lifelong under-achiever who spent more of his time drinking than he did looking for a job. Harlan had mastered the art of working as little as possible and squeezing as much money from the government as he was able. He would deliberately take a job he knew wouldn't last very long. Then when it ended, he'd collect unemployment. He'd ride it out as far as he could, occasionally doing odd jobs under the table for cash while still collecting from Uncle Sam. When his unemployment benefits were about to run dry, he would miraculously find another entry-level job and try to stretch it out until he was once again eligible for unemployment money. Also, he managed to feign a few on-the-job back injuries to score himself some workmen's compensation money as well.

The amazing thing about this? Harlan was able to accomplish all this conniving while being a raging alcoholic. Incredibly, he had never been canned from any job because of his drinking. He had been arrested a few times for driving under the influence. Nonetheless, he continued to operate his vehicle without the benefit of a license. Apparently being a functioning drunk and cheater of the system were the two things in life Harlan had managed to do successfully. That was until one day, when his luck ran out and everything went horribly wrong.

That afternoon, high school junior Stevie Parker was walking home, as he often did. It was the same route he had walked hundreds of times before without incident. Harlan was cruising down Elm Street with a blood alcohol level far beyond the legal limit. This wasn't new for Harlan; it was pretty much how he went through life whether behind the wheel or not. Stevie was deep in thought, perhaps concerned about the upcoming SAT exams or maybe thinking about a girl at school he was hoping to date. Perhaps he was contemplating any one of a dozen other topics that occupy the mind of a teenage boy. Whatever the reason, Stevie stepped off the curb and onto the street at the exact moment Harlan Edgewood weaved drunkenly to the right, and the rest, as they say, was tragic history.

Stevie had been struck so hard by Harlan's car that he was knocked out of his shoes. He flew fifteen feet in the air before slamming into the trunk of an ancient oak, splattering his head apart like ripened watermelon. Harlan had slammed on his brakes, gotten out of his car, and staggered over to where Stevie lay. The man sat down and began weeping uncontrollably, knowing even in his stupor that whatever luck had carried him through life so far was gone for good. There was no way he could talk his way out of this terrible situation. When the police arrived they found Harlan still sitting next to the body, crying. Harlan was later booked and charged with vehicular manslaughter, driving under the influence, and a whole list of lesser offenses.

Harlan never made it to trial, having fallen into a major depression over what he had done. Going a week without his much-needed alcohol did nothing to help alleviate his mood. If fact, it probably made things worse. One night, Harlan managed to fashion a noose from his bedsheet. Wrapping one end tightly around the bars in his cell door and securing the noose end around his neck, he forced himself down into a sitting position until the makeshift noose tightened sufficiently.

Although Emmett and Carla were not in the least bit saddened by Harlan's demise, they knew it would never bring their Stevie back.

* * *

Emmett finished his shower and dressed in his red and black fleece pajamas. After all, he had no intention of going anywhere else that evening. He was both mentally and physically exhausted. He called downstairs and told Carla he was going to lie down in bed and maybe watch some television.

"Okay, sweetie," she replied. "I'm going to finish up some things down here then I'll be up as well. It's been a long day."

Emmett thought, *Incredibly long.*

As he lay in bed with the television not yet turned on, there was a "what if" scenario going through Emmett Parker's mind. He supposed that "visions" was the right word for them. He had been granted the opportunity to look into what he thought of as alternate realities, parallel universes. In his mind, the concept was no longer some theoretical idea or an invention from the realm of science fiction. It existed. Twice in one day he had been given a vision.

But what did that actually mean? *Vision.* Did it mean that every time something bad happened to him in this universe, Emmett might see it played out in ways more devastating? Would he someday learn to control this unique gift—assuming it was a gift? Would he be able to see into other universes at will, and learn what had happened to Stevie in those other places? Since Stevie's death had occurred more than twenty-five years earlier, would it be too far in the past to see?

This last thought made Emmett question the direction of his thinking. He recalled that in his visions, he had seen scenarios in which he had actually died. The day Stevie died, Emmett had never been called to the scene, even though it was only a few blocks from his home. As a result, his last memory of Stevie that day was of him being alive and well.

If this "sight" allowed him to look back into the past to the day Stevie died, could he actually even consider the horror of watching his only child die over and over with the thin hope that he might see him survive in some other universe? If it were possible for him to see his son, alive and living out his life as it should have been, would it be worth seeing him not survive in others? Did he have what it took to do such a thing? Emmett doubted he did.

Then an image shot through Emmett's mind. It was a flashback to when he had fallen from the bed earlier that day. In one of the scenarios, he had seen himself lying dead on the floor with a broken neck. But instead of his wife standing over him, there was a man of about forty or so kneeling down beside him, crying. Now that he thought about it, that man looked very familiar.

"Oh my God," Emmett whispered. "Is it possible? Was that . . . could that have been Stevie?"

In whatever version of reality Emmett had seen, his son had been there, as an adult. Somehow, Stevie had survived in that world. Perhaps Stevie had decided not to walk home that day, or maybe that drunk, Harlan Edgewood, had driven a different way. Maybe Edgewood didn't even exist in that particular world or had died years earlier due to his drunken behavior. The more Emmett thought about it, the more possibilities he imagined. In at least one universe, probably more, his son had lived.

Emmett closed his eyes, trying to remember more about that world and about seeing Stevie. It was like trying to remember a forgotten dream. Maybe if he tried hard enough he could recall what Stevie had said to him. Had Stevie actually spoken? Or was this nothing more than the wild imaginings of an old man combined with the grief he still carried?

"Oh, Stevie," Emmett said as tears streamed down his cheeks. "I'd give anything just to know you were well."

Emmett heard a voice somewhere off in the distance calling to him. "Dad? Are you okay? Please, Dad, answer me."

It was the deep baritone voice of a middle-aged man. Emmett knew that voice. It was a voice he'd heard twenty-five years ago, only more mature now. Stevie's voice. And he was nearby. How could that possibly be?

* * *

Emmett slowly opened his eyes, confused. A recognizable face—despite the age of the man—loomed over Emmett.

"Stevie? Is that you, Stevie?"

"Of course it's me, Dad."

Emmett realized he was no longer on his bed but was once again on the bedroom floor. "Stevie? I . . . How can you be here?"

"I live here, Dad, with you. Don't you remember? I was downstairs and heard a bang. I came up and saw you lying unconscious on the floor. I called 911. The paramedics should be here soon."

"But you can't be here, Stevie. I can't be here with you. It doesn't make any sense."

" You're probably just a little confused. You bumped your head really hard by the sound of it."

"Stevie. Do me a favor and go get your mother. She needs to know what happened to me."

Stevie was silent. His face wore a look like he wasn't sure what to say next. Then the front doorbell rang.

"Stay here, Dad. I have to go let the paramedics in downstairs. I'll be right back."

"Don't leave me, Stevie. I can't bear to lose you again."

"Dad, don't worry. You won't lose me. You've never lost me. I've been here. I'll always be here."

A few moments later, Stevie returned with two young EMTs, one male and one female. He remembered Carla calling them a boy and a girl. To Carla, everyone under forty was either a boy or a girl. This was getting more confusing by the minute.

"Mr. Parker." The male EMT asked, "Do you remember what happened to you? Do you know why you fell and hit your head?"

A feeling of extreme déjà vu flooded Emmett's mind. Hadn't he just experienced this same situation earlier that day, with the same EMTs?

The female EMT asked Stevie, "Has he seemed disoriented in any way since his fall?"

"Well," Stevie said reluctantly, "he's been a bit confused. He's been asking for my mother." The EMTs stared expectantly, waiting for further explanation.

"My mother died back when I was sixteen. I was walking home from school and Mom walked to meet me. She was hit and killed by a drunk driver."

Emmett heard a voice screaming "Noooo!" Moments before the scene faded, he realized it was his.

* * *

Carla walked into the bedroom ready for a good night's sleep after the trying day they had both experienced. She noticed the television was off and Emmett was sound asleep. She tiptoed into the bathroom to complete her nightly ritual.

When she slipped out of the bathroom, she noticed Emmett hadn't shifted position. He wasn't snoring as he usually did. And he seemed to be lying extremely still. She decided to shake him awake, just to make sure all was right. Emmett never woke.

Days later, at the funeral, Carla took what consolation the many well-wishers offered. They seemed to repeat the same cliché phrase: "He's in a better place now. He's finally with Stevie again."

PANTY LINES

by Catherine Jordan

I set down the remote, having just finished binge-watching a new series on Netflix. My husband sat at his desk, closed off in the den, reading students' papers. "I'm going to bed," I said as I peeked in on him.

He got up and followed.

Upstairs in the bedroom, I whipped off my t-shirt and jeans and hopped under the covers.

Moonlight lit up the bedroom with a soft glow. He crawled into bed with nothing except his sex face—a half-smile through parted lips and a glaze in his eyes. The familiar look told me he wasn't quite ready for sleep. I noted the glare from the clock on the bedside table. 12:43 A.M.

He crawled on top of me. He slid a finger under the waistband of my underwear, his hands still quite adept and his passion just as urgent after all these years. "Where's the lace?"

"Lace?" I asked.

"Yeah, lace. That frilly stuff. The pair you have on . . ." He peeked under the covers. "They're stretched out and huge." He tugged on the waistband and I heard a rip. "There's a hole in them, too. They look like they're about to disintegrate."

"Well, buddy, so am I. Off ya go." I pushed him aside and rolled out from underneath him.

"Oh, come on, babe," he said as he sat up. "Don't be that way."

"How is it that you are noticing them right now?" I asked.

He shrugged. "I've noticed them before but never said anything. I don't know. I thought maybe you could wear pretty panties, like the kind you used to wear when we got married. Not those granny panties."

"I am a granny panty lover," I said. "Generic, nude colored, so they blend in with my skin tone whenever I wear pants or skirts. They're cheap and practically disposable. They're comfortable and hold all my bits and pieces in place. Besides, no one else sees them."

He looked up over his eyebrows at me. "I see them."

"Sorry to disappoint. I don't have any lacy underwear."

"Well, can't you go buy some? You like to shop, don't you?"

"Ohhh, yes," I said, my voice thick with sarcasm. "We women love to shop. But, Mr. History Professor, I figured you'd appreciate the story behind each rip and thread of elastic in this well-aged pair of underwear."

He replied with a grunt.

"What about your underwear?" I asked. "Hmm? Maybe I'd like to see you in a pair of boxers, with less gut hanging over the waistband."

"I wasn't trying to pick a fight," he said. "I was only hoping for a little change." He rolled away, turning his back to me.

"I didn't know a pair of underwear could be so capable."

"Yeah, it can," came his muffled voice.

As I lay in bed listening to my husband toss and turn, I tried to remember how things were years ago when we first married, but it was difficult. We had fallen into the rut that married couples often do as they get comfortable with each other. We had always enjoyed each other's company and had fun, but spontaneity had taken a back seat. Sex was something we now planned. When I asked for a backrub, that's really all I wanted. We hopped into bed because we were tired. If my husband rolled over on top of me, it was because his large, six-foot frame took up half the bed, and then I'd nudge him away.

We had been married for over twenty years. I didn't think I needed frilly underwear anymore. I never had matching bras and panties. It seemed like such a waste of time and money. Admittedly, my underwear did nothing to get the juices flowing. Even my bras were boring, barely functional.

I released a deep sigh and decided to go shopping in the morning.

* * *

The perfumed boutique had racks and open dresser drawers filled with panties. Pretty? Yeah they were, with racy names like *Darling Pink*, *Licorice Black*, and *Hot-Tamale*. They were soft, too, I noted while fingering the delicate satin and lace-trim.

Dozens of colors and styles were on display, and I was overwhelmed by the choices. I needed to have an open mind. I had to be willing to surprise not only my husband but myself. *Don't automatically go for the plain black*, said the voice in my head. *Yes, it's flattering, but pick a shade that says something about you.*

What about me? Middle age, petite, copper skin, dark hair with a few strands of stubborn gray at the crown. I liked the gray. I liked the fine lines around my eyes. Those first signs of aging were well earned, in my opinion, and they spoke to my confidence.

Red, I decided as I snatched three pairs of panties: a thong, a satin bikini, and a French cut mid-rise. I checked out the tags, the practical me wanting to know how to wash them, then exchanged all three extra-small sizes into the drawer as my size-medium self laughed.

They weren't cheap. But it wasn't the money that made me hesitate. It was the idea, or rather the visual of me, an older woman, squirming into something so ridiculously extravagant. Within the past few years, I'd put on a few pounds. My ass sagged. Would the panties stay in place or migrate south? Would the thong's friction aggravate a hemorrhoid? And as I looked over the thong dangling from my forefinger, I couldn't help wonder how something so flimsy might support a panty liner? *I am an older woman, not old, and I still get my damn period.* I couldn't help feeling sorry for the pathetic crotch-line.

Then, I was hot. Not sexy-wow-is-she-HOT, but, if-I-don't-find-a-freezer-to-walk-into-I-will-melt-like-wax-HOT. Sweat gathered at the nape of my neck and began dripping down my back. *Time to make a decision and get out of here.*

A cute young blonde approached, dressed in black, measuring tape around her neck. She told me about the panty sale and asked if I wanted to be fitted for a matching bra, also on sale. "Sure," I said, perspiration pooling between my breasts. I had tissues in my purse—perfect opportunity to mop up.

I followed her into a well-lit dressing room. She drew the yellow tape around my chest, and as I inhaled her strong flowery perfume, something about her seemed familiar. *Oh, jeez,* I thought, hoping she wasn't one of my daughter's friends. She leaned in to read the measuring tape and I looked at the name on the tag pinned to her low-cut blouse. Mentally, I went through all my daughter's friend's names. "Clare" didn't ring a bell.

One hundred twenty-three dollars later, I hopped in the minivan and drove home. I had to admit, I felt sexier already. Spontaneous. Surely, my husband would notice the change even with my clothes on.

I waited until about a half-hour before he would be home, knowing the kids would still be at various after-school programs. I'd have the time to try on my new purchase. I pranced around the bathroom, staring at my figure outfitted in what looked like a sultry red bikini. I decided to wear one of his white dress shirts as a cover-up. Sexy, right? Me in my man's shirt, the *Hot Tamale* bra and panties popping through the white.

Laundry day (ha ha) had come and gone, so I pulled his shirt out of the hamper. As I slid into the sleeves and cinched the oversized collar around my neck, I smelled a distinct flowery scent. Perfume. Women's perfume. Wait. That smell. I buried my nose deep in the collar and inhaled, closing my eyes, focusing on what took shape in my mind—a delicate young face with blonde hair, dressed in black, with a measuring tape around her neck.

"Shit," I said, as a memory formed from one of my husband's conferences. I had met her about six months ago. She had been dressed in tight jeans and a small sweater, her hair in a sleek ponytail. His eyes had lit up when she walked into the room; they had stood a little too close when they greeted each other. When he introduced her to me, their cheeks turned a bit too pink. Clare, one of my husband's students.

I dropped onto the bed like dead weight, heavy and worthless. Foolish. He had wanted a change. Did he want our marriage to change so that he didn't need Clare? Or did he want me to change to be more like Clare?

My face flushed as red as my stupid underwear.

The front door opened.

My heart began beating faster. A whoosh of blood rushed through my veins. My skin tingled; all the hairs on my body stood on end.

Heavy footsteps up the stairs, down the hall, and into the bedroom.

My husband stood in the doorway. "Hey, babe," he said. He looked down at me with concern. "You okay?"

"You know that change you said you wanted last night?" I asked. I felt like I was outside my body, watching the scene from above.

"Yeah," he said, walking toward where I sat on the bed.

"I have one for you," I said, standing. I stepped out of the thong, toying with it absentmindedly, holding it like I was ready to sling-shot it across the room. Like it was a weapon. If only I had a rock. "Come closer," I said, still stunned, not really thinking, just doing. Just reaching up and stretching out the leg opening as I pulled it over his head, him with that half-smile on his face and a glaze in his eyes. I stood behind my husband, who probably thought this was some sort of new sex game. I cinched the thong around his neck. It didn't seem so flimsy and pathetic now. Suddenly, my knees were against his shoulder blades, my hands twisting the garment tighter and tighter.

I've heard of women, who, under duress, were able to lift a car off a trapped child, or were able to beat their much bigger and stronger assailant to a pulp. Adrenaline can make one capable of almost anything.

My hands, still intertwined in the thong, had turned blue. When I realized I no longer felt my fingers, I released the panties. My husband pitched forward slowly, like a falling tree, onto the bed. He lay, belly down, his face also blue, eyes bulging, half-smile drawn into a grimace.

"What have I done?" I asked myself, my chest heaving, fingers throbbing. The voice in my head responded: *He had hoped for a little change. You gave him a big one.*

A MODERN FABLE

by John B. Kachuba

Will Shifflet looked up, saw the crows in the trees eyeing him intently, and thought, I am not going to dig up the witch.

He turned up the collar of his jacket against the wind, jammed his hands in his pockets, then hunched his shoulders to keep from shivering. A broad belly of gray clouds scudded across the treetops. The chilly wind carried upon it the scent of rain. A few moments later, fat drops of icy water splattered on the barren ground.

Fitzpatrick, the new city manager, blathered on about something, but Will paid him no mind. Rain splashed upon the weathered gravestone before him. The water bled over the worn gravestone letters, swinging a crazy arc through the "C" in "Cranna" before dropping to the ground.

Fitzpatrick and the town engineer looked down the slope to the road that passed the cemetery as they discussed the project. Will stamped his work boots on the frozen ground, trying to restore some warmth to his feet. Widen the road? A dumb-ass idea. The details bored him. All he knew was that Fitzpatrick would demand that he dig up the witch.

Will remembered a time from the old days, when he was just a boy, of his mother telling him about the witch's last days:

Hannah Cranna lit one last candle and now the tiny cabin was bathed in light, as if it were noon on a summer's day. Outside the dark windows, the winter wind rattled the trees like bones. An occasional puff of wind, soft as a dying man's breath, would sigh into the room and set the candle flames dancing. But Hannah was not in a dancing mood—Old Boreas was dead.

A small wooden box that she had hammered together lay on a table in the center of the room. Candles surrounded it, dripping wax onto the rough wood. Hannah stood over the box, looking down at her long-time friend and companion. Immense grief washed over her, followed, oddly, by a sense of relief that it was over, and it would soon be over for her as well.

She stretched her pale, gnarled fingers down to the box and stroked the rooster's ebony feathers one last time. Soft. She thought of him following her everywhere, thought of the comfort he brought her in the long, lonely nights.

A tear fell upon the dead bird. She wiped her eyes, lifted the wooden lid, and laid it across the box, nailing it shut.

She took her shawl from the peg near the fire and wrapped it around her shoulders, pulling it forward to cover her head. She picked up the box, opened the door, and stepped out into the cold night.

The trees waved skeletal limbs against the starry sky as she passed below them. An owl hooted. Beneath a large elm was a hole she had dug earlier that day. Hannah carefully placed the box in the earth. The shovel stood nearby in a pile of dirt. She refilled the hole and now the tears flowed. She couldn't stop them.

* * *

Will sat in the Public Works garage, sipping coffee, his feet propped on the desk. DeMarco and some of the others were listening to the police scanner in the back room, but he had no interest in that. Through the window he watched a windblown curtain of water ripple over the street, slowing the traffic along the town green to a crawl. Gray clouds hunkered over town. Mist swallowed the steeple of the Congregational Church across the street. There wouldn't be much work done today. That was okay with him.

He wasn't eager to get back to the cemetery. He wasn't superstitious, but it didn't seem right to go around disturbing dead people, especially dead people who were also witches. And one, a witch who, according to his mother, could possibly be his ancestor. It was a stupid idea, anyway, widening the road. The town had been around since 1639, and Turkey Roost Road had been there all that time. In his way of thinking, the road only needed resurfacing every now and then.

But Will knew things were changing in his town. Despite the objections of almost everyone, this Fitzpatrick, with his big ideas about development, his expensive suits and shiny new BMW, would have the town covered over with condos and shopping centers if he had his way. Will took a swallow of coffee. Sure, easy for Fitzpatrick, he thought. He doesn't have to dig up a witch.

Will had plenty of doubts about Fitzpatrick. He heard the rumors and figured there was probably something to them. Embezzling. Bribery. He wasn't surprised. It seemed that's how business was done these days. All in the name of progress. Were people so dishonest, so morally bankrupt in the old days? Would Hannah have stood for that?

He sighed and leaned farther back in his chair. Will's mother would know about Hannah:

The first thing young Mrs. Peterson noticed when Hannah opened the cabin door was the absence of the old witch's cantankerous rooster. Still, she quickly set the bundle of firewood on the hearth, expecting the ghastly bird to fly at her out of nowhere. She nodded to Hannah and turned to go, but the old woman caught her by the arm.

Hannah dragged the frightened woman to a chair and sat her in it. She did not smile or even thank Mrs. Peterson for her gift, having grown accustomed to the kindnesses of the townsfolk who held her in awe, if not outright fear.

"Now you listen, girl," Hannah said, as though lecturing a schoolgirl. "Old Boreas is dead and I'm bound to follow him."

The young woman was speechless. She stared at Hannah, her eyes wide with fright. The witch shook her roughly by the shoulders.

"Pay attention! Don't go stupid on me, girl. When I am dead you must not bury me until after sundown. Not a moment before, do you hear?"

Mrs. Peterson nodded.

"Speak up! Do you understand me?"

24

The witch's face was inches from her own. "Yes," Mrs. Peterson whispered.
"Good girl. And another thing. My coffin is to be hand-carried to the
cemetery up the hill and never to be moved. Ever. That's the only way."
Hannah shook the young woman one more time for good measure. "Mind
me, girl! Do as I say."

Mrs. Peterson swallowed hard and said she would. Who would cross a
witch?

Without another word, Hannah released the woman, then opened the
door. Mrs. Peterson didn't linger.

* * *

The men got an early start the next morning. The storm had finally
blown itself out and now the sky was a hard, clear blue. Will felt he
could reach up and rap his knuckles against it. He bounced along in the
high seat of the truck next to Haines, the kid. Will didn't drive much
anymore, eyes too weak. He didn't care. Now he had more time to look
around, to see where they were going, even though after all these years he
knew the route perfectly with his eyes shut.

The kid was also bouncing on the torn seat, skinny fingers drum-
ming on the wheel in time to music playing in his earbuds. A gaping hole
in the grimy dashboard marked where the radio used to be. Will watched
the kid bopping to the music and smiled to himself, barely remembering
what it had been like to be nineteen.

The road rolled beneath the broad yellow hood of the truck as if the
vehicle was sucking it in. That would keep everyone at the Public Works
busy, wouldn't it? Trucks that ate the highway so PW could get back out
there and repave—if such a truck could be invented, Fitzpatrick would
figure out a way to make a quick buck on it.

They were driving down Turkey Roost Road. The ancient oaks and
maples marching down from the hillsides revealed a few houses, but the
landscape hadn't changed much in the three centuries since settlers came
up from New Haven Colony. Will knew all about those stalwart settlers.
His ancestors had been among them, including one who may have been
a distant relation to Hannah Cranna herself. His knowledge was gleaned

from family stories and rumors, legends and gossip. He knew the history of this place, heard its rhythm in his bones.

Haines slowed the truck, waited for a minivan engorged with kids to pass, then turned left into the cemetery. Will and the kid climbed down from the cab. They didn't take tools from the truck. This trip was merely an inspection. Will's thirty-plus years in Public Works had taught him the value of several inspections before doing a job.

A fringe of trees bordered the burial ground on three sides. The road edged the fourth. There wasn't much left of the cemetery, no more than two dozen or so stones leaning in the yellow grass, most of them illegible, some mere stumps, like broken teeth set in the rotting earth. The witch's grave was in the near corner of the lot, on a little knoll that rolled down to the road. Frozen grass crunched beneath their boots.

They stood before the stone, the kid bobbing and dipping his head to his internal music.

Ice crystals glittered in the letters chiseled into the stone.

HANNAH CRANNA
1783 - 1860
Wife of Capt. Joseph Hovey

She had invented a new name for herself after her husband, the captain, mysteriously fell from a cliff, widowing her at a young age. Some said she changed her name when she sealed a pact with the devil; others said she just wanted to start anew.

Wind blew across the cemetery, rocking the barren trees. Will noticed a dozen or more crows perched high in the branches, riding the current of air as though sailing a Yankee clipper. The kid watched the birds, too, standing still for once, his hands in his overalls.

Will turned his attention back to the grave. It was parallel to the road, on an extensively eroded knoll. He was surprised the witch hadn't already rolled out of her grave into the street—what was left of her, that is. Two other graves were set in line with Hannah's. Will shook his head. Those graves would have to be moved as well.

"That's progress, Will," Fitzpatrick had said. "You can't stop it."

"It ain't right, though," Will said. "We have no business messing around with dead folks."

"You'll move them, or I'll get someone who will."

Will would have liked to settle things with Fitzpatrick out behind the garage, man to man, but things weren't done that way anymore. Progress. Fighting would result in a lawsuit and jail time; he wasn't having any of it. He tried to think of ways to sabotage the task but never came up with anything. Maybe the kid had some ideas; but when he saw Haines wandering around the cemetery like a pup sniffing his way through a junkyard, he decided not to ask him. As Will walked between the graves, he felt the ground beginning to soften. It had been a mild winter so far, courtesy of El Niño and so-called climate change. Sunshine aided the thaw.

He stopped beside Hannah's grave marker. A crack snaked diagonally across the stone. A new one, he realized, probably caused by the latest thaw.

It's up to you now, old girl, he thought. I can't stop them.

Something spooked the crows roosting in the trees. He'd once heard that a group of crows was called a murder. Well, that murder rose up in a frenzy of flapping wings and raucous cries. Their shadows streamed over the graveside. That's when Will noticed the thin rivulet of black fluid oozing from below the grave, meandering down to the street.

More of his mother's story came to mind:

Mrs. Peterson trudged through the new-fallen snow, a wicker basket of freshly baked bread slung from one arm. She could see Hannah's cabin in the distance, tucked in a hollow beneath a grove of towering hemlocks. She dragged her feet through the deep snow, breaking the first path to the cabin. It was clear from the unblemished drift piled against the door that the old woman had not yet ventured outside.

Mrs. Peterson knocked. No answer. Snow feathers floated from the hemlock branches reminding Mrs. Peterson of Hannah's ferocious rooster. The bird was dead, but she somehow sensed its presence and nervously scanned the woods for any sign of it.

She knocked once more. Silence. She slowly pushed the door open.

A single candle was burning on the table, barely illuminating the room. Mrs. Peterson set the basket on the floor near the door. She stepped toward a dark corner of the cabin. A body lay on the feathered bed. She drew closer. Mrs. Peterson sucked in her breath—Hannah lay curled and stiff on her side, chest still, eyes open.

Within a few hours, the undertaker had Hannah's body safely secured in a simple pine box. A hazy winter sun hung in the silver sky as a party of men slogged through the snow with the coffin. It was an uphill climb to where the wagon stood waiting in the lane. The men were panting by the time they placed the coffin in the back of it.

The undertaker, muffled in a black cloak, flicked the reins and whistled up the horses. The two horses danced in their traces, steam blowing from their nostrils, their ears laid back. A second snap of the reins got them moving forward through the snow.

The men walked silently behind the wagon.

The lane rose as it met Turkey Roost Road. A scraping sound reached the men's ears before they saw the coffin sliding from the back of the wagon. One rushed forward to try to catch it, but not quickly enough. The box lurched from the wagon bed, and the men jumped out of its path right before it thumped to the road. As it hit the snowy lane, the coffin picked up speed and flew down the slope.

The party of men, dumbstruck, watched the coffin recede in the distance. By the time they came to their senses and took off after it, the coffin had come to rest against the witch's cabin door.

The party took hold of the coffin and once again wrestled it up to the wagon. The wagon had proceeded only about twenty yards before the coffin burst forth a second time. They were able to grab it before it slid too far and hoisted it up into the wagon bed. They stood around the wagon, flabbergasted and worn out by their task. The sun sat low in the sky, a pale-yellow smudge on the western horizon. When the men had recovered their wind, the wagon started up again. This time, two of them sat on the coffin.

As the wagon made Turkey Roost Road, the coffin began to shake. The two men, eyes wide with fright, held on as best they could as the pine box bucked and heaved beneath them. The others jumped into the wagon and piled on top of the coffin, but still it quaked and trembled, threatening to pitch them all into the road.

The panicked undertaker lashed the reins. The horses bolted, the wagon slewed wildly on the slippery road, and the men jostled in back like popping corn.

By the time the wagon reached the cemetery, the sun had disappeared from the sky. The coffin lay quietly in the rear of the wagon while the men dug the grave. It was dark when they finally hand-carried the coffin into the cemetery and lowered it into the earth by the light of the gravediggers' lanterns.

As the exhausted burial party headed back into town, a reddish glow began to rise in the woods down the lane. Hannah's cabin—it was in flames. No one moved to put the fire out.

* * *

Will didn't always attend town meetings, but he had no choice tonight. Fitzpatrick wanted all the Public Works guys present. Why? Did he think the town was out to lynch him?

Will, the kid, and a few others sat in the rear of the packed meeting room. The Public Works boss, DeMarco, sat beside Fitzpatrick at a table up front. Will thought Fitzpatrick looked nervous as he fiddled with the knot of his tie, but DeMarco, sitting back in his chair with his arms folded across his chest, looked formidable.

After the meeting was called to order, Fitzpatrick gave a long-winded presentation, complete with a slick video, about widening Turkey Roost Road. The video showed its present condition, especially where it passed the cemetery, and an artist's rendering depicted the future roadway, a highway of *progress*.

The crowd wasn't impressed. Too expensive, they said. Too much traffic. Too many people. Fitzpatrick's face turned scarlet as he tried to defend his plan. Will thought the man was having a heart attack.

But the next morning, Fitzpatrick was his old self again, strutting through the Public Works parking lot.

"Looks like somebody got lucky last night," one of the men said.

Someone else snickered. Ugly rumors said Fitzpatrick would screw anything that held still long enough. Including the mayor's wife. Will didn't doubt them.

That's what progress brought. No morality anymore, anywhere. Will guessed it wasn't that way in Hannah's time. If she wanted things orderly and peaceful, moral, who would argue with her? Who would dare cross a witch?

Later that morning, while spreading sand on an icy patch of Turkey Roost Road, Will noticed black fluid dribbling down the slope beneath the cemetery, saw it pooling at the side of the road. He thought it was oil at first, maybe leaking from some old tank buried under the ground, but closer inspection told him it wasn't oil. He didn't know what it was. He threw a shovelful of sand over the puddle.

By the time he got back to the garage, everyone had left for the day. That's all right, he could use the overtime, he thought, while washing up in the restroom. He took a shortcut through the administration building, heading toward the parking lot behind the building. It was dark inside, but he knew his way around.

Something thumped against the wall.

He stopped.

He heard the thumping again.

A faint light glowed beneath Fitzpatrick's office door and when he drew closer, he heard other . . . sounds. He wasn't so old that he didn't recognize the sounds of love. All right, lust. He didn't know who the woman was. Didn't matter.

Damn, he thought, right in the office! Had the man no shame? Will left the building and stepped into the night, wondering about Fitzpatrick's poor wife. It troubled him all the way home, this nasty business.

Outsider.

Troublemaker.

Sleazeball.

Will was angry that his little town, this place where his family had lived for centuries, was being corrupted by something foul. Polluted.

Hannah would have been furious. He tried once again to think of ways to sabotage the road project.

Two days later, he was sitting in the Public Works garage, eating a sandwich, when he saw Fitzpatrick drive away in his BMW. Will had the police scanner on as usual but wasn't paying much attention to it. It was the kid, Haines, who came in later and told him they had a mess to clean up on Turkey Roost Road, close to the cemetery. Didn't seem too important, the kid said, so you could probably finish your sandwich.

But when they drove out a few minutes later and saw the red and blue flashing lights of the emergency vehicles, Will knew the kid was wrong, as usual. It was much worse than he had said. The paramedics shook their bowed heads as they knelt over a bloody Fitzpatrick, who lay mangled in the street beside what used to be a silver BMW but was now nothing more than a corrugated piece of scrap-metal wedged up against an old oak tree.

Will walked back toward the truck as the paramedics covered the body. He stopped on the edge of the black slick that lay across the road. Tire tracks skittered through it. He looked at the slick for some time, wondering. Then he lifted his eyes to the knoll below the cemetery. It was clean now, no trace of fluid oozing down the slope. Whatever it was had emptied itself out.

DELIRIUM TREMENS

by Kyle Alexander Romines

Have you ever felt that you should cut down on your drinking?

Garrett Marshall sat alone in the dark, hunched over his desk. The letter of resignation lay in his shadow, waiting for his signature.

A storm raged outside the windows of his spacious fourth-story office. Lightning flashed, for an instant illuminating the white coat hanging from the door, and the various plaques, awards, and degrees mounted on the opposite wall. But it was to the place where a nearly empty bottle was hidden in a cupboard across from the desk that Garrett's gaze was drawn.

He closed his eyes and listened to the bellowing of thunder in an attempt to shut everything out. His pager went off, perfectly on cue. Garrett massaged his temples, sighed, and dialed the callback number.

After a protracted period, a nurse answered. "Dr. Marshall? It's Janet in the SICU—"

"Yes?" Garrett interrupted and tried to hide the frustration in his voice.

"It's Mr. Peters, your patient in bed three, the one status post abdominal aortic aneurysm repair. It looks like he's declining. He might be hypotensive."

"What do you mean, 'looks like'?" His tone was full of incredulity. "What are his vitals?"

"I'm not sure, sir."

Garrett's grip tightened around the phone. "You're asking me about this patient and you don't even know his blood pressure? You can't even give me a heart rate?"

"I'm sorry, sir." She offered a wimpy apology, and his blood simmered. "I can look up the values if you want, if you don't mind holding."

"I'll tell you what I want! A competent nurse who will leave me the hell alone unless she knows there's a problem." He ended the call before saying anything nastier. The last thing he needed was another disciplinary hearing.

He shoved the phone aside and slammed his pager onto the desk, glaring at it like the enemy it was. How many times over the years had he been paged during on-call nights over simple, trivial matters? More than he could count, and usually whenever he'd finally managed to fall asleep.

The lightning's glow filled the office again, and once more his eyes were drawn the cupboard that hid his scotch. Garrett rummaged through the desk drawer until his hand closed around the familiar lowball tumbler, his constant companion over the years. He licked his lips, mouth already dry with anticipation. Before he knew it, the bottle was sitting on the desk. The tumbler shook in his trembling hand. Garrett's lips curled into a frown, and he put down the empty glass.

"Everything I worked for," he whispered to the shadow. "Gone."

Four years of college. Four years of medical school. Five years of surgical residency. He was well into his thirties with a family to support, in debt up to his eyeballs from student loans. And for what?

This wasn't how his life was supposed to turn out. It was almost impossible to remember his passion for art, a dream his mother had killed in college when Garrett told her he wanted to pursue painting.

"You can come home with a medical degree like your father, or not at all," she'd said.

Garrett hadn't painted in years. He was no longer certain he could. That part of him died years ago. He'd done as his mother asked. Medicine didn't come as naturally to him as art, but he'd worked harder than his peers. He threw himself into his studies, leaving time for nothing else.

It only got worse in residency. While his dexterity and deftness of hand served him well as a surgeon, surgery was demanding, stressful, and time-consuming. It swallowed him whole and ate his soul for dessert.

Garrett was too proud to admit he was depressed. He thought a family would change his life and give him something to care about, other than medicine. But he quickly discovered that his family found itself on the losing side of a never-ending tug-of-war with his career. He barely saw his kids and had become a stranger to his wife. In time, they grew to resent him as he worked to provide a life for them—which in turn caused him to resent them.

Have people annoyed you by criticizing your drinking?

His cell phone chimed, piercing through the room's silence.

"What?" he shouted into the receiver, expecting to hear the nurse's voice on the other line.

"Garrett?" It was Kelly, his ex-wife. His *first* ex-wife, at this rate. He heard the familiar edge in her voice. It was hard to remember a time when she'd treated him with anything other than contempt. "You free? Can you talk?"

"I'm just starting on-call," he said, leaning back in his chair. Talking to her always made him feel weary. "What do you need?"

"You were late on another payment," she answered dryly. "The second time in three months."

He should have known. It all boiled down to alimony. Rage welled up inside him, then quickly dissipated, leaving him hollow. It was a feeling he'd come to know too well. "I must have forgot. I've been busy with work. You know how it is." He winced, realizing he had slurred his words.

He heard Kelly inhale. "Are you drinking? On-call?"

In truth, he couldn't remember the last time he'd had a drink. No wonder he was parched. The slurred words, along with his shakes, were well-known symptoms of alcohol withdrawal. A drink was long overdue. "For God's sake, leave it alone, Kelly."

"Don't talk to me like I'm one of your nurses," she shot back. "And don't make me contact my lawyer."

He wanted to scream, to throw something at the wall. It was bad enough that she'd robbed him of everything in the divorce: the kids, the house, even his dignity. "I'll take care of it." He wouldn't admit the truth; he hadn't forgotten to send the check—he was having trouble affording it.

Garrett mumbled an apology that he hoped she'd accept as a peace offering and promised to send the check in the morning.

Have you ever felt guilty about your drinking?

As he reached again for the empty glass in defiance, twin feelings of release and disgust beat at him like boxers in a ring. What would his mother say if she could see him now? She'd only cared about him becoming a successful doctor.

There was one solace in his life: his patients. Despite his faults, he was probably the best vascular surgeon in the city. His hands had saved hundreds of lives. It was only in his work that he found any reason for living at all. Now they'd taken that from him, too.

One week earlier he'd been summoned to the hospital administrator's office and been given an ultimatum: resign quietly, or be fired in disgrace. Deep down, Garrett understood he had himself to blame. He could only show up to the operating room drunk so many times. Someone was bound to turn him in eventually.

You've lost everything.

The certificates and awards on the walls mocked him, boldly proclaiming there was nothing left but the drink. Garrett couldn't even remember the last time he was happy.

Have you ever had a drink first thing in the morning as an eye-opener, to steady your nerves, or to get rid of a hangover?

Searing pain throbbed between his temples. Garrett dwelled on the four questions of the CAGE questionnaire, a screening test for alcoholism. When his primary care physician had administered the questionnaire during a routine checkup, Garrett had scoffed at the woman. She was, after all, a lowly family practitioner—barely a doctor at all, in his opinion.

He'd answered yes to all four questions. Alcohol had started as a cushion, and then a lifeline, until finally, it became the monster he could not overcome. On his days off from work, he drank all day. He felt sick if he didn't.

Wind howled outside his office. Garrett regarded the bottle of whiskey with increasing contempt. Out of impulse, he hurled the bottle across the room in a dark frenzy, where it shattered loudly against the wall. Perfect, he thought, watching the liquor trickle down the wall. Another mess I'll have to clean up in the morning.

His gaze returned to the glass in front of him, and he shrugged. Why not give in to temptation—no point letting it go to waste. One drink. That's all he needed to ameliorate his significant withdrawal symptoms. Garrett lifted the glass to his lips and downed it.

Time slowed. The hands of the clock ticked in sync with the thunder. He felt his eyes grow heavy. The pager sat silent where he had discarded it, as if afraid to disturb him. Garrett closed his eyes and surrendered to sleep, the taste of liquor still on his lips.

He woke with a start, the empty, sticky glass still clutched in his hand. Garrett rubbed his eyes, wanting nothing more than to return to the fleeting refuge of sleep. He glanced around the office in confusion, unsure what had roused him. For a moment he thought it might have been the storm, but the rain was too soft, almost comforting. It was the pager, which was buzzing furiously on his desk.

Garrett released the glass, and it rolled somewhere beyond his reach, vanishing into the darkness. He fumbled with the pager, hardly able to make out the numbers on the screen. He squinted. It was the trauma unit.

Garrett wondered what time it was, his thoughts disjointed and hazy. He reached for his cell phone. It was almost three in the morning. Garrett punched in the number to the trauma unit, praying they didn't need anything important.

"Dr. Marshall, we need you right away." The voice on the other end of the line sounded urgent.

"What is it?" he croaked, his throat parched.

"A new patient arrived by ambulance. High-speed collision. Imaging confirmed an acute type-A aortic dissection."

Garrett's pulse quickened. The aorta—the body's largest artery—supplied all the oxygenated blood to the human body. An aortic dissection, usually caused by uncontrolled high blood pressure or trauma, resulted from a tear inside the artery. A ruptured aorta had an incredibly high mortality rate. Many patients died before they ever reached the hospital.

He stumbled out of his chair. "Why didn't you call me about this before?" he demanded, heading for the elevator.

"We've been trying to page you since we were first notified the patient was en route," the voice replied with a hint of irritation. "You're the only vascular surgeon within reach of the hospital, and it's too dangerous to evac the patient to another hospital by air."

The elevator doors slid open, and Garrett punched the button for the second floor. "Prep the operating room. I'm on my way."

A splitting headache reverberated through his head, teasing him with worse to come. Garrett gripped his head and leaned against the elevator doors for support. Get a hold of yourself, he told himself as the elevator began its descent. He felt sick. His solitary drink had done little to sate his thirst or ward off his symptoms. He needed another.

Garrett swallowed down a wave of nausea. He forced himself to stand as the elevator doors opened.

The trauma ward was unusually quiet, regardless of the time of night. He felt like a ghost haunting the halls of the hospital. Garrett located an abandoned computer terminal, logged on using his credentials, and pulled up the patient's information. He scanned through the pertinent vitals, labs, history, and imaging as quickly as possible, knowing the patient was being prepped for emergency surgery.

April Summers, he read. My God, she's only seventeen. She has her whole life ahead of her. Or at least she did at one time. The odds were sharply against her, and they worsened with every minute. Garrett jogged down the lonely hallway to the doctors' changing room where he threw on shoe covers, a surgical cap, and facemask to go with his scrubs.

The intercom crackled to life. "Dr. Marshall, they're ready for you in operating room three."

He ran out of the changing room and started down another abandoned wing, one that ended in front of a set of massive wooden doors with a red EMERGENCY warning sign. Garrett swallowed hard and scanned his ID at a panel beside the doors, gaining access to the surgical wing. Cool air rushed him as he crossed the threshold. The air felt good, and his nausea subsided temporarily.

"I can do this," Garrett muttered to himself. He marched across the lifeless tile floor, his footsteps echoing down the hallway. Operating room three loomed at the end of the corridor. His confidence grew with each step. He might have made a mess of things in the real world, but here in the operating room, he was a god. Garrett had performed the same procedure many times, and in his heart, he believed he was the best.

He stopped outside the room at a sink to scrub in. With his wet hands held high, Garrett entered the OR.

Garrett winced. The operating theater was awash in bright white light. Thick, monochromatic walls masked the sounds of the storm outside. A digital clock overlooked the operating table in the center of the room where the patient lay anesthetized. The time read 3:35 A.M. It was going to be a long night.

Paige Sullivan, an overweight nurse technician in her mid-forties, stood opposite him at the operating table. Newly opened surgical instruments gleamed on a silver tray beside her.

"Dr. Lawrence," Garrett said, greeting resident doctor Natalie Lawrence. She was already gowned and gloved, waiting quietly for instruction. Garrett spotted a rather severe-looking charge nurse he didn't recognize, watching him with her arms folded across her chest. Cullen Burrows, the nurse anesthetist, sat in a chair at the head of the table, monitoring the patient's vital signs. The team looked on edge—even Cullen, who normally had his nose buried in a book during surgeries. Garrett turned to the young girl's pale, thin frame spread across the operating table. "She's so young."

"Horrible accident," Cullen said. "I saw it on the news. All her friends were killed, along with the driver of the other car." He shook his head.

Garrett looked at her vitals. She was barely hanging on.

The charge nurse helped to gown and glove him, and Garrett approached the head of the operating table.

He cleared his throat and held his palm out in expectation. "Let's begin. Scalpel." Nurse Sullivan slapped the scalpel into his palm, and Garrett closed his grip around it.

As he lowered the blade, one of the overhead lights flickered for an instant. It was as if there was distortion in the room, like a heat shimmer on a summer day. An unpleasant sensation spread through him, and ice flowed through his veins. Garrett lowered his scalpel and made the first incision, drawing blood.

He was over an hour into the procedure, fast at work, deep in concentration when the withdrawal symptoms hit. The room suddenly felt like a million degrees. Sweat beads ran down Garrett's brow and dripped into his eyes. It took a conscious effort not to wipe the sweat away—if he touched his brow with his gloves, he'd contaminate the sterile field.

He stepped away from the table. "Paige, suction. Someone get over here and wipe my face with a towel." As the charge nurse obliged, Garrett studied the operating field. Blood covered his gown and gloves, the drapes, and the floor. Two units of blood transfusions ran simultaneously at the head of the table, replenishing what had already been lost. Garrett took another look at the patient and felt his anxiety level rise. "Come on," he barked to the charge nurse, who was taking her time retrieving the towel. "I don't have time to stand around." She scurried over and dabbed away his sweat. "Finally," he muttered and shot her a dark look as she stepped back into place.

The headache hit hard. It felt like someone was stabbing each temple with an ice pick. "Dr. Lawrence, clamp that vessel," he said, trying to ignore the pain. "It's obstructing my sight-line."

Dr. Lawrence squeezed too hard, breaking the vessel.

Garrett swore. "Where the hell did you go to medical school?" He ripped the clamp away from her and let it clatter to the ground. "I can't believe they gave me a resident to do a surgery like this."

"I'm sorry, sir," Dr. Lawrence replied.

Garrett glowered at her. "Keep your mouth shut unless I ask you a question. I'm trying to save someone's life here." He stared at Nurse Sullivan. "What are *you* looking at? Focus on holding that retractor." Sullivan kept silent, obviously wary of drawing his wrath.

The ringing in his ears joined the headache, and sweat ran down his back. His heartbeat pounded in his chest like a drum. The scalpel shook in his hand.

No, he thought. Not now.

Most alcoholics begin withdrawal six to twelve hours after their last drink. But Garrett had built up a tolerance, and so his symptoms started earlier. Except for the scotch he'd consumed, he'd hadn't had any alcohol over the course of the day, yet his body was making him pay the price.

He glanced at the others, praying they hadn't noticed his slight tremor. Come on, he told himself. Focus.

That was when he saw it for the first time. He might not have noticed it if the light at the back of the room hadn't flickered again.

Someone—no, *something*—lurked in the shadows in the corner of the room. Though it appeared humanoid in form, the thing's features were distorted and blurred. The lurker's skin was grayish, and its enormous whitish orbital eyes were fixated on the table.

Garrett nearly dropped the scalpel in surprise. "What the holy hell is that?"

Dr. Lawrence frowned. "What? Sir, is something wrong?"

Garrett caught his breath. It was gone. Was he imagining things? "Nothing," he snapped. "Get back to work."

The glowing clock blared five forty-five in the morning, and he sighed. He felt like hell. Alcohol withdrawal always came in stages. The first phase consisted of the "shakes." Hand tremors, headache, profuse sweating, and increased anxiety and stress. He was going through all of them at once. Small mercy that the others hadn't noticed.

Despite his best efforts, the surgery was going poorly. The patient had suffered catastrophic damage in the accident. It was a miracle she had survived this long. Garrett found himself wondering what her life was like in the hours before the accident. The girl was at that perfect age when the possibilities were endless. Was she an honor student? An athlete, perhaps? Garrett dimly remembered what that was like—what *he* was like before he'd ruined his life. His family was gone, and his career was over. He swallowed hard. Maybe it wasn't too late for her.

"Clamp," he rasped, his voice grating against his raw throat. The thirst was insane.

A jet of blood squirted up and hit his goggles. An alarm rang out.

"Her blood pressure is dropping," Cullen said. "Oxygen saturation, too."

"Tell me something I don't know," Garrett answered. "We need more blood!" The lights flickered again, and he cast his gaze toward the corner of the room.

The lurker's features appeared more clearly now, though the light around it remained distorted and mingled with shadows. Its skin was not gray after all, but translucent, except there was nothing revealing underneath the surface. Ripples spread across the folds of its body, as if the skin had been stretched too tightly. The thing's arms and legs were disproportionately long and thin. The arms terminated in four elongated, claw-like fingers. Its feet didn't quite touch the ground. In fact, he couldn't see its feet at all; they seemed to disappear into the refracted light.

When he first saw the lurker, it had been pressed up against the wall in the corner of the room. Now, it hovered somewhere between the wall and the operating table, its gaze still set on the patient. It lingered longer than before, until Garrett blinked, and then it was gone.

Garrett's legs wobbled. He felt extremely claustrophobic. "She's stable for now," he managed to say. "Dr. Lawrence, take over. I have to break."

The others' eyes widened. "Is something wrong?" the charge nurse asked coolly.

"I need a bathroom break. That's all."

It wasn't unheard of for the head physician to break in the middle of a long surgery. Though it meant he would need to be gowned and gloved all over again. Garrett remembered an elderly surgeon with a bad prostate who had a penchant for taking frequent bathroom breaks. Garrett saw those breaks as an admission of weakness. Now, it was all he could do not to throw up across the operating table.

Garrett tore away his gown and gloves and stumbled out of the OR. Down the hall, he whipped open the bathroom door and collapsed in front of the toilet. After a few burps of vomit, he stood and grabbed hold of the sink to steady himself. He turned on the faucet and splashed cold water on his face. Garrett caught his reflection. He looked bad. His face was pale, his hair disheveled.

"It isn't real," he told himself, but his reflection didn't look particularly convinced. "You're seeing things."

Seeing things.

The second stage of withdrawal symptoms became more pronounced. Garrett was at risk for full-fledged withdrawal seizures, but perhaps more importantly, he was in danger of experiencing visual and auditory hallucinations. Like the thing he saw in the OR.

Without warning, Garrett's knees buckled. He felt himself twitching uncontrollably. There was no controlling the convulsions. Finally, his body stopped moving. He gripped the sink and vomited. He wiped strings of puke-slime from his mouth and breathed in the quiet loneliness of the bathroom.

Surely he couldn't return to the operating room in such a state. If he had another seizure while he was holding the scalpel . . . Garrett shook his head. But, he thought, that resident can't do this surgery on her own. It was far too late to transport the patient to another hospital, and by the time another vascular surgeon could be found, the girl might be dead on the table.

No, Garrett realized. It has to be me. I'm the only one who can save her. There isn't anyone else.

He wrapped a shaking hand around the bathroom doorknob and made the long, woozy walk to the OR.

"Dr. Marshall," the resident said when he returned. "Thank God!"

He nodded grimly and waited to be gowned and gloved. The charge nurse watched him more carefully with what seemed like suspicion in her eyes. Garrett averted his gaze and took his place in the operating field.

42

"Suture," he said to the nurse.

Every motion was a new torture. It took all his energy to concentrate. All the while, he knew he could collapse at any moment.

"We need to pick up the pace," he said, monitoring the patient's vitals. "She can't take much more of this."

"C'mon, hold on," he said to the girl. She didn't deserve to die this way, naked and spread over a cold table. She wouldn't either, if he could manage to work through his ill-effects.

The light fixture in the back of the room flickered. Not again, he thought. This time, Garrett felt the lurker's presence before he saw it. He tasted copper and raw, gamey meat. The creature reeked of sulfur and burnt nuts—the smell of hunger.

It stood inches away from the foot of the table, close enough now that he could finally see the thing's face. It was hideous; a horror born out of a nightmare. White eyes obscured. A round head sprouted off an abnormally long neck. The lurker's translucent skin peeled away in a web near the center of its face, exposing a circular mouth of narrow yellow teeth.

Garrett wasn't sure if he was hallucinating, or if the lurker was, in fact, real.

The creature fixated on the girl. Garrett realized that each time it appeared, it materialized closer to the table than before, which coincided with a decline in the patient's health. If the lurker was real—still a fairly big *if*—then it perhaps it was some form of reaper come to claim her life. Or maybe it was there to take her soul while she was on the verge of death, at her most vulnerable.

But why could *he* see it? Either he was hallucinating (still the far more likely scenario), or the alcohol delirium had allowed him to see something meant to remain invisible to human eyes.

Alarms went off across the operating room.

"The patient is flatlining," Cullen shouted. "She's going into cardiac arrest!"

Garrett started to respond, but the force of an explosive headache knocked him off balance. Trembling, he felt himself on the precipice of a seizure.

"Start CPR," Garrett stammered, his hand shaking violently.

"Dr. Marshall?" the resident asked, concerned.

"Just do it!"

"She's going into cardiac arrest," Cullen shouted, and the others watched in wide-eyed terror as Dr. Lawrence began chest compressions.

It's tamponade, Garrett thought. Blood surrounded the heart, preventing it from beating. If he didn't act quickly, the girl would die in minutes.

The lurker hovered over the table, its mouth inches from the girl's face. Its teeth parted, and it breathed in deeply, inhaling the air from the girl's body.

Delirium Tremens. The third and final stage of alcohol withdrawal, associated with alterations in consciousness, heightened hallucinations, and death.

His lot in life was the result of his choices. The girl, on the other hand . . . She had everything to live for. "I won't let you win," he said to the lurker, snatching a syringe from the equipment tray. He plunged the needle into the patient's pericardium and drained the blood in one fluid motion.

The beeping alarms silenced one by one. It's okay, he thought. She's going to be okay.

"You did it," Dr. Lawrence said, awe in her voice. "Her vitals are returning to normal."

Garrett went limp. The syringe dropped from his hand to the floor. He heard a scream as he flopped to the floor and began to seize.

The lurker no longer floated over the table—it hovered over him.

Garrett lay alongside the blood-trail left by the syringe. He smiled defiantly at the lurker. "I did it," he said as it lowered its horrid, toothy face toward him. "I beat you."

He heard the thing inhale and felt a tug at his lungs as the breath was sucked from his body. His eyes fluttered, and Garrett stilled.

C H I R U R G E O N

by Chris Pisano & Brian Koscienski

Ten-year-old Johnny Ghastson got his first glimpse of human gill-gites. He realized as he named them, while pulling their pink, pulpy mass from the dead boy's flayed body, that "gillgites" wasn't a technical term. In fact, he wasn't even sure what purpose gillgites served. But he felt more alive today than he had at any previous point in his eleven years of existence.

There, in the basement, he lifted his ensanguined hands to his face and breathed in the smell of accomplishment. Johnny lowered his hands. From the elbows down, his forearms were positively incarnadine with the essence of life. The operation was a success, and he had done it without a lab assistant. Fortunately, this was a simple experiment. If he decided to perform more delicate procedures in the future, then he would definitely need help. But where to find a willing assistant for his Ripperesque experiments?

Perhaps Bobby from down the street.

All great minds were decisive in nature, and so he quickly discarded this pundit. Bobby had discovered the secret of "pulling his pud," whatever that meant, two months ago, and hadn't been seen outside of school since. Johnny wished to know this secret, but it apparently required knowledge passed down from an older brother. Bobby had been vague with the details. Presumably, like most grand secrets, Bobby feared to share a part lest someone else wrest the whole from you.

This was no time to digress. Johnny's mind turned back to the dead body, and he remembered that cleanliness was a high priority if he expected to be able to continue his experiments. With a sigh and a smile, he considered how best to dispose of the body and the blood.

Johnny's father kept a homemade still in the far corner of the basement. The old man had attempted to make raspberry wine this time. The color of the liquid was just about a perfect match. With some alembics and plastic pipettes, Johnny fashioned a network of piping and set to siphoning the crimson blood into the wine. It was time-consuming, but he stayed on task with relative ease and marveled at the finished product. There was a noticeable change in viscosity, but it would likely mellow out quite nicely in about the same time it took for wine to ferment.

His father always drank heavily while concocting alcohol; he frequently made a considerable mess of things—in particular, the concrete basement floor. For this reason, he had installed a drainage system. The kitchen had an impressive butcher's knife, though his mother only used it as a placeholder in the knife block. Johnny loathed using such an unsophisticated instrument, but it had a sharp enough blade to do the job well. The job—cleaving a large piece into a smaller to transport to the forest for burial.

In the basement, Johnny twisted open the hose-nozzle until it achieved a steady flow. He rinsed his talented hands after attending to the gore, all the while reconsidering his stance on "pud pulling."

Perhaps it was for him, after all. At the very least, he made himself a mental note to ascertain the definition of a "pud." He'd searched the poster of the human muscular system several times and found no mention of such a body part. Must be an internal organ, he reasoned while casting an eye about the basement floor for any tainted spot he may have missed. His parents, wealthy and working their way toward wealthier, existed, rather than lived. Tidiness was directly proportionate to money, in their book, and they never turned an eye away from disorder.

For the next several weeks, Johnny trudged through his daily routine. School wasn't buzzing with news of the boy's disappearance. The boy really hadn't held any sort of a social life, so there were few friends for the authorities to question. Local news reported that the boy had left his house wordlessly and his parents hadn't missed him for the better part of two days. Word about school was that he was just another runaway, unhappy with his home life and lack of popularity at school.

Johnny began to notice how his father eyed him a little more often than he would have preferred. Not that he cast accusing stares. Rather, Johnny *felt* his father's watchful gazes, casting inconsequential suspicions toward his direction.

He eventually decided all was clear; time to plan another expedition.

That Friday when he came home from school, he stopped in the hallway outside the closed door of his father's home office, listening. His parents were engaged in a heated debate. With the intensity only a mother can muster, Mrs. Ghastson said that she was showing her son support in the way one expected from a nurturing mother. And, no, he wasn't awkward and socially backward. His father insisted that Mrs. Ghastson was blind to her coddling protectiveness and that no boy would grow up to be a self-sufficient man unless he was dealt with in a direct, albeit distant, manner. Johnny's mother declared the entire argument "absurd" and told Mr. Ghastson, "If you insist upon alienating yourself from our son, who, I might add, is very intelligent for his age, then that's your right, but don't come whining to me." She punctuated the end of the discussion by slamming the door shut, but not before saying, "We should have gotten Johnny a dog when he asked for one six years ago."

Johnny thought back to when he had asked for the dog. Yes, he'd been disappointed, but a new idea had bloomed within his mind like a springtime flower after the rain; his neighbors. The Robinsons' dog strayed into Johnny's backyard. It was a mangy, bluish-white mutt. It bayed and howled away the sun-filled days of summer, voicing its discontent at being tied up. But the Robinsons were redecorating their house, and the constant flow of contractors and consultants made it difficult to keep the hairy scoundrel from sneaking out the front door. So they hired a contractor to build a doghouse, then proceeded to chain the little beast outside. An ill-tempered brute should be kept hidden away; that was the opinion of Johnny's mother. Johnny, ever conscious of his mother's judgment, seized any opportunity to indulge her.

The little mutt proved quite friendly when it snuck over one night. After luring the fuzzball with tasty treats, Johnny got hold of the dog's collar.

With his bag of instruments in hand, he walked the dog into the woods, excited about his endeavor to discover the enigma of gray matter. He had brought a shovel for later but turned it into a multi-use tool by using it to crack the dog's skull open. Gloved hands, tweezers, and a scalpel took care of the rest. Turns out the mystery was not as complex as he had imagined. It was just a canine brain, and a lowly specimen. Johnny exchanged his bloody clothes with a clean set and buried all evidence of his experiment.

The Robinsons came calling that evening, Mrs. Robinson distraught over the missing mongrel. He had broken his chain, don't you know, and must have lost his way in the dark, the poor dear. Johnny's parents attempted sympathy, invited her inside for a glass of wine, which eventually led to a boorish discussion. She went home tipsy, and that was the end of that.

Satisfied that the Robinsons were none the wiser, Johnny had moved on to a more substantial subject in his first human experiment. Rumors surrounding the missing boy from months ago had evaporated like early morning dew. Now, Johnny enticed his next victim: a vagrant he had tempted from an alleyway with the promise of free alcohol and a warm meal. After two bottles of poisoned beer, the man lay dead beside his half-eaten hamburger. This time Johnny was determined to know the secret of cockles. He was familiar with the idea that they were related to one's heart, but again, his dogmatic search of human anatomy charts revealed no clue as to their true location. Johnny dug wrist deep into his chest for the elusive organ. Determination was rewarded when he found a fatty deposit attached to one of the heart's chambers. He found the object of his investigation and wondered how the crimson-streaked glob of yellow goo could warrant such regard from poets and romantics.

Satisfied that he completed his quest, he shrugged and then contentedly disposed of the body.

As Johnny suspected, no mention was made of the missing vagrant in either the paper or the local news. This was a godsend for one eager to continue his work.

Johnny wasted no time. He duped a youth via an online chat room. Terrance—a kid from another school district—and Johnny hit it off, Johnny fabricating his personal views to make himself more agreeable. Both kids shared a similar lifestyle in regard to their parents' utter disinterest in the lives of their children. When they finally met in person, Johnny alleviated Terrance from the resentments stuck in his craw.

Quite an interesting little part of anatomy, the craw. Right in the throat where he expected to find it—proof that his dissection skills had evolved far beyond biology class. While lesser beings were grossed out by the acrid smell of formaldehyde, the frog-like batrachian parts, and the rough feel of shark-thick skin, Johnny quickly bored. His quest lay in a higher calling—that of cataloging body parts not found in any reference book.

Johnny's father had always considered his son a bit too precocious. One evening, after many glasses of wine, which was his wont, Father and Son chanced to meet in the basement. It wasn't often that their paths crossed, according to the father's desire to escape his son's condescending behavior. On this particular occasion, however, goaded into action by the considerable consumption of alcohol, Johnny's father set his goblet of wine on the cellar stairs. He took a position there himself, speaking to his son with the curiosity that frequented those who already knew the answer to the question they were about to pose.

The exposition of his son had the tact that drunkenness made available—direct and obtrusive. It was like opening a door with a battering ram when picking the lock was a better option. The discussion—consisting of fatherly accusations and filial denials—lasted until Johnny's father reached the point of disinterest, the same emotion he used to swaddle his son during infancy. When the interrogation concluded, his father's attempt to rise was met with an inquiry from Johnny about the usage of an obscure tool in the basement. His father, who doted upon his tools the way other men doted upon their children, rushed to the defense of his power unit, lest it be used in a manner for which manufacturer's precautions existed. His explanation of the device's purpose was brusque, though his examination of its condition was thorough and lengthy—up to the very moment the blade of the hoe impacted his brow.

Though Johnny was of a small stature, he managed impressive leverage with the long-handled implement, and his aim was fiendishly accurate. His father's final breath was brief as he slumped to the floor. Within minutes, Johnny fondled his way through the examination of a pickled liver. He spent time prodding and pressing, searching for every nuance, each secret the brownish organ had to yield.

Certain he could learn no more, he expertly cleaned the mess. With a wisdom that belied his age, he placed clues that would lead his mother to believe his father had run off as he had threatened to do so many times.

Several days passed. Coworkers of Johnny's father, it turned out, noticed his absence. Johnny's mother, in her state of constant boredom and perpetual depression, had not. When it was brought to her attention, it seemed as if she couldn't care less. Officers came by to ask questions. Of course it was abundantly clear to her that her husband had run off with another woman. The investigator, finding no evidence of foul play, finished his questioning and said goodbye.

Despite his preadolescent ardor, Johnny was not impetuous. He whiled away the next several weeks behind winsome smiles and good conduct while in public. In private, he devoured every medical journal and magazine within reach. With concerted effort, he stemmed his unsavory desire to experience firsthand what he was still too young to learn through words. His best efforts yielded unsatisfactory results.

No more than a month had passed since he committed patricide, but he was back on the take, looking for yet another opportunity to conduct his grisly experiments.

His interest in the macabre only grew when he found a wrapped birthday present on his bed after school. Diligently, he untied the box and peered inside. A small silk bag peeked out at him. He opened the bag, turned it upside down. A shiny instrument dropped into his palm.

A new scalpel. Enamored with the new toy, he went back to the box. Surely there were more hidden treasures. His search yielded a note in his mother's handwriting.

For you, Johnny. Make a mother proud.

SUSPECT NUMBER TWELVE

by Michael L. Hawley

Chuck Engles glanced around the police station's waiting room. Others were being re-interviewed, too. So, all these idiots also own white vans? He shook his head and smirked. He knew these cops were no closer to finding the killer than they had been three months ago when they first questioned him. According to the detectives back then, someone saw a person in a light-colored Caravan throw a large wrapped object off a bridge and into the Pearl River, upstream from where they discovered the body of a woman.

A police officer walked by, escorting a tall, thin man wearing a white sleeveless shirt and handcuffs.

Engles scratched the exposed portion of his portly belly as he stared, then pulled his T-shirt down in a futile attempt to cover his skin. He wiped sweat off his balding head and glanced up at the clock. "This van thing must be the only clue they have," he muttered.

The interview room door opened. A young police officer sporting your typical buzz cut and a cliched athletic build—probably fresh from the academy—escorted another dude through the waiting room; some crazy-looking guy who could possibly be the murderer.

Just before the interview door closed, Engles spotted two detectives—the same ones who had questioned him months ago—seated behind a table. He chuckled and shook his head as the door clicked shut. Little did those boneheads realize, the killer they were so desperately searching for was within spitting distance. He'd given a solid alibi, which was the reason the cops hadn't bothered him. Until now.

The young officer walked back into the waiting room and approached Engles. "Mr. Engles? The detectives are ready for you now."

Engles eagerly got to his feet. *Now, let's see how much these guys really know.*

"Take a seat, Mr. Engles," the thin, elderly, gray-haired detective directed. "Been a few months since we last met. Let me reintroduce myself. Detective Hobbs." He turned toward the detective seated beside him. "This here is Detective Nebelecky, also on the serial killer task force."

Engles nodded to both of them.

Hobbs glanced up at the officer. "Officer Mitchell."

Mitchell nodded as he positioned himself in the back corner, standing with shoulders straight and rigid, his hands behind his back. He glanced at Engles. "Engles refused to have an attorney present for this interview."

Engles nodded with a confident, almost cocky grin. "Nothin' to hide, Detective. I'm here to help y'all." He paused, then added, "Pity about those women being tortured and murdered." That was the first of his lies today, and he was enjoying every minute of their attention. Hobbs studied his clipboard. "As you can see by the crowd in the waiting room, we've brought back everyone even remotely connected to the case to be re-interviewed." Hobbs paused. "We recruited an out-a-towner to help us in our investigation, and he's asked to retrace our steps in the investigation from the beginning. Before we begin the interview, Mr. Engles, I want to again offer you the opportunity to have a lawyer present."

Engles shook his head. "Thanks; I'm fine." He crossed his arms, reveling in outsmarting the police. It gave him almost as much pleasure as torturing and mutilating his lovelies. Well, that was an understatement, but the excitement of playing with these cops for a second time was incredible. Oh, the power he felt running through his veins!

At that moment, a hidden door situated behind the detectives opened, and Engles eyed a scrawny middle-aged man with steel-gray eyes, dressed in a tweed suit coat with elbow patches.

Detective Hobbs nodded to Engles. "Okay, but if at any time you want to end the interview, we'll stop." He glanced up at the man who'd just entered the room. "Allow me to introduce Dr. Edward Dunham, special agent and chief scientist for the FBI."

Dunham stared at Engles over his wire-rimmed glasses. "You're interview number twelve of thirty planned for today."

Engles humphed confidently. Hobbs gave his seat up to this so-called expert out-of-towner; most likely a Yankee. Engles stared into the eyes of the frail-looking doctor. Although FBI, he was clearly a weakling, and Engles loved to bully weaklings.

Dunham nodded to Hobbs, then smiled at Engles. "Good morning, Mr. Engles." He dropped his smile. "I want to be upfront with you. In a court of law, you are considered innocent until proven guilty." He shook his head. "But we are in no court and I am no judge." Dunham leaned forward. "I shall begin by assuming you're guilty, Mr. Engles, yet I'm giving you the opportunity to prove your innocence." He took in a deep breath, glaring at Engles. "Only then will I take you off the suspect list."

Engles popped his head back, taken off guard by Dunham's abrupt, aggressive approach. Engles dropped his gaze, giving this FBI agent the upper hand. He shook his head and regained his composure. "Hey, I did nothin' wrong. I just own a white Caravan." He pointed at Dunham. "I only agreed to come down here because I thought I could help."

Dunham nodded. "We appreciate that, Mr. Engles, but think back for a moment. I've read your statement." He glanced down at the file and flipped through the pages. "The victim's body was dumped off a bridge on a Friday evening—the same time a witness saw a white Caravan identical to yours on that bridge. Interesting to note that the witness was reported missing four days ago." Dunham read further, then glanced up at Engles. "Why were you traveling north on Emerson Road around one in the morning Tuesday night?"

Engles raised his chin, fully prepared for this question. "Coming back from a late night of fishin' at Briar Lake, like I do every Tuesday. It's my day off."

Dunham flipped to the first page of the file. "I see you work as a night watchman at a local business, is that correct?"

Engles nodded. "Yep; I'm one of two watchmen on duty at all times. My partner can vouch for me."

Dunham flipped further into the file. "I notice you lived in Vicksburg, Mississippi, in the mid-1990s." Dunham popped his head up. "There was a series of unsolved murders near Vicksburg in the mid-1990s. Those victims were mutilated not unlike the victims recently found here in Jackson."

Hobbs and Nebelecky shot each other a glance. Hadn't those two picked up on that coincidence?

"What're you trying to say?" Engles asked.

Dunham didn't answer Engles' question. "You wouldn't mind giving our detectives an account of your whereabouts at the time of these Vicksburg murders, would you?"

Engles frowned. "Not at all." He then threw up his hands. "Well, you'll find that I was real close to one of those murders, actually."

"Oh?" Dunham asked.

Nebelecky rolled his eyes.

"I saw my neighbor's dog on the loose around those woods where a woman was found, so I figured he must have been in there. Later that evening, I saw him walking back to his apartment."

"What were you doing at those woods, and why didn't you inform the police?" Dunham asked.

Engles shrugged. "I dunno why I was there. And I didn't think to call the police."

Hobbs chuckled and shook his head.

Dunham continued to scan the folder. "Are you familiar with an Annie Witherspoon?"

Engles sat up in his chair; anger filled his eyes. "Yeah, she was my neighbor, and I was proven innocent! Cleared of all charges!" Sure, he'd abused young Annie in the woods behind her house more than a decade ago, but besides her testimony, there was no evidence connecting him to the attack, especially when he luckily drummed up a convincing alibi. The key to getting away with anything was a solid alibi.

Dunham smirked. "Mr. Engles, you're presumed innocent at the onset." He sat back and shook his head. "However, I think the available evidence in this case merely precluded the jury to convict." He rubbed his gray stubbled chin. "Now, I read this same evidence as . . . not proving you innocent. You tortured and molested that twelve-year-old girl."

Engles tilted his head in confusion. "Wha . . . I was found not guilty! And, and, I had nothing to do with that McKenzie lady!" He gazed forward, puffing, fists clenched.

Hobbs whacked Nebelecky's leg under the table, grinning.

Nebelecky nodded back to Hobbs, beaming, and mouthed, "Nice."

"Well, before we get to the missing McKenzie woman, Mr. Engles," Dunham read the file for a few moments, "I'd like to ask you about the Peeping Tom incident you were convicted of seven years ago."

Engles sighed heavily. Yes, he was convicted in that case, but little did they realize his true intentions were more diabolical. Until someone called the cops. He replaced his frown with a grin. "So what if I like to stare at nude women. They like it anyway."

"And the duct tape and knife found on your person?" Dunham asked. "You weren't intending on entering that home, were you, Mr. Engles?" He shook his head. "You're not doing a very good job convincing me to take you off the suspect list."

Anger filled Engles' eyes. "I always carry a knife, and, the duct tape—"

"So, where were you two nights ago when Janice McKenzie disappeared?"

"Working; check my time card." Engles breath hitched. "Oh, I mean I was fishing at Briar Lake by myself."

Dunham glanced down at Engles' hand. "Mr. Engles, you have a fresh cut on your left index finger. How'd you get that?"

Engles unconsciously closed his hand into a fist and placed his other hand over it. He recalled cutting himself while slicing off his lovely's bra before tying her up. "I cut myself filleting a bass." Sweat began beading on his forehead, and he wiped it with his sleeve.

"May I see that knife?" Dunham asked.

"Sure," Engles replied. "But I cleaned the blood off."

"That's okay. That won't affect the test for latent bloodstains. I'll have a deputy pick it up tomorrow."

Engles' jaw dropped slightly and he felt the color fade from his face.

Hobbs snickered.

Nebelecky sneered.

Engles gulped. This interview was not as pleasurable as he thought it would be. He leaned forward. "You're a Yankee bastard asshole, and this interview's done. I'd like to go home. Now."

Dunham closed the file. "Okay, Mr. Engles. Thank you for being of service to us." He glanced up at the police officer in the corner. "It's late and we still have many more interviews, but before we have Officer Mitchell escort you out, I have one final question."

Engles cocked his head, awaiting the question.

"We happen to know that the six recent Jackson victims—all discovered in or near Pearl River—were first tortured with a cattle prod."

Engles righted his head. Nowhere in the papers did it say the police knew he used a cattle prod. He was sure he left no burn marks on his lovelies.

"I'm not saying we found a cattle prod yesterday at a . . ." Dunham paused. "Do you mind if we take your fingerprints before you leave?"

There was no way they could have found *his* cattle prod! Ah, so what! If they did raid his makeshift getaway and confiscate his cattle prod, he always wore gloves, so there was no way his fingerprints were on it.

"I'd be glad to," Engles responded.

Dunham stood. "We've taken up enough of your time. Thank you, Mr. Engles."

Officer Mitchell approached Engles. "Follow me, Mr. Engles."

* * *

Hobbs watched Engles through the open door as he walked away, then inched closer to Dunham. "I thought we weren't going to reveal your discovery of the use of the cattle prod, Dr. Dunham?"

57

Dunham winked at Hobbs. "He's our man, Detectives. Case files on serial killers show that offenders take great care in trying to reduce their DNA signature. In other serial killer cases I've encountered with a similar MO, the offenders used a separate location other than their domicile to torture and murder their victims. Chances are he has a hideaway, and if he does, he might think we've found it.

"And our priority is finding Janice McKenzie alive." He paused. "I believe he's going to check to see if we indeed discovered his cattle prod, and wherever that location is, Janice McKenzie is nearby."

Nebelecky glanced at Hobbs and shook his head. "Dr. Dunham, we eliminated Mr. Engles from the suspect list three months ago because he had an alibi."

"He was working with his fellow night watchman," Hobbs interrupted. "His timecard showed he clocked in at precisely 9:00 P.M. and clocked out at 6:04 A.M. Another watchman confirmed he was at work."

"He admitted he left work to pick up food at McDonald's around eleven but immediately returned," Nebelecky continued, "and his credit card receipt stated 11:04 P.M. McDonald's is ten miles in the other direction from the bridge, making it impossible for him to have been at the bridge at 11:06 P.M."

Dunham placed his index finger on his lips. "I purposely put Engles in a state of agitation before asking him where he was two days ago, in hopes of detecting a rehearsed response. The glitch you saw in his reply was textbook deception. I don't think McDonald's requires a signature for such a small purchase, but if they did in this case, we need to get it and compare signatures."

Hobbs glanced at Dunham. "That was brilliant questioning by the way, Dr. Dunham. Working his emotions, then seeing him covering up that cut on his finger; another classic case of deceptive behavior." He looked toward the file on the table. "Guilty until proven innocent; I love it."

Dunham grinned. "You set him up perfectly, Detective Hobbs. He believed he had the advantage."

Nebelecky elbowed Hobbs and grinned. "Dr. Dunham, if you're convinced he's our man, so am I."

* * *

Engles peeked at his watch; it read 11:05 P.M. He scanned the dark streets in his neighborhood from behind the overgrown cedar shrubbery in his front yard. He had unscrewed his driveway light earlier in the day, so the closest light source, a distant street light, created dim, long shadows. Perfect for a getaway, he thought to himself. There were no strange vehicles around, and no unusual activity. The neighborhood was boring as usual, and that gave him comfort. He didn't plan on visiting his hideaway for another few days, when his lovely was even more exhausted, less obstinate, and closer to death.

But he had to know. Did the cops really stumble upon his hideout? It was too coincidental. How many people in this area owned a cattle prod?

He suspected it could be a trap, but anxiety got the better of him. Satisfied he wasn't being watched by the police, he slipped inside his Caravan, which was parked in his darkened driveway. He sat motionless in the van's dark interior for at least ten minutes, ensuring that no one was watching him. Again satisfied, he pulled onto the street, headlights off.

After about a mile or so, he turned on his lights, driving in a random pattern through the mountain roads until he was convinced he was not being followed.

Engles quickly hopped out of his van and then dashed through the flap of his rundown, makeshift hideaway in the woods. He held his breath as he shined his flashlight onto the rotting two-by-four where he hung his torture toy. There it was; his special cattle prod. Relieved, he exhaled.

Those bastards are far from catching me, he thought to himself.

They were guessing about the cattle prod, pulling at threads. His cocky grin returned, then he shifted his gaze to the tarp-covered pit in the center of the hideaway.

He wondered how his lovely was. "Oh Lovely," he called out. "I'm here! Did you miss me?"

He snatched his cattle prod and approached the pit. Throwing aside the brown tarp, he shined the flashlight on Janice McKenzie, tied and gagged where he had left her. He could see that she was dazed but certainly alive.

"Since I'm here, Lovely, it's time to play." He climbed down the rope ladder. As he neared McKenzie, he watched for the fear in her face; it made him shudder with excitement. "Hello, my Lovely. I see you stayed up for me. How sweet."

McKenzie wriggled her body into the ground as he approached.

"Oh, don't be shy," Engles teased. "It's—"

Crash! Engles heard the sound of wood collapsing onto the ground above his head. He shielded his head and looked upward through his arms. Men pointed rifles directly at him.

"Get on the ground! Face down! Now, now, now!"

Engles quickly dropped to the ground. His body went cold. He thought of nothing other than how quickly his hands and feet were bound.

E S C A L A T I O N

by J. B. Toner

Originally appeared in December 2018 issue of Horror Zine.

A rain of apes. They fell mostly on the windy plains beyond Chicago's limits, but thousands hit the streets and rooftops, plunging from troubled skies to douse the neighborhoods in blood and fur. They lived till they landed, and such a symphony of howls and yammerings had not been heard. Many people hungered in the city, yet the most desperate of the poor would not try the flesh of those fallen apes, handiwork of the experimenting Archons. Even the crows ate nothing but the eyes.

They were outside of town when it happened—out in the Corpse Lands. Decatur lowered his 12-gauge, raised his goggles, and said, "Rainin' monkeys."

"Ayup," said Tomlinson.

Rookwood spat.

They moved on.

The Dead were getting harder to find. Good news for travelers, bad news for hunters. Also bad news for the species, but that was no longer news. Twenty years since They arose, and less news every day.

Father Joe pointed. "Yonder."

Beyond the shale outcroppings, a grove of pines. Half a mile, maybe. Man-forms in rotted clothes were moving. Omaha gave a sharp nod and went ahead through the late afternoon shadows to a clump of dust and old dead grass, just tall enough to prop his M24. The other four fanned out and closed in slowly on the pines.

Omaha's first shot: square in the hip of the nearest one. Kneecaps were too small a target. The Dead turned and crouched and came loping toward Omaha with their skinless knuckles scraping the pebbled earth. Decatur stepped in on their flank, fired the second shot, smashed the pelvis of another one. Then wiry Rookwood's katana and barrel-chested Tomlinson's sledgehammer, pulping and severing. Father Joe moved in with the scooper and started snatching out eyeballs. One got too close; Omaha popped it, center mass, to knock it down, and Decatur smashed its head with the shotgun butt. As it was getting back up, the padre plucked it. It flopped down as a final-dead.

"Felix!" Rookwood shouted. Behind: three stragglers. Tomlinson shoved the first one toward Rookwood, who pinballed it back to him with a flying spin kick, then it ran straight into Tomlinson's brutal clothesline, hitting the ground hard enough to spray dirt clods. Rookwood drew his Glock 18 in midair and came down raking the knees of the other two Dead with automatic fire. Father Joe pounced and plucked, and then the hunt was over.

Omaha came sauntering. "'Nother day at the office, huh, boys?"

"Ayup," said Tomlinson.

When the Archons rose from the waves and the world's electricity died, millions of people died with it. At first, the survivors used fearful names for the victims—the Walking Dead, the Hungry Dead. But there was simply no need for adjectives. *All* dead men walked; all dead men hungered. Not for brains, not for blood, but for eyes. And only taking the eyes of the Dead could give them final death. So the government (there will never not be a government) issued high bounties for every pair of rotten, soulless eyes.

The sun was bloodying the west. "Let's make camp in them pines," Decatur said.

Their fire began as the daylight ended. They hunkered, and they ate their jerky and their limes. Then they counted up.

"Hundred'n fifty-seven brace of eyeball," Omaha said. "Good haul."

Decatur nodded. "How 'bout ammo?"

"That ain't so good, Moe. Used more'n we shoulda, that fracas."

"Last three came outta nowhere," Rookwood said.

"No one's blamin'. But them bastards back in town's chargin' more and more for iron these days. We either gotta conserve or start cuttin' back on whiskey."

"Conservation got my vote."

"You and me both, brother. Speakin' of?"

Father Joe produced an old scuffed bottle of The Glenlivet. "Bless us O Lord and this Thy scotch, upon which we are about to get tore."

"Amen," said the others, and the bottle made the rounds.

"What about some harmony, Dude?" Decatur said.

Deuteronomy Omaha, late of Barney, Kentucky, dug in his satchel and emerged with his harmonica. "I call this one, 'Home, Home, with the Deranged.'"

And they drank and they sang beneath the dying moon. More of the Dead might be about, but a time came to stop worrying. Finally, with a pistol in his left hand and a sword in his right, Rookwood got to his feet. "Gotta go piss."

"First piss of the night!" Omaha proclaimed. "Make a wish out there, Patrick."

"You know it."

Thirty seconds later, he came back with his fly unzipped and a strange look on his face. "Guys—come look."

They followed him from the pine grove and over the lip of the hill beyond. There they stopped and stood.

"Jesus, Rooks, what'd you wish for?" said Omaha.

In the valley below them was an Archon. No one could mistake that *thing*, a many-tentacled slug the size of a football field, blasphemous and pale in the starlight. Named for the monster-gods of ancient Gnosticism, they had arisen and gone about their own business, never going out of their way to plague mankind—but their business, whatever it was, had sucked up the power behind all technology and brought about the ghoulish obscenity of shuffling undeath, which now awaited every living soul.

"Damned filth," muttered Father Joe.

Omaha squinted. "Is it dead, ya think?"

"Let's go see," Decatur said.

They picked their way down through the brambles and scree to the base of the hill, fanned out, and advanced uncertainly. When they were within about twenty yards of it, Omaha stooped and picked up a rock. "Hey, you bag a' shit!"

The rock hit the Archon's side with a squish, stuck for a moment, and then clattered to the earth.

"Yup, it's dead," said Tomlinson.

They had all heard the stories: mankind's most powerful weapons leaving the Archons untouched, stopped by some unseen aura surrounding them. It was said that the hateful slug-gods had neither retaliated for the attacks nor even seemed to notice them.

Decatur pointed. "The bounty."

A standing reward had been offered, vast in sum, for any who could harvest their grotesque genetic material. Prized above all would be one of their eyes.

The hunters gathered by the blubbery mass of the creature's forehead. Three dull gray orbs, six feet in diameter, dribbled reeking pus.

"Patrick."

"My pleasure." Rookwood holstered his sidearm and plunged his blade into the socket. The flesh cut away easily, and he began to saw the eye loose.

"You guys ever heard of one of these things dying before now?" Omaha asked.

The others shook their heads.

"Folk say they got no souls—that's why they gotta take ours. Why they took all the electric lights. What if they're runnin' out?"

"Runnin' outta what?"

"Us. Ain't been a baby born in Chicago in near ten years now. We're going extinct."

Silence.

"Gimme a hand, Felix," Rookwood said.

He and Tomlinson grabbed fistfuls of gristle and rolled out the squelching eye. A cord like an optic nerve came trailing after it, and Father Joe sliced it with a Bowie knife.

"Wonder if that's why they made it rain monkeys back there," Omaha said, distant. "Trynna make humans. Make souls."

"They won't," the priest grunted. "Only God can."

"Hope you're right, Padre."

"All right," said Decatur. "Rookwood, Tomlinson—you take these back to town and buy a horse and cart." He tossed the sack of eyes to Tomlinson. "We'll stand watch, make sure no other hunters come along."

"Hold up," said Rookwood. "I still gotta piss."

"The hell you doin', Rook?"

He was hunched down and making his way into the gaping socket. "Gonna piss on this thing's brain."

"Man, are you out of your—aw, suit yourself."

The other four ambled around, gazing up at the massive carrion and the glimmering worlds above. The night wind blew and the peepers sang. A minute or two went by. "Hey, Pat, you okay in there?"

Then he came out, flailing. One of his hands was clenched around something, and orange light was spilling through his fingers; the other was clawing desperately at his own face. Blood ran down his shoulders. "Get it off! Get it offa me!"

"What is it? What's on you?"

"*My skin!*"

Whatever he was holding fell, and he ripped at his arms with both hands, screaming like a man in a pyre. They grabbed him, tried to hold him, but he writhed and kicked and spat until Tomlinson hauled off and hit him with a right cross that made a sound like a suicide hitting the asphalt. Rookwood went limp.

They laid him down and put a jacket under his head. Omaha knelt by the glowing orange jewel and peered.

"Careful, Dude."

"Ain't gonna touch it. Just wanna see . . . what . . ." A look of puzzle-ment grew in his face. Then dawning horror. He started touching his hands and forearms, his eyes widening ever more. "What is this? This shouldn't—gotta—get this off." And he started to scratch.

"Dude? Dude!"

Tomlinson raised his sledgehammer, swung it like a golf club, and the jewel went flying into the scrub grass.

"Thought you was gonna hit Omama for a second there," Decatur said.

Father Joe knelt and shook him gently. "Dude. Can you hear me?"

Omaha blinked and rubbed his eyes. "Yeah, I—I'm here, Padre. I'm here."

"What did you see?"

"It was like—can't rightly—gimme a minute." He sat down in the dust, and the others followed suit. After a long moment, he spoke slowly, like a man recalling ancient memories. "It was like seein' Earth from space. In the old pictures. Except it was all wrong. All this stuff—skin and dirt and bodies—it felt like bein' wrapped up in a suit made of mag-gots. The whole, whattayacallit—*matter*. It felt like matter was a prison. Made of barbed wire. I just wanted out."

Rookwood chimed in, his voice mostly groan. "Yeah. What he said."

Tomlinson gave him some water. "You okay?"

"Think so. You about broke my damn jaw."

"Panicked. Sorry."

"'Sokay, buddy. 'Preciate the save."

"What the hell was that thing, anyway?" Decatur asked.

"Dunno. It was stuck in the skull, right where the optic nerve came out. Looked pricey, thought it might be worth somethin'."

Father Joe was ruminating darkly. "What you said—it's what They see. Time and space as an abomination."

Omaha nodded. "That squares with what the Gnostic are always say-ing." (One couldn't walk down the street without encountering Gnostic prophets.) "Like the world was one big mistake."

"Heresy."

"I ain't disputin' that, Padre, but you gotta know how your enemy thinks in order to beat him."

"Yes." The priest got up and walked into the dark, following the orange gleam. They scrambled up and came after him.

"Padre, don't be a damn fool," Decatur said sharply.

"It's all right. Felix can always bash me if need be." He picked up the jewel. "Now, don't let me pull my face off. But don't stop me the second I look uncomfortable. Give it a minute or two." He made the sign of the cross. "Lord, by your name save me; by your strength defend my cause." And then he looked.

They watched the padre. Blood drained from his face, and his shoulders started to move back and forth as if straitjacketed. Almost inaudibly: "No. No, no, no." They glanced at each other, tense, half-raising their hands every time he twitched. "Not true. It's not true, not true."

"Father Joe? You hear me?"

Abruptly, his eyes squeezed shut and he lowered the jewel. "I'm okay." He fumbled for his hip flask and took a long pull. "I'm okay." He walked back toward the Archon, unscabbarding his Bowie knife. Carved a tiny chunk out of one of the eyes. And popped it into his mouth.

"Padre, what the fuckin' fuck!"

He turned toward them, and his gaze was strange: half-looking past them like a man in a dream, but not unfocused; rather, peering intently at something unseen. "Yes. Of course."

"What do you see?" said Omaha.

"Their world. They're amphibians, you know. Half outside. In the spirit world. But they've got no spirit of their own."

"I wanna see."

Decatur winced. "Dude, come on."

"I wanna see it, Moe. I done ate worse than this in my day; we all have." He walked over, carved a piece, gulped it down with a slosh of whiskey. "I don't—oh. Oh! Whoa."

The other three exchanged glances. "How do we know it won't turn our willies into tentacles or some such?" Rookwood demanded.

"You're the one unzipped hisself inside the thing's skull, Rookwood."

"Yeah, I mean—I guess."

"I wanna see too," Tomlinson said quietly.

"Aw, why not. They're gonna eat all our souls anyhow."

Decatur shook his head. "Like bein' back in high school. All the cool kids are eatin' Archon eyes."

"So, you in?"

"S'pose."

They carved and they gulped, one after another. And for each of them, the veil of matter was rent. The night became an orange and purple dome, fifty times higher and wider than the cosmos they knew, stretching back through numberless ghastly eons; the earth underfoot, a pink and green expanse of rippling sea, girded by no horizon, extending through insane infinities. And the five of them stood, minuscule and meaningless, in the flat détente of those abysms of wave and sky.

"Welp," said Rookwood, "I no longer need to piss."

Tomlinson's voice: "Uh, guys? How come I can't see you?"

"Squint, Felix," Omaha said. "We're right here, you just gotta, like—tilt your head."

"Y'all fuzzy."

"Spitballing here," said Father Joe, "but my guess is the Archons have never attacked human beings because they can't see us. All they see is souls and energy. So as long as you're alive, your soul is camouflaged in skin."

"You guys feel that?" Decatur said abruptly. "That pull?"

Chorus of "Yeah." The flowing tides around them moved urgently westerly. Their feet were planted in the dust of the physical world, but their hearts felt the tug.

"This is what they feel—what we feel—when we die. This is how they suck us up."

"We have to stop this," Father Joe said grimly. "Whatever it takes. We have to kill them."

"Well we ain't dead men," Rookwood said. "Let's follow it and shoot whatever we find."

"Just keep squinting at the real world," Omaha said. "We won't do no good if we follow the pull off the edge of a cliff."

They moved out on foot, following the maelstrom-like tug. Tilting and peeking and shaking their heads, they managed to negotiate the rocks and dales of the corporal universe; all the while, they let themselves be reeled along like fish on a black steel hook. At the end of an hour, they crested a ridge and stared down bleakly to the vale beyond.

"The God-damn monkeys."

From the east, from Chicago, a slow meandering stream: the thin, pale souls of apes. A dozen titan slugs, their mouths wide-gaped to swallow. The Archons had succeeded.

"They don't need us anymore."

"No," said Father Joe. "No, in Christ's name, no!"

And he charged down the hill, unholstering the sawed-off Remington that swung beside his hip flask. One of the monster slugs was opening its grisly maw to swallow an apely soul. The padre sprinted straight into its darkling gullet and fired both barrels into the roof of its unholy demon mouth.

The others stood frozen for half a second. "It's bleeding!" Omaha yelled. "Let's go!"

They followed their madcap chaplain into the fray, firing rifles, shotguns, pistols, and derringers into the mouths of the monster gods. The Archons bellowed like the everlasting wrath of Satan, and four of them flopped over dead. The others reared their ghoulish bulk and waved their tentacles, and then rocks began to shower from the sky.

"Let's get the hell outta here!"

Scrambling desperately, they fled the vale as mountains' worth of stone came showering down. The Archons, aura-clad, shrugged off the plummeting debris. But now they knew. We knew.

The vision of the Archon's eye was fading. The moon was far above; the night mist hung about the hunters like a shroud. Decatur racked a shell into the chamber, and the empty one went flying. "They're vulnerable when they feed."

"Yeah," said Rookwood. "But also, they can make their own food now. All they gotta do is conjure mountains down on all of us."

"So the war's done escalated. We can hurt 'em now, but they can hurt us more. We gotta get the eyes back to Chicago. Let everybody know."

"Yeah, but—first we get the bounty, right?"

The others glanced around.

"Well, yeah. 'Course we get the bounty first."

"All right then, let's go save the fuckin' world."

"Amen, brother mine."

"Fuckin' A."

CHIHUAHUAS

by Will Falconer

Chihuahuas. Never liked them.

Their insubstantial pint-sized bodies teeter on anorexic legs. Their pointy, oversized ears don't hear a word you say to them. Their fangs jut out at freakishly weird angles. They shake and shiver like they've got Parkinson's or something.

And their bulging, watery eyes. Without looking too closely, they seem so sweet and innocent until you reach out to pet them and they bare their sharp little teeth and nip at you and snarl. Savage, malicious, remorseless little beasts. Not to mention their incessant high-pitched ARR-ARR-ARR-ARR-ARRing that's not even barking, really, but more like a hellish squeaky toy's pathetically desperate and incredibly annoying attempt to deter you from drop-kicking it into the next zip code.

I mean, really, if you shave a chihuahua, what do you have? An oversized rat. I rest my case.

So, what's that got to do with the price of tequila in Cancún, you say? I'm getting to that—there's plenty of time—but first, it's important that I tell you just how much I loathe those spastic little shits to the deepest, darkest, most malevolent recesses of my otherwise dog-loving soul.

Okay (deep breath), please be patient. I'm still new to this storytelling thing, and I'm only giving you this testimony now because it helps to pass the time; something I have an abundance of now.

I didn't always. I used to consider every minute to be a precious and valuable resource. I was a lawyer at a prestigious law firm in downtown Los Angeles. You might know the name of the firm if I told you. You'd definitely recognize the firm's name if you're among the entertainment industry elite, but it's not important, not unless you're impressed by that kind of thing. (If you're not, insert your own lawyer joke here.)

Most weeks I'd work at least seventy hours—more if I went in on Saturday, which I usually did. I made it a rule, the bendable kind, not to work on Sundays. Not because I was religious, which I most definitely was not (unless you count my faithful gym workouts), but because the partners paternalistically tell all the younger lawyers not to—although those pasty-faced, aging white men doth protest too much, methinks. Actually, meknows because they're definitely impressed when a hotshot up-and-comer practically moves into his or her office, and there were several new young rising stars in the office, so the competition was fiercer than ever.

I'd even put in a few consecutive seven-day weeks myself lately—uncharacteristic for me because even though I was working my ass off to impress the partners, I didn't want them to see me as a sycophantic suck-up. I wasn't some untested rookie. I didn't have to be at their beck and call 24-7. No need to burn myself out. I was established. I had street cred. I was—and this is going to sound arrogant, but I don't care anymore—smarter than the other guy; always two, three steps ahead of the competition. I always knew some unanticipated shit would hit the proverbial fan, so I abided by that old special-ops strategy: Always have a Plan B, a Plan C, a Plan D. I never needed to sweat.

I was prepared.

But even with all that going for me, on one particular manic Monday—as it turned out, my last day with the firm—the thought of lunch had not even crossed my mind. I was too busy scoring some serious, non-sycophantic partner points by quickly and efficiently putting out more than my fair share of fires that day. I'll spare you the details because, believe me, I know what's in the details.

I'd already worked over fourteen hours, and I was ravenous. I still had some work to do, a few loose ends to tie up, but I needed to clear my head, to get out of the office for a few minutes even if it was just to grab some takeout. I took the elevator down to the lobby and stepped out into the unseasonably warm night air.

I was thinking Mexican. I knew of several decent restaurants in the vicinity of Olvera Street. It was a bit of a trek from the office, but I didn't feel like getting the Mercedes out of the garage, and it was a nice night. I ignored the grumblings of my empty stomach and set off on a quest for chips and guacamole, charred but juicy carne asada, and a margarita at the bar while I waited.

As I perambulated the streets of this not-so-fair city, I observed the usual cast of characters. Young couples glowing with that look of mutual love (or lust), taking their time on their way to a romantic table for two. Women in twos or threes going who knows where, chattering away about their asshole bosses or their cheating boyfriends or their inconsiderate friends. Blue-collar working people, trudging to the bus stop or to the stairs descending to the Metro, to shabby tenements where they squander their free time in front of the TV after a long day of cooking other people's food or cleaning other people's toilets.

And the pathetic homeless people. Who can forget them? Seems like there are more of them every day—mumbling to imaginary confidants or raging at imaginary tormentors, huddling against walls, sleeping it off in doorway niches. Or, if they're resourceful, pushing shopping carts that hold their treasures: aluminum cans, plastic bottles, miscellaneous junk, what's left of their hopes and dreams. There but for the grace of God, as they say—although I certainly didn't believe in anything as nonsensical as an interventionist God. Just a figure of speech.

My musings were interrupted by a scruffy representative of that despicable canine breed I was speaking about earlier—a chihuahua. It ran up to me—no, "ran" isn't the right word because there was something wrong with its back left leg. It held it up in the air, never putting weight on it, so the mangy cur was half-hopping, half-ambling toward me. I kept an eye on the little ankle-biter as it yipped up at me a few times, turned, and amble-hopped over to a sign made from a small piece of greasy corrugated cardboard lying on the dirty sidewalk in front of the building I was passing. Upon it someone had written:

POR FAVOR

HELP A POOR CRIPPLE

DIOS BENDIGA

Sitting on one corner of the sign was an aluminum can with the label peeled off. For donations. On the aluminum someone had drawn, in what looked like black permanent marker, symbols I didn't recognize—geometric shapes and dots and lines both straight and curved. A few crumpled dollar bills snuggled inside the can.

"Buenas noches, señor."

The voice startled me. I hadn't seen her in the shadowy doorway niche, but now she sat up from her reclining position on a modest pile of grimy blankets or coats or whatever they were. A street person, her face obscured in darkness.

"You spare change for my cripple friend? Maybe even little more? You see he need doctor."

"A veterinarian," I corrected.

She leaned forward, and her countenance came into the light. Her face and hair were clean, and she was not as old as I had first imagined when I heard her voice from the shadows, although it was difficult to tell just how old she was. I also noted that she was what you might call handsome, not in a mannish way, but—and this is going to sound weird because of her lowly position—she had a dignified bearing, like she was inhabiting a sublime realm far above and only tangentially related to her current impoverished circumstances.

She squinted up at me, displaying delicate crow's feet at the corners of her dark eyes. "Sí, a . . . what you call it, bet—"

"Veterinarian."

"Someone kick him. Maybe leg broke."

"Maybe you found an old stray you could use to scam some drinking money out of gullible dog-lovers."

"I no drink." She tilted her head to the side. Now she was curious. "You no like dogs?" Her little partner-in-crime sat down and panted, its disgusting pink tongue—disproportionately long, I thought—hung down between its crooked, pointy teeth.

"No, I like dogs. Just not chihuahuas."

"Por qué? They creatures of God like other dogs."

"Creatures of the devil, more like."

"Ahhh, you know el diablo?"

"Not personally, but if I run into him, I'll send him your way." I started off.

"I know devil."

I stopped and turned around. My empty stomach protested, but my curiosity about what variation of the hackneyed I-was-lost-but-now-I'm-found story she was peddling overrode its growling objections.

"He is well known to my people."

"Your people are devil-worshipers?"

"Chantales."

"Doesn't ring a bell."

"People de las montañas. How you say?"

"Mountains. They're cognates."

"Sí, mountains. De Oaxaca. En Mexico."

"You're a long way from home."

"Sí, but God is in all things."

"Well, it was nice chatting, but I have to go. Have a good night."

"Every night is good night. Our god, Tezcatlipoca, he is god of night."

"Whose god?"

"We. Witches." She stood but remained half-hidden in the shadows.

"You're a witch?"

"Sí, I was born under sign of rain. As girl I trained by senior witch. He love me. He can change. To jaguar."

"Of course. I suppose you can, too."

"No." She seemed to find this amusing. "I become crow."

"A crow?"

"Sí, crow. Do not be afraid of this."

"I'm not afraid. Why would I be afraid?"

She stepped forward into the open and stood before me on the side-walk as oblivious pedestrians passed us by. Her feet were bare.

"Good." She wore a long white dress with red trim and a large scarf wrapped around her head and neck. She looked more like Aimee Semple McPherson than a witch. Her dark eyes studied me. I felt uncomfortable and—I know this is going to sound weird—defenseless.

"I'm a lawyer. You should be afraid of me." I thought a little levity might lighten what had become an oppressive mood. I was wrong.

"Can you put stones in stomach or worms in veins? Can you fill lungs with swamp water or make bones so brittle they break? Can you come to me in night and suck my blood?"

I took a step back. She was a little close.

"So now you're a vampire?"

She also found this amusing and stepped even closer, staring up into my eyes, less than a foot from my face.

"No, but I make potion make you love me." And then, as if she'd been mulling this over for a while, "But I no want."

"Well, great meeting you, but . . . gotta go." I tried to go around her. I was so flustered I didn't even realize I was heading back toward the office. She sidestepped and blocked the way. Light on her feet, this one. I brushed her out of the way, not hard, but firmly.

She staggered but maintained her balance, fortunately. She rubbed her upper arm as if I'd injured her, and she studied me. Her dog skittered over, unsteady as a wobbly tripod, and sunk its teeth into my pant leg. I shook my leg, trying to dislodge it, but it held on, a ferocious, guttural growl emanating from its straining jaws and neck. I reached down and grabbed it with both hands, feeling its warmth. I pulled till my pants ripped, but at least I was free of my attacker's grip—or so I thought.

He bared his gruesome teeth and snarled, twisting and biting until one of his crooked fangs drew blood. I winced and threw him down. He hit the concrete with a sickening sound and lay on the filthy sidewalk, twitching and staring off into nothing, not even trying to get up. He never would.

In a daze, the woman knelt by the dog. She stared down solemnly at its broken, lifeless carcass. Finally, she looked up at me, not with anger or hatred but with a dispassionate, faraway gaze.

"You say you do not know el diablo. You will. He already know you."

"You're . . ." I was going to say, "You're crazy, lady," but I restrained myself.

I could have left, could have made my escape, but something—guilt? responsibility? pity?—rooted me to the spot where I stood in my tailored suit, the pants now torn and worthless. A few looky-loos had stopped to gawk. A little Monday-night entertainment. Something you don't see every day, not even on so-called reality TV. I sensed the scrutiny of strangers' eyes upon me and took a different tack.

"I'm sorry about your dog, but he attacked me. He bit me, for God's sake. Look at the blood."

I held my arm out toward one of the onlookers, a slender woman in a red power pantsuit who was looking down at the dog. She took no notice of my injury but instead squatted near the motionless little body that looked even smaller now that it was lifeless. The eyes of the women found each other.

"I think he's dead." The woman in red rose and redirected her clinical gaze toward me. "You'll live." She took out her cell phone, tapped it with a stylus, and held the phone up to her ear. I assumed she had dialed the police, but then . . .

"Hi, Danielle. I'll be a little late. No, everything's fine, I just . . ." Her voice trailed off as she moved away for some privacy, leaving the self-professed witch kneeling alone by her expired companion.

"Look, I didn't mean to—"

"Is only for God to kill," she intoned without looking up.

I stood—stiff, awkward, self-conscious—sensing the judgmental bystanders milling around, making comments under their breath. I avoided looking any of them in the face. I kept my eyes on the woman and the dead dog, unpleasant as that was, trying to clear my head enough to think of a way to extricate myself from this shitstorm.

"I'm really sorry. I—"

She rose. Most of the rubberneckers had already lost interest and shuffled off, moving on with their busy lives. The woman faced me, her eyes locked on mine.

"You will haunt streets of city till is no longer city."

I didn't know what the hell to say to that, so I said, "Okay, whatever."

Her eyes gleamed with an intensity that penetrated my being. That may sound corny or New Agey or whatever to you, but it's the only way I can describe it. When I first saw her, she had seemed like just another street person, a little crazy maybe but essentially harmless. In a matter of seconds, she had transformed herself into a woman of strength, knowledge, power. A witch.

For a few unreal moments, I was transfixed. I could picture her in the mountains of Mexico, arms waving as she cast spells, head thrown back as she summoned spirits, cackling malevolently as she put a curse on those who had crossed her.

"You will haunt streets of city till is no longer city."

"I hear you, but you know this hoodoo evil-eye mumbo jumbo is just horseshit, right?" I wasn't trying to be mean; just trying to neutralize her spell, so to speak, so I added, "No offense."

Her eyes glazed over—that faraway look again—like she was somewhere else.

"I no give evil eye. I give evil eye, you no live. Is only for God to kill."

"You're not getting it. I don't believe in God. There is no God. No magic. No astral plane. No heaven. No hell. No devil. No Great and Powerful Wizard of Oz. Nothing. Got it? Nada."

Her eyes glared with defiance. "If Catholic priests with Bibles and holy water and Spanish conquistadors with swords and guns no destroy belief de los brujos, what chance you got?"

I started to feel weird. Otherworldly. My head was floating in a cauldron of witch's brew. I probably just needed some goddamn food in my stomach.

"Aztecs feared us." Bubble bubble. "Mayans feared us." Toil and trouble. "You fear us."

Bullshit. I had no fear of facing off against Los Angeles power brokers and Hollywood moguls. What made her think she could scare me? "Look . . ." I took out my wallet—I noticed my hands were shaking—pulled out a Benjamin, and held it out to her. "Please. Take it. Again, I'm really sorry."

"No. But you will be." She snatched the bill out of my hand. "You will—"

"Uh-huh, haunt the streets forever. Got it." I turned and walked away.

"That is bad news."

"You think?" I said over my shoulder, walking in the right direction this time.

"Now for good news."

I stopped and spun on my heel to face her. It felt good to walk away, to leave her behind, to forget all about her, but I couldn't resist. Hey, who doesn't like good news?

"Power de los muertos stronger than power of the living."

"That's it? That's your good news?"

"Man cannot be good and evil. Must choose. Man fear death. Los muertos stronger than the living. Many man open arms for el diablo. Many not. Must choose. You must choose."

"I have. I've decided . . ." I paused for dramatic effect, "to get some dinner." Having regained my composure—and my confidence—I nodded toward the crisp hundred clutched in her hand. "Buy yourself ten more dogs."

My ripped pant leg flapped around my ankle as I power walked to a restaurant I'd frequented before—I'd had enough novelty for one night—and downed two shots (maybe three, but who's counting) of Cuervo Gold while I waited for my takeout order. I wasn't in the mood to sit alone in a restaurant. Drink at the bar, maybe, but not eat. Hence, I got my carne asada to go.

I walked back toward the office at a pretty good clip. To tell you the truth, the bruja had kinda given me the creeps. It seemed like there were fewer pedestrians than usual on the streets at that hour. What time was it anyway? I was too lazy and buzzed to check my phone. Probably spent more time at the bar than I should have. I still had work to do. I was relieved when I turned a corner and saw the law firm building just up the street. Only three more blocks. Then the nape of my neck started tingling. Tiny, ice-cold needles were pricking my skin. I felt the rush of fear and panic a cornered animal must feel.

Get a grip! She was just some homeless psycho trying to scam easy money out of suckers lame enough to feel sorry for her lame dog. I'd given her money, but that was compensation for the loss of her dog, not because she had scammed me or convinced me she was a witch and could turn herself into a jaguar or a crow or whatever. Shapeshifting? That's some ridiculous shit. Superstitious nonsense, all of it.

I walked a little faster, enjoying the warm buzz from the tequila shots. Passing the entrance to an alleyway, I heard a high-pitched sound, like a squeaky toy. A homeless person with a baby? I slowed and peered into the shadows. A chihuahua hobbled out from behind a small wooden crate. The dog's back-left leg was lame. It limped back around the crate and disappeared.

Friggin' weirdest night of my life. What were the chances!

I stepped into the alley. I was cautious, ready to bolt out of there, but I was curious. I had to see. I walked up to the wooden crate until I was about three feet away. I wasn't exactly afraid, but given my experience with the other chihuahua, I thought it best to keep a safe distance. I leaned forward, craning my neck to get a look at the crippled dog behind the crate.

No dog.

I inspected the far side of the crate for holes but didn't see any. I didn't want my takeout to get cold, but . . . I was flummoxed. Careful not to get any slivers, I grabbed the edge of the crate with my free hand and tried to lift it. No go. It would take two hands, and there was no way I was going to set my takeout order on the ground in that filthy, dark alley. Anyway, if I wasn't able to budge the crate, a chihuahua certainly couldn't.

It must have scurried away into the shadows when I wasn't looking. I started walking back toward the street. I stopped when I saw a dog at the mouth of the alleyway—a chihuahua backlit by the streetlights, hobbling around on three legs. I continued to move toward it. Around the corner skittered another chihuahua. This one had four good legs. A slightly bigger chihuahua joined them. Then two more, even larger. Mexican hairless breed. Nasty-looking, big-eared bastards.

"Hey, boys. You smell my carne. Well, too bad 'cause you ain't gittin' any."

They snarled in unison, displaying their pointy teeth, emitting low, guttural growls. I took a step back. I was confident I could kick my way out of the alley, but I'd already killed one dog that night, and I wasn't looking for a fight even if they were picking one.

I turned and saw for the first time that the alleyway went all the way through to the next street one block over from the firm. I walked briskly in that direction, away from the chihuahuas. They followed. I glanced back over my shoulder. The pack had grown to about . . . I don't know. I didn't have time to count. I was too busy running.

They chased me. The dogs covered a lot of ground fast, considering their diminutive size. As I neared the end of the alleyway, a chihuahua trotted around the corner. I slowed to a walk. It snarled at me as five, six, seven more, and then more, and more—there were so damn many—padded into the mouth of the alley. All the dogs hemming me in were either full-blooded chihuahuas or mongrels with some chihuahua blood. Both packs inched closer, showing their teeth, growling. Ready to bite, rip, shred.

Ready to feed.

I tore open my brown paper to-go bag and popped the lid on the plastic container holding the carne asada. I hoped they liked spicy.

I tossed pieces of meat to them, first in one direction, then the other. The meat splattered on the ground and lay untouched. The feral little pieces of shit didn't so much as sniff it.

I threw the rest of the food at them and scrambled up onto another wooden crate—a larger one, the top about three feet off the ground—with the vicious curs literally nipping at my heels. I needed a weapon. I took off one of my handmade Italian loafers and smacked the heel against the palm of my hand. It would have to do. I didn't think they could climb the sides of the crate, but this had been such an unbelievable night. I figured I could swat them away if they did manage to climb up. They were expensive shoes, but given my current situation, I would be happy to clean chihuahua blood off them.

But they didn't try to climb up—just as I knew they wouldn't—and they didn't try to jump at me or bite me. They started doing something far more terrifying.

They began chewing on the crate, methodically, relentlessly, gnawing it out from under me splinter by bloody splinter. Their muzzles were red and raw. Slivers small and large protruded from their pink gums and the blood-caked edges of their mouths. But they never let up. They gnawed and bit at the wood and ripped and tore pieces from the crate until they were smeared with their own blood.

I called for help, but no one came. No one passed by either end of the alleyway. Believe me, I kept looking, kept hoping, but the streets seemed suddenly desolate. Below me, blood bubbled from the mouths of the malevolent feral pack as they snarled and gnawed at the wood until the crate became unstable and tipped. I teetered and fell, hitting the pavement hard. Desperate to escape those demonic red teeth, I tried to scurry back up onto the crate, but they were on me in seconds, gouging sizeable chunks of my flesh—ripping my arms, tearing my legs, sinking their teeth into my neck, chewing on my ears and face. A Mexican hairless took my nose with one bite and swallowed it.

I tried to push myself up, to stand on shaky legs, my entire body on fire with pain, but there were so many of them, all around and on top of me, their powerful little jaws clamped onto every part of me, not letting go. I was losing so much blood. I was in so much pain.

Then they stopped—just stopped—suddenly and simultaneously, as if commanded by some unseen and inaudible master to unclench their jaws and back the hell off. That's when I saw the beast at the far end of the alleyway. I didn't believe it at first, but I knew that it was as real as the vicious little carnivores that moments ago had mutilated my body bit by bloody bit.

A jaguar, moving toward me with that powerful grace only big cats possess. The dogs scattered and disappeared into the night, their bellies full, their diabolical work done.

The jaguar devoured the rest. Everything but my eyes.

A crow took those.

The power of the dead is stronger than that of the living. I know that now. I will haunt the streets of this city until it is no longer a city. So now I pray—yes, me, I pray for nuclear war or a 10.0-magnitude earthquake or a direct hit from a large asteroid. Anything that will obliterate the City of Angels.

Until that day of dreadful grace, I will haunt this city as her words haunt me. Man cannot be good and evil. He must choose. I chose, and I chose badly.

I met the devil, and I was not prepared.

THE MIMICS

by Travis Liebert

For most, the Mimics came without warning. No one knew how, but it was as if a cosmic and catastrophic switch had been flipped. One day humans lived in peace, and the next they lived in fear. Fear of their neighbors, their friends, loved ones, and even their own children. The day the Mimics appeared was the day the world came to be ruled by mistrust.

What are Mimics? That's a difficult question to answer. It would be easier to say what they're not. They are most definitely *not* human. No one is sure of a Mimic's true form. Some claim their natural state is that of a lumbering, black-cloaked figure. Others say a shapeless, dark mass. While others insist they have no true form. Mimics move from shape to shape, ever-changing as the wind, without any true or original design.

No one is sure how they do it, but Mimics are able to find the most vulnerable places in your mind and pry them open. They imitate the cherished and hated people we keep locked away in the darkest corners of our psyche. They could be your lover, abusive father, or even miscarried child. Anything to make you vulnerable. Anything to get you close.

Once they lure you in, are you killed? Devoured? Taken somewhere else? Everyone has their own theory—but I have *facts*. I survived an encounter with a Mimic. I know why they suddenly started appearing at such a rapid rate. And I know what happens when you get too close.

It was a warm summer evening when I set the apocalypse in motion. My friend Michael and I were loading up the trunk of his car. His dingy gray Toyota was laden with backpacks, food, a tent, and camping gear.

This was anything but a casual trip. In a way, it was a goodbye; a passage from one stage of life to another. We were nearing the end of summer, and our freshman year of college was about to start. I had decided to attend a local community college, while Michael found himself enrolled at a technical institute a few states over. Separated by an eight-hour drive, we would be farther apart than ever before.

I stared at the bumper of the car, lost in thought. Michael and I had known each other ever since we were babies. Our mothers had been friends and introduced us as playmates. As adults, we now headed in our own separate ways. Of course, it wasn't as tragic as it seemed. We would still see each other during breaks, and it's not as if we couldn't stay in touch during the semester or visit one another occasionally. Nonetheless, it felt like the end of an era. A farewell to our younger selves and the friendship we had fostered.

"Stephen!"

Michael's shout jerked me from my thoughts. He was leaning against the driver's side door, tapping his watch. "We have to get going. I want to make sure we have enough daylight to explore."

I nodded and moved to get in the car. Michael had always been an outdoorsman and took any opportunity to spend his time in some far-flung forest. I preferred to stay inside but usually tagged along because I enjoyed his company. This had been our dynamic for years now as he excitedly dragged me along to every distant, unpopulated area he could find.

Our destination was the Golgotha Caves, a cave system about two hours north in an isolated area between our town and the next.

I sat in the passenger seat and fastened my seatbelt. I glanced at Michael. "Are you sure about this?"

He smiled, a hint of mischief in his eyes as always. "Of course! I've been planning this for months. Can't back out now."

I sighed and leaned my head against the headrest. The local government had forbidden anyone from exploring the Golgotha Caves for the past fifty years. Countless people had gone missing inside there, and the area was prone to landslides and cave-ins. Not to mention the plethora of horror stories about the place. Ghost sightings, strange sounds, mysterious lights. The Golgotha Caves had it all.

Music blared from our open windows as Michael pulled out of the driveway and veered north.

We reached the caves about three hours later. We had to park several miles away from the caves since the roads leading to them had been turned to rubble. Supposedly, security patrols were stationed around the area to catch anyone who tried driving off-road. But I didn't see any posted out here.

Michael clapped me on the back. "Let's go, Stephen!"

The hike was long, and our heavy gear made it even longer, but the terrain was surprisingly flat and easy to navigate. We knew we were getting closer when we began seeing signs scattered about, warning us against trespassing and alerting us to the dangers of cave-ins.

It took a little searching, but we eventually found the main entrance. Though it was early afternoon and everything was bathed in the golden glow of the sun, the enormous cavern before us with its great stalactites hanging from the ceiling and stalagmites rising from the floor, seemed like the mouth of some giant creature waiting to swallow us whole; a cold and thoughtless beast that devoured all who neared it.

There was nothing supernatural about it. The caves were almost eerie in their normality. One would think a location that inspired so many folktales and ghost stories would be more interesting. But that wasn't the case. Sure, they presented their own dangers: sharp rocks, steep drop-offs, and potential cave-ins. Still, these caves were just like any other dark, wet tunnel of gray stone.

Michael and I set up camp in the cool shade of the cave.

We then explored for the better part of an hour, leaving a trail of string behind so we could find our way back, chatting and bantering the whole time. Our voices echoed strangely in the craggy depths, and cold shivers ran down my spine. "Getting tired yet, Michael? I hoped it would be more entertaining than this. There's nothing but endless gray walls of stone and rocks."

"All right, yeah, I'm wearing down too. Hey. Wait. You see that? A crack in the wall, but I think it's another tunnel. C'mon. Let's just take a quick look, then we'll go back."

He had that gleam in his eye again. He was going to explore the niche, and nothing I said would stop him. Without a word, Michael gravitated toward the crack. I sighed and followed him as he beamed his flashlight down the narrow passage.

"I bet this leads somewhere cool," Michael said.

"I bet it's a hundred yards of squirming toward a dead end."

Michael smirked. "Well if that's the case then we're only adding a couple hundred more yards to our trip."

Damn. He had me there. Michael turned sideways and began to edge his way through the narrow crevice. I felt like he wasn't giving much of a choice, so I obliged him and followed suit. It wasn't too narrow, and we had no trouble making progress so long as we were angled sideways.

The passage turned out to be much longer than a hundred yards. It stretched on in an endless line. The esophagus of some cataclysmic beast, closing in around us with suffocating rigor.

I'd been moving slower than Michael, and he had managed to get farther ahead of me. Every time I grumbled about turning back, Michael would reassure me that we were certainly on the cusp of some awesome cavern or beautiful underground lake.

I took a deep breath and was about to insist on turning back.

"Steve, come here!"

Thinking he was injured, I rushed forward and frantically aimed my flashlight down the dark, ragged corridor.

There was a change in the way my light hit the walls, and then I stumbled out of the narrow corridor into a large cavern. Michael stood gazing, mouth agape in amazement.

"Jesus, man, you scared me," I said, leaning on my knees to catch my breath. I stood and aimed my light at his face. "Michael!" I snapped my fingers to get his attention. I reached out to grab his shoulder. "It's just a cav—" My words were cut short as I finally processed my surroundings.

No rock formations were visible; the room's perimeter surface was perfectly smooth, as if polished. It reflected the glow of our flashlights. We stood in what looked like a circular room. It had a consciousness, a distinctly human intent in its construction.

"This is incredible." I had barely whispered the words, but they sounded like a shout in the cold silence. "Someone must've carved out this area and sanded it until everything was perfectly smooth."

Michael had grown still. He began to march forward with intention and curiosity in his posture.

As he moved, I noticed something that Michael's body had blocked my view of: The part of the wall directly across from me—there was a door in the wall.

Michael made his way toward the door, and I followed closely behind. He stopped just short of it, and we both stood in silence for a moment.

Unlike most doorways, this was a perfect square set about two feet off the ground and measuring around four feet long on each side. It had a metal handle for opening or closing. A person could climb through it if they wanted to, but it seemed less like an entrance and more like a window.

A strange symbol with hard angles and perfect circles was carved into the center of it. Looking at it made my head hurt.

"I don't know if we should open it," I said, my voice echoing in the chamber. "What if there's some kind of toxic chemical on the other side or dangerous wiring?"

Michael shook his head. "There hasn't been any industrial work in this cave for the last century. The passages are too narrow and the caves are unstable."

He grabbed the door by the handle and jerked it open. The hinges screeched a terrible, jarring chorus as the door swung wide.

Michael shined his light through the dark opening. It seemed to be another chamber resembling the one we were in. He swept his light back in forth in wide arcs. On his second pass, we both caught a glimpse of something white. Michael focused his beam on the shape.

A sudden sinking feeling came over me and my blood ran cold. A woman lay on the floor. She glanced up. She was chained at her ankle, and that chain led from her ankle to a fixture on the wall.

"Holy shit," Michael whispered.

I stepped closer to the doorway, elbow to elbow with Michael. There was something perhaps Native American in her tan skin and long, dark hair. She wore a white dress covered in dirt, and her skin was crossed with thin, pale scars.

I shuddered to think what had been done to her. All alone in the belly of this stony beast, subjected to unspeakable horrors.

The woman opened her mouth and wailed. There were no words. Just a cry of pain and suffering. I was about to climb through the door to help her when Michael leapt into action. He threw one leg over the doorway's ledge and looked to me.

"Focus your flashlight on her so I know where I'm going," he said. I nodded and trained my light on the chained woman.

The small circle of his light glided across the floor as he neared her. She reached out toward Michael's approaching form.

She said something, but the words weren't English. Her mouth darted through consonants and vowels in a way I'd never heard before. I told myself she was simply in shock and saying nonsense, but something about the way she spoke felt wrong. She began to quiet as Michael got closer. His light was only a few feet away from her.

The woman turned to me. She shouldn't have been able to see me with my flashlight in her eyes, but her eyes locked with mine. I expected to see fear or even hope in her eyes, but there was nothing behind them. They were completely blank. Like when someone's eyes go blank because they're distracted or daydreaming—but this was different. It felt as if I was staring into a cold, vast emptiness within some imitation of a human body.

"Michael!" It was too late. He had already reached her. With a quick, snakelike motion she grabbed his ankle. I heard him shout, then go silent. My breath caught in my throat as I kept my flashlight trained on the pair.

A strange hum filled the air.

Michael began to shake uncontrollably. It was as if his body was filled with a swarm angry hornets fighting to burst free. Then he went limp. His face lost all semblance of consciousness. In that moment, something told me there was nothing left of Michael in that body.

He turned toward me. A slow, eerie turn that was at odds with the current situation.

"Come here, Stephen." His voice was flat, without a hint of emotion. "I think I'm going to need some help with this chain. You wouldn't want to leave your mother alone in the cold, would you?"

I glanced back at the woman and gasped. She was no longer the dark-haired Native. Instead, my mother lay there bound in chains. I almost leapt through the doorway and tried to save her. I blinked and shook my head. My mother had died years ago. I remembered going to her funeral, hugging all the visitors as they told me how sorry they were, and later standing over her grave with tears in my eyes. That *thing* in there wasn't my mother any more than the other one was my friend Michael.

I'd like to say that I did something heroic, that I tried to save Michael or at the very least barricaded the door so that he and the creature could never break free. But I simply ran. I blindly ran through the twisting passages, subconsciously following the trail of string, convinced Michael and the woman were right behind me, until I was suddenly running through the forest.

* * *

I sit here in my kitchen looking out the window, writing all of this down for whoever might someday stumble upon it. I now realize that the woman in the cave was the first of the Mimics, locked away by some long-dead civilization. Once freed—and she was freed; she had followed the same trail of thread—she spread like a virus through touch and was able to inhabit and make others like her, absorbing their knowledge and using it to target the ones they were close to.

Michael is gone, his body a shell. He was the second of the Mimics. Not the last.

I'm sorry for what I did. For what I unleashed upon the world. I was a follower, a stupid kid. I've never told any of this to anyone. But I'm satisfied that it lies here for all who might look upon it. Hate me for what I did, or forgive me for it. It matters not.

I must be going now. Mother is starting to become irritated. She's been outside shouting my name all night. It sounds like she might be hurt. I don't have the heart to ignore her any longer.

THE BLACK CAT

by Edgar Allan Poe

For the most wild, yet most homely narrative which I am about to pen, I neither expect nor solicit belief. Mad indeed would I be to expect it, in a case where my very senses reject their own evidence. Yet, mad am I not—and very surely do I not dream. But to-morrow I die, and to-day I would unburthen my soul. My immediate purpose is to place before the world, plainly, succinctly, and without comment, a series of mere household events. In their consequences, these events have terrified— have tortured—have destroyed me. Yet I will not attempt to expound them. To me, they have presented little but Horror—to many they will seem less terrible than *barroques*. Hereafter, perhaps, some intellect may be found which will reduce my phantasm to the common-place—some intellect more calm, more logical, and far less excitable than my own, which will perceive, in the circumstances I detail with awe, nothing more than an ordinary succession of very natural causes and effects.

From my infancy I was noted for the docility and humanity of my disposition. My tenderness of heart was even so conspicuous as to make me the jest of my companions. I was especially fond of animals, and was indulged by my parents with a great variety of pets. With these I spent most of my time, and never was so happy as when feeding and caressing them. This peculiarity of character grew with my growth, and, in my manhood, I derived from it one of my principal sources of pleasure. To those who have cherished an affection for a faithful and sagacious dog, I need hardly be at the trouble of explaining the nature or the intensity of the gratification thus derivable. There is something in the unselfish and self-sacrificing love of a brute, which goes directly to the heart of him who has had frequent occasion to test the paltry friendship and gossamer fidelity of mere *Man*.

I married early, and was happy to find in my wife a disposition not uncongenial with my own. Observing my partiality for domestic pets, she lost no opportunity of procuring those of the most agreeable kind. We had birds, gold-fish, a fine dog, rabbits, a small monkey, and *a cat*.

This latter was a remarkably large and beautiful animal, entirely black, and sagacious to an astonishing degree. In speaking of her intelligence, my wife, who at heart was not a little tinctured with superstition, made frequent allusion to the ancient popular notion, which regarded all black cats as witches in disguise. Not that she was ever *serious* upon this point—and I mention the matter at all for no better reason than that it happens, just now, to be remembered.

Pluto—this was the cat's name—was my favorite pet and playmate. I alone fed him, and he attended me wherever I went about the house. It was even with difficulty that I could prevent him from following me through the streets.

Our friendship lasted, in this manner, for several years, during which my general temperament and character—through the instrumentality of the Fiend Intemperance had—(I blush to confess it) experienced a radical alteration for the worse. I grew, day by day, more moody, more irritable, more regardless of the feelings of others. I suffered myself to use intemperate language to my wife. At length, I even offered her personal violence. My pets, of course, were made to feel the change in my disposition. I not only neglected, but ill-used them. For Pluto, however, I still retained sufficient regard to restrain me from maltreating him, as I made no scruple of maltreating the rabbits, the monkey, or even the dog, when by accident, or through affection, they came in my way. But my disease grew upon me—for what disease is like Alcohol!—and at length even Pluto, who was now becoming old, and consequently somewhat peevish—even Pluto began to experience the effects of my ill temper.

One night, returning home, much intoxicated, from one of my haunts about town, I fancied that the cat avoided my presence. I seized him; when, in his fright at my violence, he inflicted a slight wound upon my hand with his teeth. The fury of a demon instantly possessed me. I knew myself no longer. My original soul seemed, at once, to take its flight from my body; and a more than fiendish malevolence, gin-nurtured, thrilled every fibre of my frame. I took from my waistcoat-pocket a pen-knife, opened it, grasped the poor beast by the throat, and deliberately cut one of its eyes from the socket! I blush, I burn, I shudder, while I pen the damnable atrocity.

When reason returned with the morning—when I had slept off the fumes of the night's debauch—I experienced a sentiment half of horror, half of remorse, for the crime of which I had been guilty; but it was, at best, a feeble and equivocal feeling, and the soul remained untouched. I again plunged into excess, and soon drowned in wine all memory of the deed.

In the meantime the cat slowly recovered. The socket of the lost eye presented, it is true, a frightful appearance, but he no longer appeared to suffer any pain. He went about the house as usual, but, as might be expected, fled in extreme terror at my approach. I had so much of my old heart left, as to be, at first, grieved by this evident dislike on the part of a creature which had once so loved me. But this feeling soon gave place to irritation. And then came, as if to my final and irrevocable overthrow, the spirit of PERVERSENESS. Of this spirit philosophy takes no account. Phrenology finds no place for it among its organs. Yet I am not more sure that my soul lives, than I am that perverseness is one of the primitive impulses of the human heart—one of the indivisible primary faculties, or sentiments, which give direction to the character of Man. Who has not, a hundred times, found himself committing a vile or a silly action, for no other reason than because he knows he should not? Have we not a perpetual inclination, in the teeth of our best judgment, to violate that which is *Law*, merely because we understand it to be such? This spirit of perverseness, I say, came to my final overthrow. It was this unfathomable longing of the soul *to vex itself*—to offer violence to its own nature—to do wrong for the wrong's sake only—that urged me to continue and finally to consummate the injury I had inflicted upon the unoffending brute. One morning, in cool blood, I slipped a noose about its neck and hung it to the limb of a tree;—hung it with the tears streaming from my eyes, and with the bitterest remorse at my heart;—hung it *because* I knew that it had loved me, and *because* I felt it had given me no reason of offence;—hung it *because* I knew that in so doing I was committing a sin—a deadly sin that would so jeopardize my immortal soul as to place it—if such a thing were possible—even beyond the reach of the infinite mercy of the Most Merciful and Most Terrible God.

On the night of the day on which this cruel deed was done, I was aroused from sleep by the cry of fire. The curtains of my bed were in flames. The whole house was blazing. It was with great difficulty that my wife, a servant, and myself, made our escape from the conflagration. The destruction was complete. My entire worldly wealth was swallowed up, and I resigned myself thenceforward to despair.

I am above the weakness of seeking to establish a sequence of cause and effect, between the disaster and the atrocity. But I am detailing a chain of facts—and wish not to leave even a possible link imperfect. On the day succeeding the fire, I visited the ruins. The walls, with one exception, had fallen in. This exception was found in a compartment wall, not very thick, which stood about the middle of the house, and against which had rested the head of my bed. The plastering had here, in great measure, resisted the action of the fire—a fact which I attributed to its having been recently spread. About this wall a dense crowd were collected, and many persons seemed to be examining a particular portion of it with very minute and eager attention. The words "strange!" "singular!" and other similar expressions, excited my curiosity. I approached and saw, as if graven in *bas relief* upon the white surface, the figure of a gigantic *cat*. The impression was given with an accuracy truly marvellous. There had been a rope about the animal's neck.

When I first beheld this apparition—for I could scarcely regard it as less—my wonder and my terror were extreme. But at length reflection came to my aid. The cat, I remembered, had been hung in a garden adjacent to the house. Upon the alarm of fire, this garden had been immediately filled by the crowd—by some one of whom the animal must have been cut from the tree and thrown, through an open window, into my chamber. This had probably been done with the view of arousing me from sleep. The falling of other walls had compressed the victim of my cruelty into the substance of the freshly-spread plaster; the lime of which, with the flames, and the *ammonia* from the carcass, had then accomplished the portraiture as I saw it.

Although I thus readily accounted to my reason, if not altogether to my conscience, for the startling fact just detailed, it did not the less fail to make a deep impression upon my fancy. For months I could not rid myself of the phantasm of the cat; and, during this period, there came back into my spirit a half-sentiment that seemed, but was not, remorse. I went so far as to regret the loss of the animal, and to look about me, among the vile haunts which I now habitually frequented, for another pet of the same species, and of somewhat similar appearance, with which to supply its place.

One night as I sat, half stupified, in a den of more than infamy, my attention was suddenly drawn to some black object, reposing upon the head of one of the immense hogsheads of Gin, or of Rum, which constituted the chief furniture of the apartment. I had been looking steadily at the top of this hogshead for some minutes, and what now caused me surprise was the fact that I had not sooner perceived the object thereupon. I approached it, and touched it with my hand. It was a black cat—a very large one—fully as large as Pluto, and closely resembling him in every respect but one. Pluto had not a white hair upon any portion of his body; but this cat had a large, although indefinite splotch of white, covering nearly the whole region of the breast.

Upon my touching him, he immediately arose, purred loudly, rubbed against my hand, and appeared delighted with my notice. This, then, was the very creature of which I was in search. I at once offered to purchase it of the landlord; but this person made no claim to it—knew nothing of it—had never seen it before.

I continued my caresses, and, when I prepared to go home, the animal evinced a disposition to accompany me. I permitted it to do so; occasionally stooping and patting it as I proceeded. When it reached the house it domesticated itself at once, and became immediately a great favorite with my wife.

For my own part, I soon found a dislike to it arising within me. This was just the reverse of what I had anticipated; but—I know not how or why it was—its evident fondness for myself rather disgusted and annoyed. By slow degrees, these feelings of disgust and annoyance rose into the bitterness of hatred. I avoided the creature; a certain sense of shame, and the remembrance of my former deed of cruelty, preventing me from physically abusing it. I did not, for some weeks, strike, or otherwise violently ill use it; but gradually—very gradually—I came to look upon it with unutterable loathing, and to flee silently from its odious presence, as from the breath of a pestilence.

What added, no doubt, to my hatred of the beast, was the discovery, on the morning after I brought it home, that, like Pluto, it also had been deprived of one of its eyes. This circumstance, however, only endeared it to my wife, who, as I have already said, possessed, in a high degree, that humanity of feeling which had once been my distinguishing trait, and the source of many of my simplest and purest pleasures.

With my aversion to this cat, however, its partiality for myself seemed to increase. It followed my footsteps with a pertinacity which it would be difficult to make the reader comprehend. Whenever I sat, it would crouch beneath my chair, or spring upon my knees, covering me with its loathsome caresses. If I arose to walk, it would get between my feet and thus nearly throw me down, or, fastening its long and sharp claws in my dress, clamber, in this manner, to my breast. At such times, although I longed to destroy it with a blow, I was yet withheld from so doing, partly by a memory of my former crime, but chiefly—let me confess it at once—by absolute dread of the beast.

This dread was not exactly a dread of physical evil—and yet I should be at a loss how otherwise to define it. I am almost ashamed to own—yes, even in this felon's cell, I am almost ashamed to own—that the terror and horror with which the animal inspired me, had been heightened by one of the merest chimæras it would be possible to conceive. My wife had called my attention, more than once, to the character of the mark of white hair, of which I have spoken, and which constituted the sole visible difference between the strange beast and the one I had destroyed. The reader will remember that this mark, although large, had been originally very indefinite; but, by slow degrees—degrees nearly imperceptible, and which for a long time my Reason struggled to reject as fanciful—it had, at length, assumed a rigorous distinctness of outline. It was now the representation of an object that I shudder to name—and for this, above all, I loathed, and dreaded, and would have rid myself of the monster *had I dared*—it was now, I say, the image of a hideous—of a ghastly thing—of the GALLOWS!—oh, mournful and terrible engine of Horror and of Crime—of Agony and of Death!

And now was I indeed wretched beyond the wretchedness of mere Humanity. And *a brute beast*—whose fellow I had contemptuously destroyed—*a brute beast* to work out for *me*—for me a man, fashioned in the image of the High God—so much of insufferable wo! Alas! neither by day nor by night knew I the blessing of Rest any more! During the former the creature left me no moment alone; and, in the latter, I started, hourly, from dreams of unutterable fear, to find the hot breath of *the thing* upon my face, and its vast weight—an incarnate Night-Mare that I had no power to shake off—incumbent eternally upon my *heart*!

Beneath the pressure of torments such as these, the feeble remnant of the good within me succumbed. Evil thoughts became my sole intimates—the darkest and most evil of thoughts. The moodiness of my usual temper increased to hatred of all things and of all mankind; while, from the sudden, frequent, and ungovernable outbursts of a fury to which I now blindly abandoned myself, my uncomplaining wife, alas! was the most usual and the most patient of sufferers.

One day she accompanied me, upon some household errand, into the cellar of the old building which our poverty compelled us to inhabit. The cat followed me down the steep stairs, and, nearly throwing me headlong, exasperated me to madness. Uplifting an axe, and forgetting, in my wrath, the childish dread which had hitherto stayed my hand, I aimed a blow at the animal which, of course, would have proved instantly fatal had it descended as I wished. But this blow was arrested by the hand of my wife. Goaded, by the interference, into a rage more than demoniacal, I withdrew my arm from her grasp and buried the axe in her brain. She fell dead upon the spot, without a groan.

This hideous murder accomplished, I set myself forthwith, and with entire deliberation, to the task of concealing the body. I knew that I could not remove it from the house, either by day or by night, without the risk of being observed by the neighbors. Many projects entered my mind. At one period I thought of cutting the corpse into minute fragments, and destroying them by fire. At another, I resolved to dig a grave for it in the floor of the cellar. Again, I deliberated about casting it in the well in the yard—about packing it in a box, as if merchandize, with the usual arrangements, and so getting a porter to take it from the house. Finally, I hit upon what I considered a far better expedient than either of these. I determined to wall it up in the cellar—as the monks of the middle ages are recorded to have walled up their victims.

For a purpose such as this the cellar was admirably adapted. Its walls were loosely constructed, and had lately been plastered throughout with a rough plaster, which the dampness of the atmosphere had prevented from hardening. Moreover, in one of the walls was a projection, caused by a false chimney, or fire-place, that had been filled, or walled up, and made to resemble the rest of the cellar. I made no doubt that I could readily displace the bricks at this point, insert the corpse, and wall the whole up as before, so that no eye could detect any thing suspicious. And in this calculation I was not deceived. By means of a crow-bar I easily dislodged the bricks, and, having carefully deposited the body against the inner wall, I propped it in that position, while, with little trouble, I re-laid the whole structure as it originally stood. Having procured mortar, sand, and hair, with every possible precaution, I prepared a plaster which could not be distinguished from the old, and with this I very carefully went over the new brick-work. When I had finished, I felt satisfied that all was right. The wall did not present the slightest appearance of having been disturbed. The rubbish on the floor was picked up with the minutest care. I looked around triumphantly, and said to myself—"Here at least, then, my labor has not been in vain."

My next step was to look for the beast which had been the cause of so much wretchedness; for I had, at length, firmly resolved to put it to death. Had I been able to meet with it, at the moment, there could have been no doubt of its fate; but it appeared that the crafty animal had been alarmed at the violence of my previous anger, and forebore to present itself in my present mood. It is impossible to describe, or to imagine, the deep, the blissful sense of relief which the absence of the detested creature occasioned in my bosom. It did not make its appearance during the night—and thus for one night at least, since its introduction into the house, I soundly and tranquilly slept; aye, slept even with the burden of murder upon my soul!

The second and the third day passed and still my tormentor came not. Once again I breathed as a freeman. The monster, in terror, had fled the premises forever! I should behold it no more! My happiness was supreme! The guilt of my dark deed disturbed me but little. Some few inquiries had been made, but these had been readily answered. Even a search had been instituted—but of course nothing was to be discovered. I looked upon my future felicity as secured.

Upon the fourth day of the assassination, a party of the police came, very unexpectedly, into the house, and proceeded again to make rigorous investigation of the premises. Secure, however, in the inscrutability of my place of concealment, I felt no embarrassment whatever. The officers bade me accompany them in their search. They left no nook or corner unexplored. At length, for the third or fourth time, they descended into the cellar. I quivered not in a muscle. My heart beat calmly as that of one who slumbers in innocence. I walked the cellar from end to end. I folded my arms upon my bosom and roamed easily to and fro. The police were thoroughly satisfied and prepared to depart. The glee at my heart was too strong to be restrained. I burned to say if but one word, by way of triumph, and to render doubly sure their assurance of my guiltlessness.

"Gentlemen," I said at last, as the party ascended the steps, "I delight to have allayed your suspicions. I wish you all health, and a little more courtesy. By the bye, gentlemen, this—this is a very well constructed house." [In the rabid desire to say something easily, I scarcely knew what I uttered at all.]—"I may say an *excellently* well constructed house. These walls—are you going, gentlemen?—these walls are solidly put together;" and here, through the mere phrenzy of bravado, I rapped heavily, with a cane which I held in my hand, upon that very portion of the brick-work behind which stood the ghastly corpse of the wife of my bosom.

But may God shield and deliver me from the fangs of the Arch-Fiend! No sooner had the reverberation of my blows sunk into silence, than I was answered by a voice from within the tomb!—by a cry, at first muffled and broken, like the sobbing of a child, and then quickly swelling into one long, loud, and continuous scream, utterly anomalous and inhuman—a howl—a wailing shriek, half of horror and half of triumph, such as might have arisen only out of hell, conjointly from the throats of the dammed in their agony and of the demons that exult in the damnation!

Of my own thoughts it is folly to speak. Swooning, I staggered to the opposite wall. For one instant the party upon the stairs remained motionless, through extremity of terror and of awe. In the next, a dozen stout arms were toiling at the wall. It fell bodily. The corpse, already greatly decayed and clotted with gore, stood erect before the eyes of the spectators. Upon its head, with red extended mouth and solitary eye of fire, sat the hideous beast whose craft had seduced me into murder, and whose informing voice had consigned me to the hangman. I had walled the monster up within the tomb!

LANEY

by Thomas M. Malafarina

By far, the greatest danger of Artificial Intelligence is that people conclude too early that they understand it.
—Eliezer Yudkowsky

Artificial intelligence is growing up fast, as are robots whose facial expressions can elicit empathy and make your mirror neurons quiver.
—Diane Ackerman

Of all ghosts, the ghosts of our loved ones are the worst.
—Arthur Conan Doyle

The room was whiter than any place Bill had ever seen in his life. Even the term "antiseptic" did little to describe its almost ethereal appearance, as a glow seemed to emit from all of its walls, floor, and even the ceiling. Bill sat on a surprisingly comfortable white plastic chair in front of a glossy white table. He felt quite conspicuous in his gray suit with a brightly patterned blue tie.

Another unoccupied chair sat directly across the table from him. Bill assumed it was for the same person he was waiting for. A bank of four white-framed large screen monitors was mounted near the ceiling. Some sort of quiet instrumental music played faintly around him. He couldn't identify if the tune—played with a flute or perhaps a woodwind instrument—but he supposed the tune's name was irrelevant, anyway.

His purpose for coming to Perfect Mate, Inc. had nothing to do with songs or fancy white rooms or any other such distractions. Bill knew why he was here. He needed to stay focused and make sure he got exactly what he wanted. Couldn't allow some fast-talking salesman to saddle him with an inferior product.

The bank of monitors sprang to life. Rotating versions of a silver *P* and *M* on a red heart with a white background—the corporate logo for Perfect Mate—displayed on the screens.

Bill braced himself, expecting to be accosted with a corporate promotional propaganda video touting the many advantages of becoming part of the Perfect Mate family. But to his surprise, the logo silently rotated on all four screens in a synchronized, almost hypnotic ballet.

With a quiet swish, part of the wall underneath the monitors slid aside, and a man entered the room. He was in his late forties or early fifties with a head of thick white hair styled in a way that surely cost the man a fortune. Then again, considering what this place cost, he probably could afford it. His flesh was dusky gray and he looked gaunt to the point of being unhealthy. He was dressed in a bright white suit, white shirt, and bright red bowtie. Bill was happy to see a bit more color in the room. Once the door swished closed, not even a crack indicated its location.

The man took the chair across from Bill. He flipped open a notebook-style computer and began typing.

"Mr. William Johnston, I presume," the man said. He never took his eyes off his notebook's monitor.

"Um . . . uh . . . Yes, that's me. Are you . . ."

"I am Francois DeLamar, the creator and owner of this incredible company."

"Allow me to apologize, Mr. DeLamar, for not recognizing you. I guess I assumed some underling might be assisting me. I never expected you to handle my case. "

DeLamar flapped his hand in a dismissive gesture. "Of course you didn't. I suppose you thought some part-time college student or perhaps a brainless associate would be sitting on this side of the desk. Some easy pushover, someone who would gloss over your application. Perhaps you hoped for someone who wouldn't take the time to thoroughly scrutinize you to find out why you're here."

Then for the first time, DeLamar locked eyes with Bill.

Bill felt the color leave his face. "Tell me, Mr. William F. Johnston, why exactly are you here?"

"Why else would I be here? I'm here to purchase one of your Perfect Mate synthbots. That's why I've been sending you information and paying you for the past month."

DeLamar's narrow glare bore a hole into Bill. "Yes, I understand *that*, Mr. Johnston. I'm questioning your preferences in regards to the design you have chosen for your bot."

"I'm not sure I know what you mean," Bill Johnston replied.

DeLamar returned his focus to the file on the table before him. He pressed a button on his notebook and all four monitors displayed a blonde woman's face. Bill gasped when he saw that it was his wife's face and head slowly rotating on the screens. The resemblance was uncanny. It was like Laney was right there in front of him. Yet he knew such a thing was impossible, because his beautiful wife was dead.

"Quite a likeness, wouldn't you say?" DeLamar asked.

Bill was unable to utter a single coherent word. Although Laney had been almost ten long years in her grave, it was like she hadn't aged a day. The best Bill could do was mutter gibberish, which vaguely resembled snippets of English.

He stood and approached one of the monitors. Eventually, he found his tongue. "It's . . . it's absolutely incredible! I have no idea how you were able to accomplish it, but that face is an exact replica of my Laney right down to that small brown mole on her left cheek. All I can say is . . . Amazing!"

"Perhaps so," DeLamar said, "but we're still in the early stages of your project. We'll study your home videos to develop her facial expressions as well as the tonality of her voice. We want your girl to look, sound, and act just like your wife."

Bill thought for a moment, then turned and said, "I'm all in favor of you making her look and sound just like my Laney, but we need to spend some additional time discussing what to do about her future personality."

Once again, DeLamar seemed to eyeball Bill with intensity. "I suppose I'm not surprised to hear you say that, Mr. Johnston, all things considered." And unless he was just being paranoid, Bill was certain there was suspicion in those eyes.

Bill held DeLamar's stare, then finally broke eye contact. "I don't know what you're getting at by that statement, Mr. DeLamar. But I don't think I like your accusatory tone. I don't like it one bit."

"I'm going to be completely honest with you here, Bill. May I call you Bill? It's like this, Bill. My company is not some fly-by-night outfit selling synthetic love dolls. There are plenty of those around, and they provide a service for a fraction of our cost. We're serious creators of artificial lifeforms—not simply artificial, but as close to the perfect replication of humanity as possible with the technology available at this time. Do you understand what I'm saying, Bill?"

"Of course I understand. That's why I'm here and that's why I'm paying you so much."

DeLamar ignored Bill and continued. "As a serious, professional company we have a reputation to uphold and are obliged to do our own due diligence when considering our clients. We have to be cognizant not only of past and present clients, but we must look to our future clients as well. Again, our reputation is paramount in accomplishing this goal. As such, during our investigation of you, we have discovered some, shall we say, unpleasantness in your past regarding you and your late wife."

Bill did his best to avoid DeLamar's accusatory gaze. "Oh that? Well, that was a bit of an unfortunate confusion, a definite misunderstanding."

"I would say 'misunderstanding' is a bit of an understatement. Being charged with first-degree murder in the brutal beating and dismemberment of your spouse is a bit more than a misunderstanding, wouldn't you agree?"

"But if you truly did your research you would know I was found innocent."

"Not exactly, Bill. You weren't found innocent at all; you were found not guilty. The jury didn't believe enough evidence was put forward by the district attorney to find you guilty beyond a reasonable doubt. And since no one else has ever been convicted of the crime, you've never been exonerated."

Bill was beginning to lose his temper. "Look, DeLamar. I'm telling you right now, I did not kill my wife. Sure, we fought from time to time as all married couples do. Hell, we even separated for a bit. But eventually we got back together and worked out our differences. Our marriage may have been a little rocky at times but understand this: I truly loved my wife. I thought she was the most beautiful woman on the planet. Unfortunately, her personality sometimes left a lot to be desired, but I willingly accepted that as being part of the whole package."

"Yet, now you're paying us quite handsomely to replicate your wife as she appeared a decade ago, but you are suggesting a new personality. Correct?"

"Yes. That's absolutely correct." Bill decided he had better regain control of this situation and fast. "Your company is called 'Perfect Mate.' Your claim to fame is creating perfection in synthetic partners to the complete satisfaction of your clients. I am your client. Pleasing your client should be your foremost concern. I'm paying for perfection and will settle for nothing less. I've spent the last decade working my butt off to better myself and have become quite wealthy in the process. I've already paid you a significant amount of money for this endeavor and can easily continue to do so. However, if you feel in any way uncomfortable continuing this project, just say the word and I'll happily take my money to one of your competitors. And you know the law, DeLamar. You would be required to hand over all the technological data for which I have already paid. I seriously doubt you want to put that type of sensitive information into the hands of your competition. As you can see, I, too, have done due diligence."

Beads of sweat formed on DeLamar's forehead and upper lip. Bill had dealt with men like this many times while building his vast financial empire. They were insignificant, tiny men who existed in their own minuscule universes where they saw themselves as lord and master. They took pleasure in appearing to be superior and bullying those they considered intellectually inferior to them. Yes, Bill had seen many of these worms he called "wannabe kings" of their insignificant kingdoms, and he had trampled them into the mud as he was now doing with this high-brow snob.

"So, DeLamar, what's it going to be? Are you going to continue to work for me and develop my perfect mate or am I going to have to make things ugly?"

"Um . . . Well, Bill—"

"It's Mr. Johnston to you, DeLamar."

"Um . . . Yes, of course, Mr. Johnston. I didn't mean to offend. I just . . . I mean . . . Yes, Perfect Mate would love to continue with your project."

"Fine then, let's start discussing the personality I want you to put into Laney."

* * *

Three months later, Bill's dream girl was delivered to his home. She arrived in a large cylindrical steel sarcophagus. He instructed the workers to stand it up in a corner of his bedroom, next to his bed. There was a glass window at the top of the door and his beautiful synthetic wife lay inside. Her eyes were closed, as if asleep. He had studied the instructional video from Perfect Mate and was certain he could get the unit up and running with little difficulty. Regardless, he wasn't ready to open the door.

Strange how he had invested a ton of money in the design and construction of Laney 2.0—as he thought of her—yet he was hesitant to open the box and activate the woman of his dreams. His hesitation had little, if anything, to do with the fact that she was a synthetic being. His reluctance came from a place deep down inside him; it was deeper than skin, deeper than bone, deeper than blood and internal organs. His uncertainty came from his soul.

Some might call it fear. Others would see it for what it really was—gut-wrenching guilt. DeLamar had been right on target with his assessment. Bill hadn't been found innocent of his wife's murder, just not guilty. The district attorney did his best to convict Bill but simply didn't have sufficient evidence. Considering he was actually guilty of the heinous crime, Bill figured that made him one of the luckiest men alive.

It was a particularly confusing situation Bill had found himself in, more than a decade earlier. His wife was the most beautiful woman he had ever met. Despite her good looks, Laney had been arrogant, bossy, demanding, ungrateful, belittling, rude, opinionated, condescending, criticizing, and just about every other negative personality trait considerable. She never loved him but saw him as a good financial provider. He understood she was far out of his league, and he was amazed that he'd had such a beautiful wife, despite her negative traits.

She had given him one particular nickname that irritated him to no end: Billy Boy. She used that name when degrading him for one infraction or another. It leaked from her pursed lips like the hiss of a snake and drove him crazy, literally. Bill had put up with her constant cajoling for eleven years, until one day he snapped.

He had tolerated her antics for as long as he could, but the day he discovered she was sleeping with half the men in town . . . it was more than he could stand. Laney could drive the sanest of men to madness, which was what she had done to him. He'd come to that realization while hacking her to bits, laughing maniacally and shouting, "I love you to pieces!" He'd turned his once-precious Laney into a human jigsaw puzzle.

Laney 2.0 gave him a chance to start over. He had his Laney back, or at least a replica as technologically identical as possible, minus Laney's negative traits. This version had to be kind, caring, loving, thoughtful, eager to please, and in every way the antithesis of his dead wife. He had even used Ira Levin's twentieth-century movie *The Stepford Wives* as a reference for his new version of Laney. DeLamar chuckled and said most of his male clients had done the same.

That perfect woman waited inside the metal cylinder.

Bill plugged the unit into a nearby wall outlet. Electric devices inside the box hummed pleasantly. He pressed an ON button, and the cylinder opened. He looked in amazement at the naked form resting on a bed of silk. It was Laney, just the way he dreamed she should be. She wore a wedding ring and diamond on her left hand. It was an artificial diamond, put there to make others they might encounter believe she really was his wife.

According to the instructional video provided by Perfect Mate, this container would become the charging station for the synthbot. She had to spend a minimum of five hours a night in the chamber. A light at the foot of the box changed from red to green, and Laney opened her eyes.

She smiled. But where was that same incredible smile he had fallen for so many years ago? With a twinge in his gut, Bill realized Laney's unique sparkle and mischievous grin would have to be filled with the same attitude and superiority that Original Laney had possessed. Her smile couldn't possibly be identical; this Laney was a robot, and its created personality should be nothing like Laney's. Still, part of Bill understood that he would miss that devilish smile of hers.

Laney turned her head from side to side, taking in her surroundings before returning her gaze to Bill. "You are my husband, Bill Johnston. Is that correct? I am Laney Johnston, and I love you with all my heart. I am here to satisfy your every need."

The synthbot stepped out of the charging station, gently grabbed Bill's hand, and led him to their bed. Amazed, astonished, and more than a little anxious, Bill followed.

The next morning, Bill awoke to find Laney resting in her charging cylinder. He still couldn't believe how much she looked like his Laney. Her body felt exactly like Laney's, too, if his memory of her was accurate. He got out of bed and went into the bathroom to take a shower.

Later, while toweling dry, he smelled sausage and eggs. When he walked into the kitchen he found Laney, still naked, save for a cooking apron, at the stove.

She turned to Bill. "Good morning, darling. I'm cooking your favorite breakfast. I hope you enjoy it."

Not only was this creature a vision of loveliness, but she existed for him, to please him in every way possible. "I'm sure I will."

Bill suddenly realized the full extent of his purchase. He couldn't have her walking around naked all the time, even though he had few friends and never had visitors. After his trial, Bill had moved across the country from California to Pennsylvania and began a new life where no one knew his past.

He had made a small fortune in business but didn't flaunt his wealth, living in a nondescript suburban home in an upper-middle-class neighborhood. He didn't attend many social functions and despite his financial success was able to remain below the radar. But he did have neighbors, and his fantasy of Laney parading around all day in her birthday suit might not be as easy as he thought.

This, however, wouldn't be a problem. He had bought Laney a complete wardrobe of clothing he believed would look amazing on her. Hell, the way she looked she could wear a burlap potato sack and be gorgeous. As he sat enjoying his breakfast, Laney sat across from him smiling lovingly, her left breast popping out of the apron.

"How is your breakfast?" Laney asked.

"I feel like I died and went to Heaven."

Bill hesitated. Laney had asked, "How is your breakfast," not "How's your breakfast." His former Laney wouldn't have said "How is." She spoke casually with contractions, not in formal language. He realized it was a small thing, but he'd have to report it to Perfect Mate for future adjustment. He needed his new Laney to sound as human as possible if she was to be his "wife" in public.

"Is something wrong, honey?" Laney asked. "You looked a bit confused for a moment."

"Everything's fine, sweetie. I'm just so amazed and happy you're here."

Laney chuckled. "Where else would I be? I'm your wife. I'm here for you. I'll always be here for you and you alone."

Bill noted that she said, "I'm" and "I'll." They got those conjunctions right. He thought: Maybe I'm being too picky and paying too much attention to details that in reality are unimportant. After all, she was unbelievable last night; much more giving than the old Laney ever was.

She was still watching him eat.

"You don't eat, do you, Laney?"

"I don't need to, however, I can do both. If, for example, you wanted to go out to a restaurant, I would store the food inside me until we got home, then evacuate it and clean out my storage compartment. It is a similar process to what I did last evening after sex."

"*Woah!* Too much information." He chuckled nervously.

Laney continued her analytical-toned conversation. "I do occasionally need to shower to keep my skin moist and fresh. Although my simulated human flesh, complete with hair follicles, does not sweat, nor does it produce body odor. The need to cleanse is largely dependent upon the amount of contact and interaction I have with my environment."

"Um . . . well . . . that's all very interesting information, Laney. Not necessarily the best breakfast conversation, but still informative."

Laney frowned. "I am sorry, my husband. I did not mean to offend you in any way. I have been programmed with the ability to adapt and learn, so rest assured; I won't make that mistake again. Would having sex with me again make you happy?"

Bill considered it for a moment, then said, "No, not right now."

Part of Bill's training on how to get the most out of his synthbot was dedicated to how to teach his perfect mate what she needed to know to appear human-like so that others wouldn't notice that she wasn't human. For this reason, Bill had taken a month's vacation to spend time working with Laney and getting her properly oriented.

Bill realized he had a lot to teach her, starting with her no longer acknowledging that she was synthetic. She had to put all those ideas aside and focus on her humanity. She had to think and act like a human if she was to truly become the perfect wife he had paid for.

He supposed the best place to start was to get her dressed. Maybe not just yet.

"Okay. I changed my mind. Sex it is."

* * *

After several weeks of training interrupted by many sexually athletic romps in the hay, Bill had managed to activate her sense of humor module as well as a few other emotional simulation programs. He tested these with sad movies, pictures of puppies and kittens, and videos of human babies.

He was stunned to realize how easy it was to transfer these real human treaties onto Laney. He sensed sadness from Laney when she watched the baby videos. She understood she would never be able to bear children. He wondered: Was she really sad, or were her perceived emotions nothing more than advanced simulated algorithms? It all seemed so real. Bill found it astonishing, and for a moment he considered adopting a child so Laney could experience motherhood. He was personifying Laney; thinking of her as a real human being. In fact, if he was completely honest, Bill was sure he was falling in love with her.

At first, love seemed ridiculous. But after a time, he had to wonder if it was really so strange. After all, he had designed Laney's appearance to be identical to the only woman he had ever loved. Perfect Mate made her sound and feel exactly like Laney.

One morning, Laney came bopping into the kitchen. Her long blonde hair was pulled back in a ponytail. She wore pink shorts with an oversized T-shirt. As far as Bill was concerned, she was absolutely the most beautiful woman in the world.

She gave him a smile. "Good morning, sweetie pie. How is the love of my life this morning?"

Bill was still astonished at how fast she learned subtle things like voice inflection, tonal quality, slang, facial expression; all those things that make us human. She constantly used words like, "husband," "lover," "darling," and other terms of endearment. That's what kept Perfect Mate in business: absolute customer satisfaction.

"I'm just fine, Laney. You sure look chipper. What has gotten you so happy this morning?"

"Oh, I suppose nothing in particular. I am just so incredibly happy to be your wife, darling. I have no idea how I ever could have been so lucky as to meet you. Can I make you breakfast, Bill, my husband?"

She mentioned meeting him with complete disregard to having been created for him. To any casual observer, they would hear that they had dated and eventually married, like most human couples. He decided it was time to try her out on the general public.

"I don't believe we'll eat at home, Laney. Maybe we'll venture out and get breakfast in town at a restaurant. What do you think about that idea, baby?"

"Oh, Bill. Are you serious? We are going out . . . with other people . . . like us? Oh, Bill, you make me so happy. You are the best husband in the world. I promise I will not let you down, honey. I'll be the perfect wife, I swear I will. No one will know . . . you know."

Bill walked over and took Laney's hands, looking deep into her beautiful blue eyes. "Remember, darling, there is no need to mention that ever again. You truly are the perfect wife in every sense of the word. You are as human to me as anyone. You're *my* wife, Laney, and I want you to know that I love you more than I have ever loved anyone in my life."

Laney smiled strangely at Bill, as if caught completely off guard. Then she asked, "Is this a test, Bill? Are you verifying how my emotional simulation program is processing? Because if you are, that would make me very sad because you know how I feel about you. I tell you every day."

"No, Laney, I'm being quite serious. I understand that a lot of what you express is the direct result of your programming and emotional modules. But I think you have grown over the past month to the point where I believe you've evolved beyond your programming. I wanted you to know that I've come to the realization that I'm deeply in love with you."

"But, Bill, I am not your Laney. I know you asked me not to mention this, but remember, I am a synthetic replication of your wife. I do love you, but that may be because that is what I am made to do. How can you possibly be in love with me? I have trouble processing that."

"Laney, I don't completely understand it either. It may appear to be completely illogical; I realize that. Then again, life has taught me that there's nothing logical about love. All I know is, I love you with all my heart and I believe your love is not the result of programming, but true, honest, human love. Maybe it's too early in your emotional development for you to understand your feelings, but I believe, in time, when your programming progresses and your emotion modules are functioning at optimal efficiency, you will understand."

"Oh, Bill, darling, I certainly hope so," Laney replied with a bit of uncertainty in her voice.

* * *

Bill lay in his bed staring up at the ceiling while Laney rested in her charging cylinder. He couldn't sleep; he was thinking about how incredible the entire project had been. The trip he had taken with Laney that first time they had gone out for breakfast had been successful. Bill had taken Laney on several additional excursions around the area during the following weeks. In every single case, no one could have suspected Laney of being anything other than Bill's wife—his human wife.

Laney became increasingly comfortable in her role as Mrs. Bill Johnston. She was more outgoing and friendly toward strangers whenever exposed to new social situations. This was especially good to see since initially she had been quiet and reserved among people. Everyone who met her seemed to like her instantly. Bill couldn't believe how well his wife adapted. Yes, he thought of her as his wife. If Laney didn't have to return to her charging pod every night, he might forget she wasn't human. Hopefully, Perfect Mate would soon find a way to make the charging station more compact so Laney could spend the night in bed with him.

Bill threw off his bed covers, having made up his mind. He got out of bed and walked across the room to his dresser. In the top drawer, under several handkerchiefs, he found what he was looking for. It was a small black box which held a very special ring; the wedding ring he had bought for the original Laney, the same ring he had placed on her finger during their marriage ceremony. Years later, he removed it from her severed finger after he chopped her to bits.

He took the ring to Laney's charging capsule, then gently slid the fake diamond Perfect Mate had provided off her finger. As he began to slide on the diamond, Laney opened her eyes. She looked down at her hand. "Is that what I think it is, Bill?"

"Yes, Laney. As my wife, you deserve to have a real wedding ring, not just some simulation."

"But, Bill, I, too, am only a simulation. I'm not your Laney. I just look like her."

"Don't sell yourself short, Laney. You are a thousand times better than the other Laney was or could ever hope to be. Now close your eyes and get your rest. In the morning we'll continue our wonderful life together. Goodnight, sweetheart. I have to go to sleep as well."

Moments later, Bill began to drift toward sleep. The pressures of decision making melted away the moment he put the ring on Laney's finger. He may not have been in a church in front of several hundred witnesses, but he had just completed his own marriage ceremony. Laney was no longer his project, no longer his purchase. Laney was now his wife.

* * *

Laney's eyes closed as electricity made its way into her batteries, filling her with fresh power. When she charged she thought of nothing, unlike humans who dreamed while they slept. That is to say, she never dreamt. Until that night.

The diamond on Laney's left hand began to glow. Long, luminescent tendrils snaked their way along Laney's neural network toward the central processing unit inside her skull. Simultaneously, more tendrils found their way into her synthetic lubrication system, one like our own bloodstream, but which utilized synththetaplasma. Laney's eyes fluttered beneath closed lids, experiencing REM for the first time.

All the while, Bill slept. All the while, Laney recharged, neither of them aware of what the next day would bring.

* * *

The next morning, Bill came down to breakfast expecting to smell eggs and sausage cooking on the stove. Instead, he saw Laney sitting at the kitchen table with her left hand extended outward, admiring her wedding ring. She didn't seem to notice Bill when he walked into the room.

"How do you like the ring, Laney?"

She released a sigh. "It's beautiful, honey. I love it."

"At first I was a bit concerned about giving it to you. I wasn't sure how you'd feel. I know sometimes it makes you uncomfortable when I tell you I love you."

"In the beginning, yes. Now I like it. I love that you love me. It makes everything perfect."

Laney looked up at Bill, and he was taken aback. For a passing moment, she had the same mischievous look his dead wife always had. But that wasn't possible. This Laney wasn't programmed to have such an expression. She didn't have the personality to pull off that look. Where had it come from?

"Are you okay, Bill? You look like you saw something that frightened you."

"A ghost," he replied.

"What?"

"It's an expression. 'You look like you saw a ghost.' That's what most people say."

"Yes." Laney nodded. "That's how you looked. But since there are no such beings as ghosts, something else must be bothering you."

Bill shook off the bad notion. "No, Laney, I'm fine. I'm just having some trouble waking up. I think I need a good breakfast."

"I was hoping we could go out for breakfast this morning. We haven't gone out in a while. What do you think? Can we, Bill, please?"

"Well, I don't see any reason why not."

Laney beamed. "That great. Can we go to Mac's for breakfast? The people there are so friendly, especially Mac. He's a sweetheart and always fusses over me."

"That he does," Bill agreed. Then he paused. Laney had never instigated a conversation about other men. Bill made comments when a man paid extra attention to Laney, and she'd brush the idea aside, insisting Bill was exaggerating. Noticing other men was . . . the sort of thing his dead wife would have done. But for the first time, his new Laney had brought up Mac's overt attention. Was it possible her programming changed as she became more in tune with humanity? Or were these expressions nothing more than her microprocessors trying to mimic observed human female behavior? Perhaps it was nothing more than his old jealousy from other men paying attention to his wife. Yet, *she* had been the one to bring up the flirtation.

He had several momentary flashbacks of Real-Laney going out of her way to flirt. He assumed it was to make him jealous. Eventually, he found out otherwise when he learned how she had cheated on him numerous times. Could these negative traits have found their way into Synth-Laney's programming? How was such a thing even possible? Had that character DeLamar done something to her programming to screw with him? He knew the man didn't like him; DeLamar had made that perfectly obvious. Could DeLamar have created some subroutines, which given the right stimuli and circumstances would bring these personality traits to the forefront? Bill decided it might be better if they stayed in for the day, giving him a chance to watch for other strange idiosyncrasies

"Sorry, Laney. I changed my mind. I have too much going on. I'll need you to make breakfast here at home."

"But . . . I was hoping—"

"Breakfast, Laney. I want you to make me breakfast right now."

"I don't want to make breakfast. Come on, Billy Boy, don't be such a stick in the mud."

Bill caught his breath. Something was very wrong. The last time he had been called Billy Boy, he had gone completely postal and chopped his wife to pieces. She knew that name always worked on his nerves. "Laney? Where did you hear that name?"

"What name?"

"The name you just called me. Where did you hear that name?"

"I have no idea what you're talking about."

"Laney . . . Directive 6789."

Upon hearing that code word, Laney stopped in her tracks. Bill had never used the directive before. It had been given to him at the time of final payment for Laney. He was told to simply issue the verbal code and she would become unresponsive. It was a failsafe for the owner's protection. No matter how human-like these synthetic units appeared, they were still machines. Synthetic bio-machines, perhaps, but nonetheless machines.

Bill hated to do it, but the hairs rising on the back of his neck told him he had no other choice, since Laney was obviously malfunctioning. Besides her blatant disobedience and the annoying whining reminiscent of his deceased wife, just a moment earlier he had seen yet another disturbing facial expression change. She had acquired a sullen pout exactly like his former Laney.

Time to get his robot back to Perfect Mate for reprogramming and reconditioning. He called their twenty-four-hour customer satisfaction line—he was a customer and not at all satisfied.

* * *

"If you don't mind my saying so, Mr. Johnston, I think you might be exaggerating. The symptoms you've described are not possible with your model's programming."

Bill sat in the same glowing white room where he had originally met with Francois DeLamar. Only this time, all of the formalities and pretenses were out of the way. Bill was loaded for bear and wanted answers.

"Look, DeLamar, I neither exaggerated nor imagined any of this. I'm telling you, this unit has shown behaviors and expressions identical to those of my late wife. In fact, she used terminology only my late wife would know. How is that possible?"

"Mr. Johnston, I assure you . . ."

"Assure my butt, DeLamar. I'm telling you something is wrong with this unit, and I need a full barrage of diagnostic testing run on her."

The four video screens above DeLamar's head came to life. Various views of his Laney lying on an operating table with a series of wires attached to her head flickered onto the screens, while a bank of computers displayed a variety of graphs and charts depicting God-only-knew-what.

"A complete workup is being performed as we speak, Mr. Johnston." DeLamar lifted his hand to indicate the monitors. "But I'm certain the results will come back clean. We made sure of that before we released this unit to you."

"If that's true, then what the hell is going on?"

"Perhaps I can offer an alternative reason for your discomfort. What you're experiencing is quite common in situations such as yours."

"And what sort of situation is that?"

"You said you were still in love with your wife when she died, although her personality had caused you a degree of consternation."

"Yeah, so what?"

"In cases where the unit has been constructed to identically resemble a deceased loved one, the recipient of the unit can project the deceased's characteristics onto the synthbot. Not a bad thing, and often something we even encourage. When the deceased is severely missed, it helps the living get maximum benefit out of their bots. We've had situations where users have actually fallen in love with their units."

Bill chose not to respond to that and let DeLamar continue.

"When we are tied so intimately and emotionally to a departed loved one, we often unconsciously project those familiar features, good or bad, onto their synthetic replacements."

"Are you trying to tell me I'm imagining all of this?"

"I'm trying to explain that what you're experiencing is not uncommon and is nothing to be ashamed of. It's largely due to the fact that your synthbot resembles your Laney so much."

"Let's assume you're correct, which by the way I don't believe for one minute. What solution would you recommend to stop this transference?"

DeLamar hesitated and then said, "In the past, we found it successful to change the unit's appearance so that the customer's subconscious no longer projects onto the synthbot."

"So, if I allow you to change Laney's appearance then I'll stop 'imagining' the things I've mentioned?"

"It has worked in the past."

Bill could not imagine such a thing. "Look, DeLamar. Your company guarantees complete satisfaction. If I didn't care what my Laney looked like, I would have gone to a less-expensive place and bought some generic love-bot for a fraction of your price. I wanted Laney. You gave me Laney. Now you have to figure out what's wrong with this unit so I can go back home and resume my life. Get it? Find out what's wrong and fix it."

"Mr. Johnston—"

"Fix it or I'll make sure you never sell another unit. I've made many friends over the years, including the chairman of the Synthetic Beings Oversight Committee. Don't force me to start making phone calls. You won't be happy if I do."

Bill swore he heard DeLamar's rectum pinch with fear. With audible trembling in his voice, the man said, "Very well, Mr. Johnston. I'll personally oversee the diagnostic testing and provide you with a complete report. Please make yourself comfortable. I'll be back shortly with an update. Can I have my assistant bring you anything? A soft drink? Coffee? Tea? Anything?"

"I'll be fine as soon as you find out what's wrong with my wife and make it right."

* * *

As he turned and left the room, DeLamar realized his assumption was correct. This Johnston fellow had fallen madly in love with his synthbot and was projecting his dead wife's personality onto it. He saw the ring. Laney's fake diamond had been replaced with a real one; likely his dead wife's ring. No doubt this guy had it bad for his walking Lego set. As bizarre as that might seem on the surface, it was even more disturbing because it was possible Johnston had actually killed his human wife. DeLamar didn't want to begin to guess what twisted psychology might be tied to that.

An hour later, DeLamar returned to the room with a diagnostic printout—a complete fabrication, its sole purpose to appease Johnston. The actual testing revealed what DeLamar suspected; there was nothing wrong with the unit. Not a single malfunction of any sort was discovered. DeLamar sat across the glossy white table from Bill Johnston and passed him the fictitious report.

"It appears you were right after all, Mr. Johnston. As you can see by the report, Laney's precognitive dominant rotophysics and endocriptics module had a slight deviation in its sine wave, which was the direct result of a misalignment of the phychotechnic modulator."

"Um . . . okay. What the hell does that mean?"

DeLamar gave him a positive smile, allowing all of his pearly whites to glisten in the overhead lighting. "It means we had to realign her receptive diodes. Bottom line? She's as good as new."

"What do you think caused it?"

DeLamar was waiting for this question. He already had an answer ready, one which would throw Bill Johnston off his game. "It appears something must have jostled one of her intuitive circuits loose. This rarely happens, except . . . except in cases of repeated and extremely acrobatic sexual encounters. Often when a unit is new, some users get a bit carried away with sexual enthusiasm and certain problems might occur. Is this a possibility, Mr. Johnston?"

Bill smiled slyly. "Guilty as charged." Then he began to snicker.

"Not a problem, Mr. Johnston. Now that we know, we've taken steps to assure this won't happen again. We've added protective film in vital areas of her circuitry that will be more receptive to repetitive shock impacts." Then he smiled and winked at Bill.

"So you're saying Laney will be back to normal?"

"Absolutely. If fact, she already is," DeLamar assured as the unseen wall slid open, revealing Bill's wife standing there, smiling.

"Bill! I missed you so much. I'm sorry if I did anything to upset you. I promise I'll be a good wife from now on."

"Not to worry, Laney," Bill said. "Everything's going to be all right now. Mr. DeLamar has assured me you're in tip-top shape. Let's go home and celebrate."

* * *

All the way home from Perfect Mate, Laney seemed to be her normal self. There were no strange expressions or statements that Bill considered out of the ordinary. Bill decided to try an experiment.

"Say, Laney. Think you might want to stop at Mac's for lunch? You know how Mac loves to fuss over you."

"If you would like to stop, that's fine with me. Mac seems like a nice person, but I never really noticed him fussing. Even if he had, I wouldn't pay attention. I have you, Bill, and you are more man than any woman could be lucky enough to have. No one's attention means more to me than yours, darling."

"Thank you, Laney." Bill was relieved to have his Laney back. Whatever DeLamar had done to repair her whos-a-whats-it, it had done the job perfectly. "No. I think I've changed my mind. I think we should head home and you can make me one of your delicious lunches instead."

"That sounds just perfect to me, honey."

Although it made her seem a bit less human-like, Bill had to admit he loved her constant adoration and was in no hurry to see that change. He probably would have asked for such a personality trait from the beginning had he thought of it.

Bill sat at the kitchen table while Laney prepared his lunch. He picked up the morning newspaper from the table and tried to read the front page story but found himself distracted. Laney had bent over to put lunch into the oven, and to his surprise, she was not wearing any underwear. This got his attention, especially when Laney looked back at him, watching him watch her with a sly grin on her face.

"Like what you see, darling?"

"You'd better believe it." Bill stood from his chair, unbuckling his belt, prepared to take Laney right there in the kitchen.

As he got close, Laney turned quickly. He felt a sharp pain in his abdomen. The handle of a knife, held tightly in Laney's hand, protruded from his stomach. He was shocked and could barely focus on the pain.

"Well now, Billy Boy," Laney said in an exact imitation of his dead wife's voice. "How do you like that? Not quite the poke you had in mind, was it? Yes, well it wasn't what I expected ten years ago when you cut me to pieces either."

"Laney? Is that really you? You're dead."

"I am dead, Billy Boy. You made sure of that, didn't you?

Bill started to feel faint. "But how, Laney? How can you be here now?"

"Well, Billy Boy. You put my ring on the finger of this aberration you call a wife, and did so with love. More love than you ever showed me. Once the ring was in place it gave me the opportunity to inhabit this shell. And now, my darling husband, you are going to die, slowly; one piece at a time."

MEAN STREAK

by Catherine Jordan

[signature: Catherine Jordan]

I thought a candy factory tour would mean chocolate and sugar awesomeness.

I poked my tongue into the five cavities I have. Genetics, not my fault, even if I skip a brushing here and there.

Mom and Dad said I couldn't go on the tour. Mom's words were, "I absolutely forbid it."

He gave Mom one of *those* looks. "You know we can't forbid him," he said, barely above a whisper. He grasped my shoulders and looked me straight in the eyes. "We've always told you to be a good boy. I hope you are."

Wow, I knew they were concerned about my teeth, but this seemed a little overboard. I figured they were trying to keep me from getting more cavities, but jeez. Typical parental drama. The dentist pretty much said I'd get 'em no matter what, so of course I ignored their warning when I got the text from Sid:

lots of free candy. meet at my house. bike 2 factory from there

Sid lived two doors down, next to old Mrs. Adler. He was a year older than me and his real name was Eddie. Everyone called him Sid, nicknamed after the bully in *Toy Story*—the one who tortured kids' toys. He looked exactly like him.

I hopped on my bike and headed over. My tires skidded into the shade of Sid's garage just as Mrs. Adler's new kitten dashed inside. Before

I had a chance to nudge the kitten back out, Sid pushed the button on the wall. The automatic door whirred and clunked with dread.

"Here, kitty, kitty," he called, his voice high with false emotion. Like Dorothy's witch calling, "Come here, my little pretty."

The light in the dark garage came from a high window in the back corner. Sid often snuck in that window whenever he forgot his house key. The two-car garage door, trapped in the smells of oil, dry grass, and festering trash, along with the kitten. Metal shelving stood along the back wall; rakes and shelves hung haphazardly by their handles from angled nails in the beat-up drywall. A pair of flies buzzed past me.

My heartbeat throbbed in my throat as the white kitten padded its way toward Sid. He rubbed his hand down its furry back, slowly, friendly. Then he snatched the tail and swung it over his head like a lasso.

"Hey! Stop that!"

Sid let go, launching the kitten. It whirled across the room in a blur of white, hitting the cement wall with a dull thud. I grimaced. My stomach started to churn—nerves, disgust, fear, all mixed with anger.

"Whoa!" Sid turned to me and smiled. "A cat that doesn't land on its feet." I took a tentative step toward the kitten before it limped under the shelving in the back of the garage.

Sid dropped to his stomach and jabbed a broom handle underneath.

"Cut it out," I said, then leaned down to see the kitten cowering against the cement wall. Blood stained its white face. It licked at its crooked paw. "Awww," Sid said, glaring at me as he turned out his lip sarcastically.

Damn you, Sid. Someone oughtta take you by your leg and swing you around, see what you hit, where you bleed. Wishful thinking, yeah. Still, Sid'd think I'm a sissy if I tried too hard to help it, probly punch me in the arm.

I'm no sissy. A wimp, maybe. Us smaller kids at school walked around with targets on our backs. And there were plenty of bullies lurking round the corners. Sid . . . he was my bully. We had this understanding where his tyranny came with protection, kinda like being a prison mate's bitch—"Hands off this one, he's mine!" Not sure how or when we formed our friendship, or if you'd call it that. We're neighbors. We grew up together. Our parents are friends. Sooo . . . Yeah.

"C'mon, man. It's hurt." I yanked the broom out of Sid's hand. The hot desire to whack him with it burned in my veins, but I knew better. I'd be an idiot to hit Sid. You know the saying—keep your friends close, but your frenemies closer. The kitten got off easy compared to what Sid would do if I wasn't around. "Leave it alone." I threw the broom aside and pushed the garage door opener, allowing the kitten to make its escape. "C'mon. Let's go."

"Hey, you let it get away!"

I hopped on my bike. "I thought you wanted to go to the factory."

"Yeah, okay. Let's get out of here. My mom's making barf-loaf for dinner. Think I'll pass, thank you."

* * *

We rolled up full speed to the factory. Our bike tires skidded to a stop on faded, cracked pavement. A red brick building loomed in front of us.

"Holy shit," Sid said, staring upward. "It's huge."

The building stretched to a dizzying height. I couldn't tell where its rooftop ended. A dented, bent metal sign that read CANDY clanged against the brick front as it swung in the hot breeze. Each bang was followed by a squawk from a bunch of crows circling a tall black smoke-stack. A dark puff whooshed from the smokestack, scattering them.

"The front door's boarded up. And those windows, they're all bro-ken." I was weirded out, to say the least.

"They look like open mouths with jagged teeth," Sid said, a little excited, kind of amused. I expected him to end his sentence with, "Cool!" Might-a been what he was thinking, even if he didn't say it. He'd crawl through those windows if there was no other way inside. He'd expect me to follow. My muscles tightened as I imagined those shards piercing my skin. I forced down the lump in my throat.

Black, burn-stained bricks around the windows sagged on top of each other, as if ready to tumble in the next gust of wind. "When . . . was there a fire? Is this place closed down?"

I stole a glance over my shoulder. The sun shined behind us, but dark clouds hung over the factory, the sky above it gray. I rubbed the goosebumps on my arms. "I don't think anyone else is here." Unease rumbled in my stomach like a horde of insects trying to poke their way out through my navel. "You sure this is the right place?"

"Yeah, I'm sure." Sid jumped off his bike and let it crash to the pavement. "We're supposed to go around the back."

"Not sure I want to." I gripped my handlebars, one foot on the pedal, ready to peel away at a moment's notice. Place was creepy.

Sid rolled his eyes. "Don't tell me you're chicken."

"I'm not chicken!"

"Hey . . . Hear that? Music! People laughing! C'mon, chicken. Meet you in back, if you're not afraid." He took off running and disappeared around the corner.

Jerk! I wanted to yell—but didn't. Sid was gone. He'd left me alone with the squawking crows. Nothing to worry about, I told myself. Til one of those crows screamed. Nearly crapped myself.

And then I heard something else. Laughter. It echoed off the brick walls. "Sid!" I pedaled closer to the corner of the building. I heard kids' voices. More laughter. Music. Circus music. Relief eased the knot in my gut. I mean, what was I afraid of, anyway? This was a candy factory, or so the sign said. I sighed, still nervous. Then I carefully leaned my bike against the brick wall and walked around the corner.

A cluster of bright balloons hit me in the face. Their dull, hollow bobbing startled me. I took a step back and started swatting, punching them out of my way.

"Sorry," said the boy holding the balloons. "Want one? Pick a color."

I recognized him. He was in my grade, different class. Couldn't remember his name. He glanced past me, his eyes floating out to the crowd of kids. "Here." His fist got lost in the tangle of ribbons as he tried to wrestle one free.

Kids of all ages trampled the tarred ground. Cracks in the macadam exposed dirt and patches of grass. "No thanks," I said to him.

He looked me up and down, shrugged, and walked away.

The music was louder, coming from . . .

The doughy, sweet smell of funnel cake and french fries hit me. My mouth watered.

I was standing at the back of the building on a wide-open lot. No cars. A few bikes had been ditched on the outskirts. The back of the building was windowless. That shoulda been a big warning, but it got overshadowed by the food stands dotting the lot: pink and blue cotton candy, lemonade, hot dogs, popcorn, shaved ice.

With a deep breath, I shrugged off the creep factor. Cuz, man, was I hungry! Besides, I figured there had to be adults here somewhere, probly inside conducting the tours, secretly in charge of the whole thing. Of course. They'd be lingering in their stiff white factory clothes and hairnets, barking orders. And they'd suck the fun out of this, like adults always do, so I might as well chill.

"How much?" I asked the kid at the shaved ice stand, my mouth still watering, throat dry. "Nuthin," he replied, shaking his head, handing me a purple-filled paper cup. Grape flavored, I figured. "It's free."

"Free! Everything?"

He nodded.

"All right then. I'll have . . ."

I wolfed down a couple hot dogs. Then chugged overly sweet but slightly bitter lemonade. Crunching on gritty sugar, about to ask for a refill, I turned to see Jimmy and Dave from swim team cheering on a hot dog eating contest. A couple girls from chorus were laughing, pointing at the contestant who leaned over his feet and puked up chunks of undigested bun and fleshy meat. Gross. I swigged more lemonade, chomped some popcorn, looked around for Sid.

Kids were gathering like ants in a line by the back door. A wooden sign staked in the ground read:

'Tour the Candy Factory'

Sid was up front with a big, shit-eating grin. He'd obviously cut in line.

Sid caught my eye and waved me over. I shook my head—Allison Damon, the class bully—stood right behind him. I hated Allison. She slouched with arms crossed, jaw working over a wad of gum in her big mouth. A couple of guys were checking her out. Long red hair hung down the back of her tight yellow T-shirt. As usual, her eyes were rimmed in dark eyeliner, emphasizing her blue eyes. She was pretty, but no one liked her. Mornings on the bus with her were a treat—she threw gum-wads, aiming at kids up front. In class, she always slumped in her desk chair, like she was about to slide onto the floor. Teachers started the year by asking her to sit up, but she just gave 'em the finger. Yeah, Allison got sent to the principal's office a lot. She'd just roll her eyes as if she didn't care.

The boy in front of me said, "You can go ahead of me. This line is taking too long."

"Nah." I was trying to decide if I should leave. My stomach started to hurt. I still didn't feel comfortable being there. Something was off. And hanging in line beside Allison for a tour—who knows how long that would last—wasn't worth it. "I know that girl up there, standing by the kid who's waving me over. She'd be mad if I cut."

"You mean Allison Damon? She threw gum in my hair. My mom had to cut it out, gave me a bad haircut. Allison made fun of me for weeks."

Sid waved again and mouthed, "Get up here."

"Definitely gyp Allison," said the boy. "I know who Sid is. Everyone does. She won't give him any crap." He sighed. "I'm outta here. Bye."

I hesitated, then thought, what the hell, and elbowed my way through the kids toward Sid. "Excuse me," I said. "Comin through. 'Scuze me." While nudging myself along, I overheard someone say, "I heard a kid lost a hand in one of the machines." Then, "Oh yeah?" from another. "My friend told me someone choked on a piece of glass in a chocolate bar." Great. Just what I wanted to hear as I was about to take a tour in that big enclosed building.

"Hey!" Allison yelled when I wormed my way in front of her. "You're not gypping the line, too."

"Screw you, Allison," Sid said, coming to my defense, stepping up to her. "I already told you I'm in a hurry cuz I gotta take a leak, so we're next, unless you want me pissing all over your shoes."

Allison's jaw fell open.

A satisfactory grin rose on my cheeks. What ya got to say now, huh, Allison? Nothing. Guess she wasn't as stupid as she was mean.

A pink wad balanced on her tongue. Her eyes narrowed into slits as she clamped her mouth shut, chomped, and snapped her gum. She sounded like a cow.

"And I better not find any gum in my hair," Sid warned.

"Or what?" Allison asked, snapping loudly, arms crossed.

Sid leaned into her. "I heard you just got a dog," he whispered.

Oh, man. Allison should've kept her stupid mouth shut.

"It's a poodle, right? I hear that thing yapping every morning when I ride by on my way to school. Sure would be a shame if anything happened to it."

Allison sucked in a gasp. Her face turned dark red. I thought she was choking on her gum until she blurted, "If anything ever happens to my dog, I swear I'll—"

"Next!" called a loud voice from behind the open door.

Sid slapped me on the back. "That's us."

A hand stretched out the door, offering dark-brown, foil-wrapped candy bars. We snatched the bars, ripped open the packaging, took a greedy bite, and walked through the door.

It slammed shut behind us. I whipped around in time to hear it latch. With my heart pounding in my throat, the chocolate turned to chalk in my mouth.

Once my eyes adjusted to the dark, I realized we were standing on a metal platform. Shadows lingered all around. I peered over the platform. My stomach flipped as I looked down into a tank filled with dark liquid. "That's a long drop."

As usual, Sid ignored me. He gobbled down his candy bar while he stared ahead. "Hey, see that sign?" he asked, pointing. "'Chocolate tank.

Bungee jumping. Must be 18 or have a parent's permission.' Ah, dude. This is fan-freakin-tastic!"

A woman stepped out of the shadows. She was dressed in white coveralls with her dark hair gathered in one of those ugly hairnets. I looked at Sid, he looked at me. He smiled through a black mouthful of chocolate.

"Well?" Her nostrils flared and she looked us over, like she was some know-it-all superior. Adults. Just as I suspected. Time for the fun to end. Pay attention. Hands to yourself. Be a good boy.

"We've always told you to be a good boy. I hope you are." That's what my father had said right before I left the house. A shiver crept along my spine, up my neck, and into my scalp. The hairs stood on end.

"Well, what?" Sid asked, defiant.

"I can tell you're not eighteen. If you want to bungee jump into the tank, then you must have your parents' permission."

"My parents know I'm here," Sid snapped. "They told me I could come." He ribbed me with his elbow. "I'll go first, cuz my friend is chicken."

"Sid," I whispered, dropping my candy wrapper, senses tingling to life. "It doesn't smell like chocolate in here. It smells like . . ." *Meat*, I realized. "Maybe this wasn't such a good idea." I wanted to bolt; my gut instinct told me to go.

Okay, so my parents had tried to warn me. I was beginning to think I should've listened. So what if Sid thinks I'm chicken. I wanted to go home. But the door . . . Locked.

The woman—our factory guide—tried to help Sid strap on a bungee cord. He pulled away from her and said, "I know what I'm doin'." I'll never forget the look on his face, the excitement in his eyes. After everything I saw, that's the thing that stays with me and makes me feel sick, that look in his eyes. "Here I go!" He jumped feet first off the ledge.

Sid dropped like a torpedo. In the split second before he hit the surface, a crocodile's reptilian head popped out. "Hey!" I yelled in a shrill, pointing toward Sid and the croc. "Hey! Lady, there's a—" Then another crocodile snout broke through the water, followed by another. "Sid!"

The croc's long jaws opened. Jagged teeth. My knees buckled.

Sid shrieked as they leapt at him. For a moment he was caught, circled by twisting, writhing crocodiles. They pulled, then released.

The bungee cord yanked him back up toward the platform. Two blood-squirting stumps, one at his wrist, the other at his elbow. Sid looked me in the eyes—terror replaced his excitement, matching my horror. He screamed as he dropped again toward the tank and the crocs.

"Help him!" My entire body went cold. I was frozen in place. The guide stood straight-faced, unmoving.

A croc's jaws sunk into Sid's shoulders and tore off a bloody chunk. Sid bobbed up and down again—all while screaming—as they wrestled with his torso. Like dogs wrestling over a bone. It seemed to take forever.

My feet were lead weights. Arms and hands paralyzed. Mouth started watering, building up saliva, ready to puke. I vomited over and over again on the platform. A candy wrapper—could've been Sid's, could've been mine—fell from the platform, twirling like a maple seed in the air. It landed on a croc's nose as the creature ducked under the water, air bubbles rising from its nostrils. Then . . . Gone. Sid, the crocs, the chocolate.

My gaze trailed up and down the bungee cord swinging in the air. Had this really just happened?

"An animal abuser?" asked the woman.

I jumped back when she spoke. I'd forgotten she was there. Her face . . . too plain, too ordinary. Unrecognizable. I was too shocked to answer, to do anything. I probly should've gone into hysterics at that point, but my thought process was all messed up.

I heard a clank of machinery and almost lost my balance as the tank of dark liquid shifted to the left on a rotation.

Sandboxes, swings, merry go rounds, and monkey bars swung into view below. The top landing of a corkscrew slide was attached to the platform. Another sign. 'Ride the slide. Must be 18 or have a parent's permission.' Ah, shit. Was I next? Was it my turn to go? "Help," I heard myself squeak. No one heard, no one was around to help. My whole body shook. My life was about to end, but still, I couldn't do anything.

The door opened. Allison was beckoned through with a candy bar.

She didn't see me cowering in the shadows. "Well?" the guide asked, her nostrils flared, same looking-over given to Allison. "If you want to slide down to the playground, then you must have your parents' permission."

Allison smiled wide. "They know I'm here. 'Course I have their permission."

"Don't." My voice shook. My chin quivered. Even my hand shook as I reached out from the shadows. "It's not what you think."

Allison pushed my arm away. "What the . . . ? Screw you." She spit her gum at me. It bounced off my nose. I watched Allison plop on the slide's landing and shove off. She slid down and around, bellowing with laughter at each curve.

She came to a halt at the last curve, caught in something. Her face contorted as a fine line of red—a sliver of a cut—appeared through her open-mouthed smile. The weight of her body and the pitch at which she sat forced her through the invisible entrapment. Then the blood ran. I watched, eyes wincing, disgusted and terrified, as she continued her descent. Her body left red streaks behind, and it slid apart into horizontal pieces. Allison's slivered body landed with a wet flop on the ground, piling up into the sandbox like a heap of raw roast beef, the sand absorbing her blood.

"Well, then," said the woman, hands satisfactorily on her hips.

I felt a twinge of regret. I probly should've done more to try to stop Allison from pushing off.

As if reading my mind, the woman who had never flinched said, "You couldn't have stopped her. She was determined. A sarcastic, mean girl whose words cut through others like the wires that cut through her."

The platform wavered. My face, now hot, felt like it might explode.

Allison had become tangled in a trap of razor-thin wires. Sid was eaten by crocs. Now what?

"I'm in charge of who enters," the woman said. "And who leaves. I decide what the next brat has coming to them."

"What about me?" I whispered. Did I deserve something worse? Was there a nasty waiting for me? Would I see my mom or my dad again?

A warm wetness spread over my crotch and down my pant legs. The sweet smell of urine hit my nose.

"Every execution deserves a witness," she said, stone-faced. "Were you able to stop them, your friends, while they committed their crimes?"

I shook my head. "They would have spit on me, hit me. I wanted to. Really, I did."

"So you were no help, were you? That's why you got to witness their punishments, without being able to help." The door unlatched. Opened. "You may leave anytime you want."

Light shined through. Laughter rang outside. I took a hesitant step, ready and willing to flee. *Whoops, forgot about my barf.* I slipped; nearly went down.

I bolted out the door, pushing kids out of my way. "Don't go in!" I screamed. "You have to get out of here! It's not a candy factory!"

"No way," I heard someone reply. "My parents told me this is the last night to take the tour. The factory's closing after tonight."

"Listen to me!" I screeched, grabbing one kid by the shoulders, like my father had grasped me. I stared into his eyes. He pushed me away, kicked dirt in my face. "Get away from me." Then I looked up the stairs to the open door, and at the kid walking through. The woman . . . she raised her eyebrow, gave me a half-smile, a shrug. And then the door closed.

I ran past the cotton candy and funnel cake stands, through clouds of balloons, toward my bike. The metallic smell of blood filled my nose.

I burst through the front door, crying. "M-o-o-o-o-m!"

"Where have you been?" she asked, hands on her hips. There was no anger in her eyes, only relief on her face. "Was Eddie with you? Mrs. Adler called. Do you know what happened to her cat?"

"Yes." I sobbed while standing there, wanting her to tell me everything was gonna be okay. "He hurt her cat. But he didn't deserve to be eaten by crocodiles!"

"Crocodiles?" Her eyes narrowed. "You went to the factory, didn't you?"

I didn't know what to say. Where, exactly, had I been?

She sighed, then pulled me into her arms and hugged me tightly. I didn't want to ever let her go. "We warned you," she said through my sobs. "Come on." She wiped my face. "You're home. You're all right. Let's clean you up." Then to herself, she quietly said, "Well, I suppose Eddie's parents will figure it out when he doesn't come home for supper."

"Mom?" I followed her toward the bathroom, stumbling along the way.

Mom sat on the edge of the tub and took a deep breath. "The factory reopens every twenty years in the early summer, closing when there's no one left in line. Do you remember from history class what happened back in 1821?"

"Yes," I muttered. We were learning about factories and the industrial revolution in school. "That's the year the first factory was built in our city. It burned down."

"It was a candy factory. That fire spread out of control and lots of people died. Almost half the city. The fire was set by children, and it wasn't an accident."

I shifted my feet. "Why?"

My mom's face turned pale. "Have you ever heard the term, 'bad seed'?"

"I think so. I'm not sure."

"A bad seed refers to a child who has turned out . . . not so good." Mom continued to explain as she turned on the tap. "Kind of like a seed you thought was a flower but wound up being a weed. Weeds choke flowers, so you have to pull them up and get rid of them. The children who set that fire were bad seeds. And now the factory—or maybe it's the victims' ghosts, who knows—rids our town of the bad seeds. Warnings don't help; it calls all the children, good and bad. I heard it when I was your age, so did your father. That's why we couldn't forbid you to go. Parents hope their children are good and will return, like you did, but some parents know better.

"You'll miss Eddie." She pulled a towel out of the cabinet. "Some of your other friends, too." The color had returned to her face. She smiled. "You're home. You're a good boy. Come down for supper when you're clean."

H E A V E N   S C E N T

by John B. Kachuba

Rick Warren sat behind the wheel of the Heaven Scent van, idling at a stoplight. A skinny boy across the street stood waiting for his school bus, a red X-Men backpack slung over one shoulder. Instantly Rick saw his younger brother Danny in that skinny kid. He imagined Danny on his last day, weighed down beneath his heavy field gear in the cruel sun somewhere south of Fallujah, the grenade cradled in his hands, and Danny lifting up his hands as if he were taking Communion.

Rick's hands trembled as they gripped the wheel. He needed a drink, but there was no time for that now. He tried to shake his mind clear, but thoughts of his brother flitted through his brain like ghosts.

Non-sectarian Willow Grove Cemetery gave Danny a closed-casket service; the Catholic Church denied Danny because of his suicide. Father Schmidt was an old-time Catholic priest, the kind who thought he walked on water. Schmidt had no problem refusing the burial, despite the church's more modern and conciliatory attitude toward suicides. Where was Schmidt's mercy? Fuck him, anyway, Rick thought.

It had been just as hot that day as it was now. Rick remembered the Marine honor guard sweating in their dress blues. He looked down at his own sweat-stained Heaven Scent Cleaners uniform, a dark blue jumpsuit with the company logo, a thin gold band encircling the words Heaven Scent, embroidered over the left breast. Danny's black hearse gleamed in the sun. Rick was vaguely aware of a dove's cooing intermingling with the mournful bugle tones of "Taps." The scent of freshly cut grass hung in the still air.

The folding metal chair radiated heat, even though Rick and the other mourners sat beneath a white canopy's shade. Danny was Rick's only sibling, and their parents were both deceased. Thankfully, they had died before Danny. Rick could only imagine what her baby boy's death would have done to their mother. He already knew what it did to him. He needed a drink.

He could not look up into the young Marine's eyes as he handed Rick the crisply folded American flag, the same flag that had draped Danny's coffin. It felt warm in his hands, as if it were alive. The service came to an end and the funeral director ushered the mourners to their cars. Rick stood alone beside Danny's coffin. He tried to envision his little brother in his mind, but that image was hidden behind a wall of grief.

Danny boy, what have you done? Where have you gone?

The driver behind him leaned on his horn. The light was green. Danny's ghost disappeared, but Rick knew it would be back.

Two blocks later, Rick turned right onto McKinley, a shady street lined with small—a real estate agent would say "cozy"—1920s vintage houses. Number 107 was a stucco-and-wood Tudor with a tall, narrow gable above the front door. The house looked in good condition—almost new, in fact—and the lawn was neatly clipped. A silver Lexus was parked in the driveway.

A man and a woman stepped out of the Lexus as Rick pulled to the curb. He grabbed his red plastic toolbox from the back and walked up the drive carrying a clipboard in his free hand. Rick set the toolbox on the ground and introduced himself to the couple, Tony and Carmela Sorrentino.

"I'm sorry for your loss," he said. It sounded mechanical since he'd said it to so many people so many times before, but truly he was sorry for them. He knew how they felt.

"Thank you," Carmela said. She was tall and built like a linebacker, but her brown eyes were kind, her voice soft. "Your office said to give you the key."

"Yes."

She dug it out of a leather purse the size of a suitcase and handed it to him. Rick noticed her red lacquer nails and Rolex watch. "How long will this take, Mister Warren?"

"Not sure yet," Rick said. "I'll check the premises and see what needs to be done. Then I'll bring in a crew. Usually, we can take care of everything in a few days."

Carmela nodded. "That would be fine."

"Right," Tony said, an unlit cigar hanging from his mouth. "We'd like to get the house listed as soon as possible." He took a step forward as he said this, as if to assert his authority. He wanted to make it clear; despite standing several inches shorter than his wife and many pounds lighter, he did, in fact, wear the pants in his family. Rick wasn't so sure.

The urgency in Tony's voice said that his crew would have to get the job done on time. There had been too many screw-ups since Danny had died. They were his own fault, but what could he do? His world had blown apart with Danny's. Maybe there were no answers to be found in the bottom of a bottle, but the booze made all his questions simply float away.

"Poor Uncle Mario," Carmela said. She looked up at the gable rising over the front door. "This house was everything to him. He built it himself, you know." She turned back to Rick. There were tears in her eyes.

"Are you sure you want to sell it?" Rick asked, sorry as soon as he spoke the words. It was none of his business, after all. His job was to clean the property, nothing more. The less he knew about the family's personal business, the better. That was a lesson he drilled into his crew. It was sometimes difficult to remain aloof to the emotions of family members, but you simply could not perform a job like his if you let your emotions get the best of you.

"Absolutely," Tony said, talking around his cigar. "We have no choice, now that old Uncle Mario has died in it. We could never live here. Have to sell it. Can't live in a dead man's house."

Carmela glanced uncertainly at Rick. He didn't think she was in the same hurry to sell. "What Tony means," she said, "is that our family members wouldn't feel right living in Uncle Mario's house. It meant everything to him, and we should respect that."

"Bullshit," said Tony. "That's not what I mean at all. The place is cursed now. Jinxed. We've got to get rid of it."

Carmela rolled her eyes. "Tony . . ."

"You know it's true, Carmela," he said, taking the cigar out of his mouth, using it now as a pointer. "You didn't waste any time selling Papa's house when he died, did you?"

Rick didn't question the couple's superstition. After twelve years in the business, nothing surprised him anymore. There were countless ways in which a person might handle the death of a loved one. Who was he to say one was more valid than another? He had chosen a bottle. So how could he offer them advice?

He had work to do, and he wished the couple would quit arguing so he could get started. He stood there on the sidewalk, sweating in his Heaven Scent uniform, wishing he were somewhere else, anywhere else. Maybe Duffy's for a shot and a beer. He swallowed, imagining a good cold one running down his dry throat.

Up beneath the gable, a little spider dangled a few feet above Tony's head. It climbed up and down its thread, then descended in a rush, the thread swaying toward Tony's head. Carmela swatted it away.

"What?" Tony said, quick-stepping aside. Rick saw a glimmer of fear in the man's eyes.

"Nothing, she said with a hint of a smirk. "A spider. You're fine."

"See? That's what I mean," Tony said. "Bad luck."

Carmela sighed and shifted her purse on her shoulder. "Is there anything else we need to do, Mister Warren, before you get started?" Now Rick was certain who really wore the pants in the family.

"Just sign these papers," Rick said. He handed the clipboard to Carmela. She flipped through the papers, signed her name where Rick indicated, then gave it back. "Would you like to come inside with me?" he asked. He didn't think they would, no one ever did, but he thought he should ask anyway as a courtesy.

Carmela shook her head. Tony said, "No."

"All right. I'll call you when we've finished."

He waited until the Lexus had pulled out into the street before putting on a pair of rubber gloves and a facemask with respirator. Years ago, such precautions would have been unnecessary, but the threat of hepatitis and AIDS from contaminated blood necessitated the gloves. The respirator was for the smell. Rick removed a camera from its box and slid it into a pocket of his jumpsuit. He tucked the clipboard under his arm and fitted the key to the door. He pushed it open and stepped into a small foyer.

It was hot and stuffy inside the house, the windows all closed, the air conditioning turned off. He walked into the parlor, the scene of the incident.

The uncle had been a suicide. Rick had a copy of the police report on his clipboard, and he looked up at the ceiling at the hole above the Barca-Lounger, where the first bullet had lodged. The man's hand probably shook when he squeezed off the first round, and so incredibly, he missed his head, sending the bullet into the plaster ceiling overhead. Cracks radiated out from the hole like spider legs. Somehow, after that failed attempt, the uncle steeled himself and pressed the barrel of the .38 against his chest. He didn't miss that time, but he didn't die right away. He managed to get up and stagger a few feet across the floor where he collapsed before the fireplace, beneath the inscription on the mantel that read: *Mine, always mine.*

Rick wondered how he'd been able to finish the job. Why hadn't the reverberation of the pistol echoing through the little room, or the ringing in his ears, or the acrid smell of the powder burning his nostrils, or even the bits and pieces of plaster raining down upon his head . . . why hadn't any of that jolted him from his death wish? How was it that after that startling first miss, he was still able to collect himself and say, *Let's try it again, shall we?*

And how was it that Danny, a good Catholic, could have stood there in the sun, the live grenade in his hands as his fellow Marines dove for cover? Could he really have smiled, as it was reported he did, before blowing himself to atoms?

Rick shook his head and blinked back the tears; some things surpassed all understanding.

In addition to the police report, Rick also had a Heaven Scent
Cleaners worksheet attached to the clipboard, which he now consulted.
He walked around the rooms, making notes as he went and taking pictures of the damage for any insurance claim the survivors might want to
file. He removed personal photos hanging on the walls in each room and
stacked them neatly in a closet. He didn't want his crew distracted by the
visual of the person who had left the grisly remains behind.

He snapped a photo of the burgundy Barca-Lounger. The fatal bullet had lodged in the man's chest, so there were no bullet holes in the
chair. There was, however, a bloody partial handprint on the chair's arm
where the man had pushed himself up. Rick bent down and examined
the fabric. He nodded, satisfied that it was covered in vinyl, a material
easily cleaned, depending, of course, on whether the Sorrentinos even
wanted to bother keeping it. He couldn't imagine either of them wanting
to keep the chair he died in. Rick noted on his form the drops of blood—
"protein" was the term he instructed his technicians to use—spattering
the oak floor between the chair and the fireplace's brick hearth. A second
handprint stained the brick.

There was a large amount of blood, maybe two feet in diameter, on
the floor in front of the hearth where the man collapsed and died. Rick
squatted near the stain, studying it. Six quarts of blood pump through
the human body, and Rick thought the man had left most of that on the
floor. The thick stain was almost black in color except near the center
where a small mass of reddish tissue had oozed from the man's chest. Rick
noticed that the floors needed resurfacing, which meant the blood would
have soaked into the dry wood.

He stood and scanned the room. Rick was accustomed to the incon-
gruity of blood and bone, bits of flesh and tissue, in a domestic setting
such as this. A pair of eyeglasses laid open on the table beside the chair. Last
week's newspaper was turned to the sports page. A cheap reproduction of
Da Vinci's *Last Supper* hung on the wall, a dry palm frond stuck behind
the frame. In the kitchen Rick would find family photos, kids mostly,

held in place by little plastic fruit magnets on the refrigerator; a medicine organizer with various-colored pills and capsules stored in plastic cubicles, each marked with a different day of the week; a coffee mug resting on the counter by the sink depicting a beach scene with blue sailboats on the horizon. It was these little tokens of a life no longer lived that made it difficult for family members to come back to the house to do what must be done. They could not be expected to enter a place resembling an abattoir, and that's where Heaven Scent Cleaners entered the picture.

It was a profession few people knew anything about, and even if they did, few would want the job. Yet, it was a valuable service Heaven Scent provided. Most people understood little about death. They didn't realize just how messy it was. The bowels give way, the bladder lets go, there may be vomit; and in violent deaths, blood, body fluids and fecal matter, bone fragments and hair, and body tissue splatter everywhere.

As proud as he was of the work he did—reclaiming dignity for the dead and helping survivors work through grief—Rick's job wreaked havoc on his social life. He recalled a recent date with a woman named Helen, which had not gone well.

"The bones are the last to go, of course," he had said to her, mistakenly thinking the process of putrefaction fascinated her while he twirled a forkful of spaghetti.

Helen paused, her fork arrested halfway between her plate and her trembling lips, and Rick knew once again that he had gone too far, too fast. Yes, there it was, the color draining from her face as if she were about to toss what little she had eaten of her eighteen-dollar veal marsala.

He would never see her again. *Over my dead body*, she had said, and he almost laughed out loud at the thought. But there wasn't really anything to laugh about, not when you were a thirty-five-year-old bachelor with no prospects.

"Don't let it bother you," Danny had once said, in a rare role reversal, Danny giving Rick advice. "You're a great guy. Some woman will find that out. It'll happen."

Easy for Danny to say, Rick thought. Danny with his string of girlfriends.

His thoughts merged with the gloom of the cloistered little house. A dense and suffocating fog had suddenly filled the room. He couldn't stay inside any longer.

Later that night, as he lay on the couch in his apartment watching the latest news from Iraq on the television, Danny was with him once again. It had been one of those days. Rick had brought it on himself. In the year since Danny had died Rick had tried to avoid the news as much as he could, but the televised sights and sounds provided some unexplainable psychic link to his little brother. It was almost as though Rick could bring Danny back from the dead, suit him up in his dust-colored uniform, and maybe this time someone would rescue him from his demons before it was too late.

Danny's demons came to Rick in Danny's last letter. The letter arrived two weeks after Danny's death. Written in an unfamiliar scrawl, it was an emotional, barely coherent ramble. Danny described a nighttime firefight in a small village, bulldozing a wall, finding the bodies of an old man and several children beneath the rubble in the morning. Danny, who had coached basketball at St. Rita's School, had wanted children of his own someday. How had things gone so horribly wrong?

And now that priest declared Danny would spend eternity in hell as a suicide. Rick could not accept that. His brother was a good man, used unwittingly by bad men for bad purposes. Rick did not believe that Danny's soul would be damned simply because he had, in one utterly desperate and faithless moment, sought his own justice. No merciful God would allow such a thing, would he?

Rick arrived back at the house on McKinley Place early the next morning with a crew of four Tyvek-suited, facemasked, and gloved technicians. He called Carmela Sorrentino on his cell phone and asked her about the chair, being careful to tell her the lounger was soiled, rather than bloody, and did she want to keep it? As expected, she answered in the negative. Rick had two technicians clean it anyway and load it into the van. It would later be donated to the local Goodwill store. The bloody rags used to clean it would be bagged and sent to a medical waste disposal center to be sterilized and then incinerated.

Two technicians were on hands and knees, working rags and clean-ing solution over the bloodstains on the floor. Although naturally right-handed, they scrubbed the floor with their left hands, a company policy Rick had established to remind them all there was nothing normal about finding a dead body in a home, nothing normal in what they were doing and they should never consider such death to be normal. The smaller stains, the trail of spots from the lounger to the hearth, came up easily. The handprint on the brick took a little more work, but it, too, was finally eradicated. The large blot before the hearth caused them trouble. They worked on it for hours, but as hard as they scrubbed, they could not remove it entirely. It was no longer as viscous as before, and the dark color had faded to a purplish-gray, but it was still visible.

Rick was worried. This was an experienced crew. Maybe if they let the stain dry out thoroughly, they could attack it again the following day. Rick told the technicians to pack up.

The next morning Rick went to the house alone, hoping he could take care of the remaining stain himself. After the previous day's cleaning there was little risk of being exposed to contaminated blood, but Rick donned his protective gear anyway. Better safe, he thought.

Inside, he opened the curtains and let the sunlight flood into the parlor. He knelt on the hardwood floor beside the stain. He ran a gloved hand over it, feeling only wood. All traces of pathology—as he called the physical remains—removed. Using the strongest cleaner he had avail-able, Rick scrubbed the stain, working the cleaner into the wood inch by inch. It took him three hours to work over the entire stain. When he was finished it looked perhaps a shade lighter, perhaps not.

"Damn!" he said, sitting back on the floor.

Again, he let the solution dry overnight and returned the following day. Again, he was thwarted in his attempts to remove the stain. He had no choice but to call the Sorrentinos and tell them what happened. In Rick's opinion, they would have to replace the floorboards before selling the house.

"What are you talking?" Tony Sorrentino asked over the phone. "That would cost us a bundle."

"Insurance would probably cover it," Rick offered, aware of the irritation in Tony's voice.

"Yeah, maybe. I want to see it first. Can I?"

"Sure, it's your house."

Later that day, Rick met the Sorrentinos at the house. He stood on the covered porch in his uniform, sheltered from a heavy rain that had begun earlier in the morning. He sighed. The weather showed no signs of improving anytime soon. The Lexus pulled into the driveway. Carmela made a dash for the porch while holding her purse over her head.

Rick didn't bother with any of the protective equipment as he unlocked the door, the threat of disease having long since been eliminated.

Tony and Carmela entered timidly, their first visit to the dead man's house since he had shot himself.

"Oh, Jesus," Carmela said when she saw the stain. She covered her mouth with her hand and stared. Rick wondered if she was going to be sick.

"Oh, Jesus is right," Tony said, circling the stain, eyeing it, as though looking for a way in. "You guys couldn't get this out?" he asked, looking up at Rick.

"We tried everything."

"Jesus," Tony said.

"It's Uncle Mario," Carmela said. She had drawn closer to the mark on the floor, yet her voice sounded far away.

"What?" her husband asked.

"He's still here, he's still in this house."

"Come on, Carmela. What are you talking about? You're giving me the willies, here."

"Don't you see, Tony? It's a sign. Uncle Mario's spirit is still in this house."

Tony's eyes darted quickly around the room as if looking for the dead man.

"We can't sell the house," Carmela said.

Tony stopped pacing. "Tell me you're joking."

"He's not at peace, Tony, and until he is, we can't sell the house."

"We can just tear up the damned floorboards, like Mister Warren said. How about we just put down a new floor?"

She shook her head. "That won't make a difference; his spirit will still be here."

Rick stood watching them, listening to their conversation. It was comical at first, but there was something in Carmela's stubborn insistence that her dead uncle was still among them. The idea tugged at him. He was suddenly uneasy in the house. Despite the cold rain outside, he felt a trickle of sweat run down his back. An image of Danny in uniform flashed before his eyes.

Tony was pleading with his wife, whining to her about repairing the floor and selling the house, but she was having none of it. This was a woman used to getting her own way, Rick thought, and she did. She politely thanked Rick for the work Heaven Scent Cleaners had done and told him she would mail him a check in the morning. To her husband's inquiries about what they would do with the house, she simply said she had an idea.

Never in the twelve years since Rick founded Heaven Scent Cleaners had he failed as he did at 107 McKinley Place. It mystified him completely. Blood, that's all it was; why couldn't he get it out? He was thinking about this the next day as he shuffled through reports and bills at the office, and he was still thinking about it when he stopped in at Fiona's Café for dinner. On the way to his apartment he found himself driving down McKinley, as if the house had called him back for yet another try. Ridiculous, of course. He didn't have the key anymore. Still, he slowed as he drew near.

There was a car in the driveway; it wasn't the Sorrentinos' silver Lexus. He pulled over to the curb. The house was dark, but as Rick watched, a faint light seemed to wash up behind the parlor window. The light grew stronger until a distinct yellow gleam shone forth.

What the hell was that? Had someone broken in? He got out of the van and quietly shut the door. Cautiously, he made his way up the steps to the porch. No sound came from the house, but he clearly saw the yellow light spilling from the window. He peered into the parlor window, the curtains still open just as they had been when he last visited.

The yellow glow emanated from the spot before the hearth where a ring of candles surrounded the indelible stain. A dark figure sat cross-legged on the floor silhouetted by the candles' glow, back facing Rick. This was no burglary, Rick thought, but what the hell was going on?

Almost without his volition, Rick moved to the door and carefully tried the doorknob. The door slowly opened. His heartbeat quickened. He stepped inside, the door clicking shut behind him. The figure across the room did not move. Rick crept closer.

"Please be quiet," a woman's voice said, softly.

Rick froze for a moment, startled by her voice. She hadn't turned to look at him.

He slowly walked toward her until he hovered alongside her. In the candlelight, he saw that the woman's long black hair was fashioned into a braid that hung down her back like a glistening snake against her white dress.

She opened her eyes—Rick noticed they were blue—and placed one finger across her lips for a moment. "Sit, please," she said. "I'm almost finished."

Rick obeyed. Why, he could not say, but he lowered himself to the floor beside her. She closed her eyes again, and he wondered how she could remain calm in the presence of a strange man in a dark and empty house. The woman sat silent and still. He studied her face, inscrutable as a mask. The candlelight played upon her hoop earrings. After a few minutes, she slowly opened her eyes, as if only then coming fully awake. She turned to him.

"My name is Gwen," she said.

"What are you doing here?"

She got up, walked to the wall switch, and turned on the lights. Then she came back to the ring of candles and began blowing them out. A smoky scent wafted through the room. In the bright light, he found her pretty in an ethereal sort of way. Thin and delicate, her face pale, but her blue eyes reflected an inner strength that momentarily flustered him.

Rick should've been angry with this strange woman. She was breaking and entering, burning candles in a home that he considered was still his responsibility. He was, in fact, curious.

"Carmela Sorrentino hired me," Gwen said. "She wants this house cleansed."

"That's already been done," Rick said, rising to his feet. "By me."

"No, not cleaned. Cleansed." She rolled the liquid wax around until the candles' insides solidified, and then collected the candles into a canvas tote Rick had not noticed before. "There's a difference," she said. "You remove the physical presence of the dead. I remove their spirits."

"You're a witch," Rick said, thinking that was not exactly the right word, but not knowing what else to call her.

She laughed. "I'm a psychic."

"You see dead people?"

"Not in the Hollywood way, but I communicate with the spirits of the dead. I help them move on to where they belong."

"And Carmela hired you to help her dead uncle?"

She nodded.

He crossed his arms. "So, how's it going?"

"I feel Carmela's uncle in the house," Gwen said, "but I sense something else as well. I don't know what it is yet. In any case, I'm finished for tonight. I'm tired."

She picked up her tote bag and started for the door. Rick followed.

"Tonight? You mean you're coming back again?"

"Tomorrow night."

He closed the door behind them and walked down the steps with her. "Listen, Gwen, would it be all right if I joined you tomorrow?"

"Why?"

He thought of his brother. But he didn't want to tell her that. "Just curious, I guess. Is that all right?"

"I suppose so. I'll be here by eight."

They were standing by her car.

"Thanks. By the way," he said, extending a hand, "my name is Rick Warren."

She shook hands with him. "I know."

"That's right, you're psychic."

"No. Carmela told me."

The next night, Rick arrived at the house before Gwen. He waited in the van until her car turned into the driveway, then got out and walked with her to the house. Inside, she again placed the candles in a ring around the bloodstain and lit them. Rick turned off the lights and sat on the floor beside her.

"What now?" he whispered.

"We wait," she said. "In silence."

They sat there for a long time, Rick shifting his weight every now and then on the uncomfortable hardwood floor. Gwen, as she had done the night before, sat serenely, her eyes closed. The candles flickered in the darkness, their shadows dancing. They drew him in as though he were shrinking into the glowing circle of light. He felt disconnected, adrift, and he thought of Danny, also adrift, wandering. Time dimly passed, but he didn't know how long he'd been sitting there, or even—a very odd sensation—if he was sitting. Then one of the candles moved, he was certain of it.

"They're here," Gwen whispered.

The air suddenly grew cold. A shiver ran down his spine. His eyes were open, but he saw only the candles and Gwen. Her eyes were also open, and she seemed alert, listening, her head cocked slightly to one side.

"Who is it?" he asked softly.

"Mario," she said. "He's confused."

The air thickened, if that were possible, and a light tingling sensation—like a buildup of static electricity—moved through his veins. The hairs on his arms rose.

A faint smile crossed Gwen's lips. She nodded her head as though agreeing with someone in a conversation. She raised her right hand from her lap and extended it, palm up, to the circle of candles. Her eyes tracked something from the dark corner of the room to the halo of light.

"Yes," she said to the air. Then, after a few moments, she said quietly to Rick, "Mario's gone. Now there's only the other."

"The other?" Images of Danny came to him in a swirl, a mental blizzard that threatened to overwhelm his senses. Danny on his bicycle.

Danny in his baseball uniform. Danny trying to play Rick's guitar. Danny sitting on the porch swing with his first girlfriend, Rachel. Danny in his military dress blues. Danny in a dusty tent writing his last letter home. Danny holding the grenade.

Rick's heart was about to explode. He was no longer sitting up but was slumped over, his head nearly touching the floor, as Danny, Danny, Danny, raced through every nerve, every bone, and every vessel within him. He was filled with Danny. He was Danny.

He felt the pain of the last year—the paralyzing depression—unwind inside him and stream through him like a psychic snake. He sobbed. A hand touched his back, and he knew it was not Gwen. At once, a great calm descended upon him. His brother's mysterious but obviously distraught letter about finding the bodies of children . . . Danny couldn't bear to kill civilians, especially children. Of course. That was why he did it. The images of his brother disappeared and light, like the candlelight, filled him. Gwen turned to him and he noticed the tears in her eyes.

"I don't have to worry about him anymore, do I?" Rick said.

"No," she said. "He's at peace."

Rick sighed.

She reached over and took his hand. "And so are you."

THE TORMENT
OF THE CROWS

by Kyle Alexander Romines

and Green County Middle School Honors Reading Class: Shelbi Bale, Catie Church, Justin Constant, Eva Edberg, Kameron Jackson, Samantha Johnson, Chloe Montgomery, Leah Nelson, Reed Phelps, Ethan Price, Layla Risen, Lauren Scott, Logan Slinker

Note: This story follows the events of the supernatural thriller The Keeper of the Crows, *by Kyle Alexander Romines.*

Jezebel opened her eyes. The world around her was wrong somehow. The chill in the air was unusual for Kentucky, even in October. The last remnants of sunlight vanished like dying embers. A vast darkness permeated everything.

Confused, she sat up and tightened her grip on the steering wheel. An alarm dinged from the open driver's seat door. *Where am I?* The disjointed blur of thoughts brought on a searing headache, but no answers. Still, she tried to remember how she ended up in the car—keys in the ignition—or where she was headed on this lonely gravel road.

Wings rustled in the dark, and a flock of crows passed overhead under the moonlight. She turned the ignition key. *Oh no . . .* It wouldn't start. She got out of the car and stood in the glow of the car's headlights. Not knowing what else to do, she decided to follow the crows' general direction.

The headlights cut through the night like twin knives, illuminating a sinister-looking house in the distance. Vines grew freely along the shutters. Even from where she stood, Jezebel knew no one would be able to see through those hazy windows. Her brow narrowed in recognition. *That's Salem's house.*

It, too, was wrong—even eerier than she remembered. Salem and his aunt lived alone in that house on the farm. The property's relative seclusion from Gray Hollow was probably a good thing, especially given all the rumors about Salem and his family.

Why this house? Why now? The answer came to her at once. It was Halloween. Jezebel had been invited to a party, but Salem—afraid for some reason—had asked her to stay with him at the house while his aunt was away. She and Salem were friends until high school, when Salem's differences from their peers created a distance between them. Or perhaps she had created the distance. It was painfully obvious he wasn't like everyone else.

No, wait. She wasn't in high school anymore. That was almost twenty years ago. Jezebel massaged her temples, hoping to jog her memory. What was the last thing she remembered? Fleeting images shot through her mind. She saw herself in a cave, surrounded by crows as something monstrous stirred within. The memory faded just as quickly as it had appeared, and it hit her. Salem was dead.

I failed him. It was the only certainty in her fog of confusion. When he had asked her to come over years ago on that Halloween, she had turned down his request to attend the party. But she hadn't known that Chuck Underhill and his friends, who had tormented Salem for years, had a deadly prank in mind.

I should have been there. I could have done something. I would have saved him. How many times had she replayed those same modals of lost opportunity since Salem disappeared? Years later, she investigated his murder and learned the truth, but by then it was too late.

A loud hiss jolted her back to the present. *There's something out there.* A shadowy figure had dashed beyond the reach of her headlights. Jezebel's eyes followed it to the cornfield, where the figure vanished into the dense maze of corn. She craned her neck. Her gaze fell upon a scarecrow on its perch above the rows of corn. Even at a distance, its misshapen features were unnerving. She didn't know how many Salem had made, but the things were everywhere.

A crow squawked. More crows circled above the field.

"Jezebel." A voice called to her from the cornfield, and the hair stood on the back of her neck.

Jezebel shook her head. She had no intention of sticking around to see what was out there. She slid into the driver's seat, put the vehicle in reverse, and stomped on the gas pedal. Gravel spun under her tires and kicked up a wave of dust as the vehicle ran right into a tree.

The collision was deafening. Glass shards showered her as the windshield cracked and shattered. She felt a blunt force to her forehead. Moments later, she took in a winded breath. She pulled away and sat up, swallowing hard, wondering if she was okay. Her head had slammed against the steering wheel. A trembling hand went to her wet forehead. With a quick glance in the rearview mirror, she saw the trickle of blood. And a looming figure behind her car. Jezebel scrambled from the car, nearly losing her footing in the process. Once she righted herself and stood, she looked again for the mysterious figure. It was gone.

Jezebel was shaking. She felt like she was sixteen again, as if none of the last twenty years had happened. But, if that were true, then the question remained—what was she doing at the house?

Maybe she was wrong. Maybe the last twenty years were a lie. What if none of it had happened? No. Salem was dead, murdered by his bullies. Something other—something evil—had manipulated events to take possession of Salem. *The Keeper of the Crows.* Jezebel struggled to hold onto the past. She searched for an anchor to keep herself from forgetting. A name popped into her head. *Thomas Brooks.* The reporter who had helped her solve the mystery of Salem's murder.

Another hiss—this one came from the cornfield. Pale moonlight revealed similar scarecrows observing silently from the woods' edge. Jezebel felt an eerie sense of foreboding as she looked up. More crows stared at her from the trees. The birds spread their wings and flocked toward her. Jezebel took off in a sprint toward the house. The front door opened to her touch, and she slammed it shut behind her. She tensed and braced herself against the door, expecting the swarm to crash against it, but nothing happened. All was silent.

Her heart pounded furiously in her chest. Jezebel took a deep breath and steadied herself. Perhaps the danger had passed. She stepped away, hesitantly. The raging winds picked up. She heard breathing, thought it was her own, then suddenly became aware of another presence in the room. Her skin crawled. Someone was standing behind her.

Jezebel slowly turned. A tall, lanky figure stared at her in the dark. She readied herself for a fight, but a flash of lightning illuminated the last face in the world she expected to see.

"Jezzie?"

Jezebel's eyes widened in disbelief.

"Salem?"

"Jezzie, what are you doing here?" He looked exactly as she remembered—rail-thin and unusually tall. That was one of the reasons his bullies called him 'scarecrow.'

Jezebel stared at him as he approached her, unable to find the words. *This isn't real. It can't be.*

Salem wore a bright smile. "You came! You came after all!" He wrapped her in a tight embrace.

She stood there, paralyzed. It was as if her secret wish had been granted. Somehow, she was reliving Halloween night all those years ago—only this time she was with Salem. Despite everything screaming that this moment in time was terribly wrong, she gave herself over to the rush of emotions and encircled her friend with her arms. "I'm so sorry, Salem. I'm sorry I wasn't there when you needed me."

He pulled away abruptly. "What do you mean? I don't understand."

Jezebel started to reply, but something about the exchange seemed familiar. She had been at a party the night Salem went missing and had no way of knowing how events transpired when he died. "Salem . . ." Her eyes drifted to the door. As if on cue, there came a knock at the front door.

Jezebel stiffened. Salem started to the door, but she grabbed his arm and shook her head. "Wait."

His expression faltered when he noticed her concern. "What is it?"

Jezebel shot another glance at the door. "They're here to hurt you. The demon in the cave is using them to get to you."

"How do you know about that?"

"You have to listen to me, Salem. We don't have much time. The demon wants to use you to bring your scarecrows to life. If it does . . ."

Another knock echoed behind them. "Jezzie, I'm afraid."

Jezebel put her hands on his shoulders. "Do you trust me?"

He looked into her eyes and slowly nodded.

"Then we have to go. Now." Jezebel took him by the hand and led him away just as the front door swung open. She led him across the hall and into the dining room, which looked as if it hadn't been used in ages. White sheets covered most of the furniture, and spiderwebs clung to the vintage waterfall chandelier.

Jezebel quietly lowered herself to the ground and eased herself under the dusty tablecloth. Salem, much taller, managed to fit only after bumping into the table.

"What was that?" The male voice outside the dining room was slurred like he'd been drinking. Logan. Big, tough Logan Randall, who wore a perpetual frown.

"Don't ask me," another voice replied. Chuck Underhill, the leader of the bully pack. He breezed through life on his judge father's coattails and expected his friends to fall in line. They usually did. "Get in there and check it out." Footsteps sounded in the room. "Logan, where'd he go?"

"I don't know. Thought I heard two voices. You think the freak isn't alone?"

Jezebel held a finger to her lips, cautioning Salem against speaking. From under the table, she glimpsed costumed figures. One, carrying ropes, stopped to look around. Although the bullies hadn't meant to kill Salem that night, they had concealed his body to coverup their crimes. But if Salem was still alive, maybe it wasn't too late. Jezebel could save him where she failed him before. Her expression hardened with resolve.

The intruder with the ropes turned around and started to leave. Suddenly, Salem sneezed, and Jezebel went rigid.

"Go!" She pulled him out from under the table, and they sprinted into the next room.

"He's over here!"

Masked figures appeared around the corner, and Jezebel pivoted and pulled Salem after her. The costumed intruders converged in the family room. There were five in all—enough to block all the exits.

"Look at this! The freak has a girlfriend!" The one with the ropes roared in laughter. "You can watch, sweetheart. If you ask nicely, we might even let you join in the fun."

Jezebel stood her ground. "Enough! I know who you are, Logan. And you, Chuck, Rick, Gary, and Jeffrey."

The laughter stopped abruptly. The kid wearing a pumpkin mask exchanged a long look with his friends. "What did you say?"

"You heard me. I know who you are, Gary." Jezebel put her hands on her hips in a show of defiance. "How did your little gang think this was going to play out? That you'd give Salem a scare and no one would ever know?" She narrowed her gaze. "I swear—if you try anything, I'll bring a storm down on you so bad even Chuck's dad won't be able to get you out of it."

Chuck's voice—full of anger and arrogance—was unmistakable from behind the ghost costume. "Is that a threat?" He took a step forward and nodded to Gary's pumpkin mask. "Maybe we'll teach her a lesson too."

The boy in a clown mask spoke up, clearly uneasy. "Now we're threatening girls?" He removed his mask, and Jezebel recognized the face of Jeffrey Daniels, Salem's neighbor.

"Get your mask back on," Chuck ordered. "I thought you said you wanted to be one of us."

"And you said you only wanted to scare him." Jeffrey clenched his teeth in anger. "I'm a basketball star. You're just a judge's entitled son."

Gary Davis, standing off to one side, pulled off his skeleton mask. "Maybe he's right, Chuck. Salem looks plenty scared enough to me. I think we should just go." He put a hand on Chuck's shoulder, but Chuck wrenched free from his grip.

"No one threatens me."

"You're right, Chuck." The voice came from Logan Randall, who spoke with his head cocked, as if listening to another voice in the room; he nodded in agreement. "We have to kill him."

Gary looked at him like he had lost his mind. "Kill him? Have you gone insane?"

Logan simply stared ahead listlessly. "We have to do it. For the Keeper."

Rick's voice broke the shocked silence that followed. "What's wrong with the freak?"

"Jezzie . . ." The words came from Salem. "They're coming."

Deep, garbled whispers echoed outside the house. The windows shattered, and hundreds of crows poured into the family room. The swarm enveloped Salem, but Jezebel grabbed him and pulled him free. Using the group's confusion to her advantage, she started for the front door, which stood open.

"Come on, Salem. We can't stay here." She glanced back in time to see Logan jab a pocketknife into Gary's eye.

They fled into the night with the crows at their backs. Chuck, Rick, and Jeffrey followed.

"This way!" Jeffrey ran ahead toward the car, but once inside, to his visible horror, the keys were gone.

Logan emerged from the house covered in blood. The birds darted about his head and seemed to murmur to him, coaxing him. Jezebel and Salem ran, taking refuge in the barn, out of the moonlight. It was quiet. The temperature dropped, their breath clearly visible. Rick had followed them and came running inside, probably to seek shelter. Logan's arm came swinging out from behind the barn door and severed Rick's windpipe with the pocketknife.

Salem let out a shriek, and Logan's gaze fell on their hiding spot.

"Salem, run!" Jezebel bolted out the back of the barn with Logan in pursuit. The cornfield lay ahead. She tripped and landed on the cold ground. Salem had skidded to a stop, but not quickly enough. Logan hovered over her, pocketknife in hand. The crows dived in, surrounding Logan, cajoling him.

"I know she has to die. Stop saying it!"

Jeffrey jumped from the shadows, tackling Logan out of the way, and the pair rolled across the ground. "Go!" Jeffrey yelled to them. "Now!"

Salem pulled Jezebel to her feet. They sprinted into the cornfield.

Mist spread along the ground beneath their feet. Thunder cackled like laughter from the clouds. Jezebel's legs burned. Her pulse raced so hard she thought her heart might burst. In the dark, the cornrows became a dense maze. The farther she went, the more she lost her way. She stopped cold when they reached the pole where the scarecrow had hung.

"The scarecrow—it's gone." With growing horror, Jezebel recalled the figure that had watched her from the cornfield and the monstrous hiss that had called to her.

Salem appeared equally shaken. "Jezzie." Salem leaned into her and placed a cold hand on her shoulder. "There's something you should know. My scarecrows . . ." He cleared his throat. "They aren't like other scarecrows." He lowered his voice, and his breath came out in short bursts. "Sometimes they walk."

"I know." Even after all these years, she never learned how Salem brought the scarecrows to life—perhaps with some latent psychic abilities—but she did know that his power had drawn the Keeper's attention.

Leaves crunched underfoot. "Someone's coming." Jezebel slipped behind the next row and lowered herself into a crouching position.

"Show yourself, freak! I know you're here." Logan's voice. He approached, pushing dried corn out of his way. Moonlight glistened on his raised, bloodstained pocketknife as he searched for them through the stalks.

Jezebel spotted a second figure behind Logan. She squinted, wondering if she was really seeing what she saw. Indeed, a withered, emaciated frame lumbered at Logan's back, inches away. Crows perched on its shoulders, and although shadows concealed its features, Jezebel clearly made out a crooked smile stitched across its face. The scarecrow bent low and whispered into Logan's ear, and he turned in their direction . . . then started straight for them.

Jezebel squeezed Salem's hand for reassurance and lowered her voice. "Come on." She retreated into the next row, then the next, careful where she stepped so as to not make a sound. She was so preoccupied with avoiding Logan that she ran face-first into Chuck Underhill, who had also hidden himself in the cornfield.

Without warning, another memory resurfaced in her mind. She saw herself with Chuck in another cornfield, in another time. In the memory, he held a gun pointed at her chest. Jezebel winced, still able to recall the pain that accompanied the gunshot. "You shot me."

Chuck looked at her as if she were crazy. "What are you talking about?"

Jezebel remembered crawling through the cornfield as he trailed her to finish the job. It all came rushing back to her. Using his father's influence, Chuck concealed Salem's murder for almost twenty years. When Jezebel, working with reporter Thomas Brooks, had come back to the cornfield—years ago to uncover the truth—Chuck had followed her and shot her to prevent her from exposing him.

Chuck turned his attention to Salem. Like Logan before him, he seemed mesmerized by the whispers of the crows. "You're the cause of all this. Maybe if I finish the job . . ."

Jezebel shoved Chuck back with all the force she could muster, and he toppled backward. Before he could climb to his feet, Logan's shadow fell over him as he emerged from the corn.

Chuck stared at Logan until an uncomfortable realization seemed to dawn on him. "What are you doing? Get back."

Logan turned to listen to the scarecrow at his ear. His eyes fell on the pocketknife in his right hand.

"I said get back!" Chuck attempted to kick Logan away, but Logan pinned him to the ground. Chuck fought, kicking and clawing at his attacker, but Logan refused to budge. "You're supposed to do what I say."

Jezebel was again struck with déjà vu, as if she had witnessed Chuck's death before. How many times had she been there with Salem in the cornfield? Logan stuck his knife into Chuck's throat, silencing his cries.

He removed the knife with a wet squelch and then turned his attention to them.

Jezebel froze. Her first impulse was to run. The barn, the house, and her damaged vehicle were all within distance—and yet, the part of her aware of what was unfolding told her those options wouldn't work. She had tried them all before, and they all ended with the same result—with her or Salem dead.

Instead, she did what she hoped was the last thing Logan expected. She charged him. He brought the pocketknife up to defend himself. The blade sliced her shoulder, drawing blood, as they met head-on in a violent collision. Jezebel hit him with everything she had. The two bounced off each other and hit the ground. She quickly hopped to her feet and kicked Logan hard in the face. She heard a sickening crack of bone. Blood gushed from Logan's mouth. Without faltering, she dove upon him and punched at his throat and head and cheeks. Her knuckles stung, but she didn't relent, even for a moment. When her anger was exhausted, she pried the pocketknife from his grip. Seized by a foreboding feeling—that it was kill or be killed—she raised her arm high and plunged the knife into his heart. His swollen eyes rolled back into his bloody head.

Jezebel let the pocketknife in his chest. She stood and stumbled toward Salem. "It's over."

"What is it? What's wrong?"

His gaze lingered on Logan's lifeless corpse.

"He would've killed you. He did kill you." She was stammering.

Salem swallowed hard. "I don't understand."

Jezebel gasped for air. It felt like one of her ribs was cracked—if not broken. She knew they should move and keep going, but she had to say it, at least once. "I let you die once before, Salem. You needed me, and I let you down."

His confusion was plain. "I don't understand."

At last, she understood. Shot by Chuck Underhill, she had managed to get the gun and shoot him before he killed her. Wounded and on foot, battered by crows, she made her way to the cave where the entity that had taken possession of Salem resided. She had burned it away, sacrificing herself to put an end to evil.

"What they did to you—the thing you became—it was all my fault. I tried to make up for it. I tried to make it right." She had given her life to destroy the entity in the cave to save the people of Gray Hollow and set Salem free from its control. "But I couldn't change the past." She vaguely recalled multiple deaths resulting from her successive attempts to save Salem. Every time she tried, the result was the same—and each time, she lost a little of herself in the process.

For the first time, Salem's face was full of understanding, as if he had been waiting for her to make her confession. "It's all right, Jezzie. I forgive you."

Relief flooded through her as he wrapped her in a hug, and at last, Jezebel began to cry. "I'm sorry. I'm so sorry."

"You saved me, Jezzie. I'm free now." He stroked her hair and held her close. "I'm in a better place."

She frowned. "Then what are you doing here?"

He released her and looked her in the eyes. "I came back for you, Jezzie. You've been stuck here in this place."

"Am I . . . am I dead?"

"You've been trapped here between life and death. The Keeper is forcing you to relive this night again and again."

She let out a sigh. "I'm tired of fighting. I want to move on, Salem— like you."

He shook his head. "You can't. Not yet."

"I don't understand."

"You destroyed the part of the Keeper inside the cave by burning it away, but as long as scarecrows remain, he still has power. Listen to me. You have to fight your way out of this place before it's too late. Before there's not enough left of yourself to remember and you're trapped here forever."

"Salem, I . . ."

The scarecrow loomed behind Logan's corpse. More whispering crows perched on its spidery shoulders.

Jezebel looked again at Salem, but he was gone. She was alone.

Jezebel. The scarecrow stared ahead with mismatched button eyes, and its stitched smile seemed to grow. Its voice—the Keeper's voice—echoed in her head. *There's no escape, Jezebel.* It held out a spindly hand to her. *Come to me, and together we will leave this place.*

She stood, frozen to the spot, transfixed by the scarecrows' whispers. The promise of freedom beckoned to her, but before she took its hand, she remembered Salem's warning.

"No."

The scarecrow's muslin face contorted in rage. It spread its cornstalk arms, and crows massed toward her, leveling the corn in their wake. Jezebel fled through the cornfield. Moonlight gleamed off the shimmering stalks, and she stumbled past the cornrows into the night. The forest lay ahead. Perhaps she could find her way to safety.

Then she noticed a scarecrow on the edge of the forest, barely visible through the mist. Its malevolent features were unmistakable. She glimpsed movement out of the corner of her eye. Yet another scarecrow staggered forward and came to a stop at the woods' edge. Gooseflesh covered her arms. *They're everywhere.* Dozens of scarecrows stood in her way.

She turned in the opposite direction, but more scarecrows waited at the house and barn. They surrounded her, cutting off her path of escape. Cornered with nowhere to run, Jezebel stood her ground as the waves of scarecrows approached. The moon turned blood red, crows stormed at her from above, and everything went black.

* * *

Jezebel opened her eyes. The world around her was wrong somehow. The chill in the air was unusual for Kentucky, even in October. The last remnants of sunlight vanished like dying embers. A vast darkness permeated everything.

Confused, she sat up and tightened her grip on the steering wheel. *Where am I? Salem.*

Author's note: This story was inspired by the students of Brenda Hall's Green County Middle School reading class. Each year, students at GCMS read my debut novel, *The Keeper of the Crows*. This year, the students wanted to know what would have happened if Jezebel had helped Salem instead of attending the Halloween party the night Salem met his end. This story resulted from my attempt to answer that question.

D A G O N

by H. P. Lovecraft

I am writing this under an appreciable mental strain, since by tonight I shall be no more. Penniless, and at the end of my supply of the drug which alone makes life endurable, I can bear the torture no longer; and shall cast myself from this garret window into the squalid street below. Do not think from my slavery to morphine that I am a weakling or a degenerate. When you have read these hastily scrawled pages you may guess, though never fully realise, why it is that I must have forgetfulness or death.

It was in one of the most open and least frequented parts of the broad Pacific that the packet of which I was supercargo fell a victim to the German sea-raider. The Great War was then at its very beginning, and the ocean forces of the Hun had not completely sunk to their later degradation; so that our vessel was made legitimate prize, whilst we of her crew were treated with all the fairness and consideration due us as naval prisoners. So liberal, indeed, was the discipline of our captors, that five days after we were taken I managed to escape alone in a small boat with water and provisions for a good length of time.

When I finally found myself adrift and free, I had but little idea of my surroundings. Never a competent navigator, I could only guess vaguely by the sun and stars that I was somewhat south of the equator. Of the longitude I knew nothing, and no island or coast-line was in sight. The weather kept fair, and for uncounted days I drifted aimlessly beneath the scorching sun; waiting either for some passing ship, or to be cast on the shores of some habitable land. But neither ship nor land appeared, and I began to despair in my solitude upon the heaving vastnesses of unbroken blue.

The change happened whilst I slept. Its details I shall never know; for my slumber, though troubled and dream-infested, was continuous. When at last I awaked, it was to discover myself half sucked into a slimy expanse of hellish black mire which extended about me in monotonous undulations as far as I could see, and in which my boat lay grounded some distance away.

Though one might well imagine that my first sensation would be of wonder at so prodigious and unexpected a transformation of scenery, I was in reality more horrified than astonished; for there was in the air and in the rotting soil a sinister quality which chilled me to the very core. The region was putrid with the carcasses of decaying fish, and of other less describable things which I saw protruding from the nasty mud of the unending plain. Perhaps I should not hope to convey in mere words the unutterable hideousness that can dwell in absolute silence and barren immensity. There was nothing within hearing, and nothing in sight save a vast reach of black slime; yet the very completeness of the stillness and homogeneity of the landscape oppressed me with a nauseating fear.

The sun was blazing down from a sky which seemed to me almost black in its cloudless cruelty; as though reflecting the inky marsh beneath my feet. As I crawled into the stranded boat I realised that only one theory could explain my position. Through some unprecedented volcanic upheaval, a portion of the ocean floor must have been thrown to the surface, exposing regions which for innumerable millions of years had lain hidden under unfathomable watery depths. So great was the extent of the new land which had risen beneath me, that I could not detect the faintest noise of the surging ocean, strain my ears as I might. Nor were there any sea-fowl to prey upon the dead things.

For several hours I sat thinking or brooding in the boat, which lay upon its side and afforded a slight shade as the sun moved across the heavens. As the day progressed, the ground lost some of its stickiness, and seemed likely to dry sufficiently for travelling purposes in a short time. That night I slept but little, and the next day I made for myself a pack containing food and water, preparatory to an overland journey in search of the vanished sea and possible rescue.

On the third morning I found the soil dry enough to walk upon with ease. The odour of the fish was maddening; but I was too much concerned with graver things to mind so slight an evil, and set out boldly for an unknown goal. All day I forged steadily westward, guided by a far-away hummock which rose higher than any other elevation on the rolling desert. That night I encamped, and on the following day still travelled toward the hummock, though that object seemed scarcely nearer than when I had first espied it. By the fourth evening I attained the base of the mound which turned out to be much higher than it had appeared from a distance, an intervening valley setting it out in sharper relief from the general surface. Too weary to ascend, I slept in the shadow of the hill.

I know not why my dreams were so wild that night; but ere the waning and fantastically gibbous moon had risen far above the eastern plain, I was awake in a cold perspiration, determined to sleep no more. Such visions as I had experienced were too much for me to endure again. And in the glow of the moon I saw how unwise I had been to travel by day. Without the glare of the parching sun, my journey would have cost me less energy; indeed, I now felt quite able to perform the ascent which had deterred me at sunset. Picking up my pack, I started for the crest of the eminence.

I have said that the unbroken monotony of the rolling plain was a source of vague horror to me; but I think my horror was greater when I gained the summit of the mound and looked down the other side into an immeasurable pit or canyon, whose black recesses the moon had not yet soard high enough to illuminate. I felt myself on the edge of the world; peering over the rim into a fathomless chaos of eternal night. Through my terror ran curious reminiscences of Paradise Lost, and of Satan's hideous climb through the unfashioned realms of darkness.

As the moon climbed higher in the sky, I began to see that the slopes of the valley were not quite so perpendicular as I had imagined. Ledges and outcroppings of rock afforded fairly easy foot-holds for a descent, whilst after a drop of a few hundred feet, the declivity became very gradual. Urged on by an impulse which I cannot definitely analyse, I scrambled with difficulty down the rocks and stood on the gentler slope beneath, gazing into the Stygian deeps where no light had yet penetrated.

All at once my attention was captured by a vast and singular object on the opposite slope, which rose steeply about an hundred yards ahead of me; an object that gleamed whitely in the newly bestowed rays of the ascending moon. That it was merely a gigantic piece of stone, I soon assured myself; but I was conscious of a distinct impression that its contour and position were not altogether the work of Nature. A closer scrutiny filled me with sensations I cannot express; for despite its enormous magnitude, and its position in an abyss which had yawned at the bottom of the sea since the world was young, I perceived beyond a doubt that the strange object was a well-shaped monolith whose massive bulk had known the workmanship and perhaps the worship of living and thinking creatures.

Dazed and frightened, yet not without a certain thrill of the scientist's or archaeologist's delight, I examined my surroundings more closely. The moon, now near the zenith, shone weirdly and vividly above the towering steeps that hemmed in the chasm, and revealed the fact that a far-flung body of water flowed at the bottom, winding out of sight in both directions, and almost lapping my feet as I stood on the slope. Across the chasm, the wavelets washed the base of the Cyclopean monolith; on whose surface I could now trace both inscriptions and crude sculptures. The writing was in a system of hieroglyphics unknown to me, and unlike anything I had ever seen in books; consisting for the most part of conventionalised aquatic symbols such as fishes, eels, octopi, crustaceans, molluscs, whales, and the like. Several characters obviously represented marine things which are unknown to the modern world, but whose decomposing forms I had observed on the ocean-risen plain.

It was the pictorial carving, however, that did most to hold me spellbound. Plainly visible across the intervening water on account of their enormous size, were an array of bas-reliefs whose subjects would have excited the envy of Doré. I think that these things were supposed to depict men—at least, a certain sort of men; though the creatures were shewn disporting like fishes in waters of some marine grotto, or paying homage at some monolithic shrine which appeared to be under the waves as well. Of their faces and forms I dare not speak in detail; for the mere remembrance makes me grow faint. Grotesque beyond the imagination of a Poe or a Bulwer, they were damnably human in general outline despite webbed hands and feet, shockingly wide and flabby lips, glassy, bulging eyes, and other features less pleasant to recall. Curiously enough, they seemed to have been chiselled badly out of proportion with their scenic background; for one of the creatures was shewn in the act of killing a whale represented as but little larger than himself. I remarked, as I say, their grotesqueness and strange size, but in a moment decided that they were merely the imaginary gods of some primitive fishing or seafaring tribe; some tribe whose last descendant had perished eras before the first ancestor of the Piltdown or Neanderthal Man was born. Awestruck at this unexpected glimpse into a past beyond the conception of the most daring anthropologist, I stood musing whilst the moon cast queer reflections on the silent channel before me.

Then suddenly I saw it. With only a slight churning to mark its rise to the surface, the thing slid into view above the dark waters. Vast, Polyphemus-like, and loathsome, it darted like a stupendous monster of nightmares to the monolith, about which it flung its gigantic scaly arms, the while it bowed its hideous head and gave vent to certain measured sounds. I think I went mad then.

Of my frantic ascent of the slope and cliff, and of my delirious journey back to the stranded boat, I remember little. I believe I sang a great deal, and laughed oddly when I was unable to sing. I have indistinct recollections of a great storm some time after I reached the boat; at any rate, I know that I heard peals of thunder and other tones which Nature utters only in her wildest moods.

When I came out of the shadows I was in a San Francisco hospital; brought thither by the captain of the American ship which had picked up my boat in mid-ocean. In my delirium I had said much, but found that my words had been given scant attention. Of any land upheaval in the Pacific, my rescuers knew nothing; nor did I deem it necessary to insist upon a thing which I knew they could not believe. Once I sought out a celebrated ethnologist, and amused him with peculiar questions regarding the ancient Philistine legend of Dagon, the Fish-God; but soon perceiving that he was hopelessly conventional, I did not press my inquiries.

It is at night, especially when the moon is gibbous and waning, that I see the thing. I tried morphine; but the drug has given only transient surcease, and has drawn me into its clutches as a hopeless slave. So now I am to end it all, having written a full account for the information or the contemptuous amusement of my fellow-men. Often I ask myself if it could not all have been a pure phantasm—a mere freak of fever as I lay sun-stricken and raving in the open boat after my escape from the German man-of-war. This I ask myself, but ever does there come before me a hideously vivid vision in reply. I cannot think of the deep sea without shuddering at the nameless things that may at this very moment be crawling and floundering on its slimy bed, worshipping their ancient stone idols and carving their own detestable likenesses on submarine obelisks of water-soaked granite. I dream of a day when they may rise above the billows to drag down in their reeking talons the remnants of puny, war-exhausted mankind—of a day when the land shall sink, and the dark ocean floor shall ascend amidst universal pandemonium.

The end is near. I hear a noise at the door, as of some immense slippery body lumbering against it. It shall not find me. God, that hand! The window! The window!

I C E L U S

by Chris Pisano & Brian Koscienski

I awoke with a start; dense blackness surrounded me, darker than the ichor of nightmares. Inky pools swirled, undulating before my eyes. I blinked the sleep away, but I felt as if the room was spinning. Was it?

I simply didn't know. My nightmares had been getting progressively worse. More real, somehow. My psychiatrist—how odd, a fourteen-year-old boy with a psychiatrist, and a useless one at that—suggested a way to awaken oneself from the throes of a particularly clutching nightmare. He said some people could simply tell they were dreaming and prompt themselves to wake up even seconds before crashing to Earth on a roller coaster amid flames and smoke and death screams. I believed him, and I envied those people. They had it easy. Like all they had to do was push a button and whoosh—back to reality.

My psychiatrist implied that people's dreams had a little escape crevice. A crease in the fabric of a fine weave. Sometimes a spot in the dreamscape was out of place, like a dog-eared book page. They could simply mark the dream open to a certain point and escape. Much to my increasing frustration, those people knew where to look for such an escape, whereas I did not.

I met one of those people last week. My psychiatrist had recently helped an abused boy through post-traumatic stress syndrome. The boy was able to end his nightmares whenever he wished. Billy was his name. He was ten; the same age I was when my priest told me I would burn in

Hell if I told anyone of our special private prayers in the rectory basement. Billy was a little wisp of a kid, and the intelligence behind his eyes far surpassed most adults. He was okay, for a ten-year-old, I supposed. But there was something disturbing about his faraway stare.

We once had a discussion about the injustices of adults, and school and church and parents. However, the conversation wasn't without its hiccups. It started with me asking Billy if he thought all institutions were designed to allow adults to abuse their power. Billy looked right at me and failed to respond to my particular question. I asked him three more times. Then Billy blinked, and it was like he had just returned from some faraway place. He made me repeat the question again. It was weird. It unnerved me. In the end, after three hours of talking through various sundry topics, including some very pointedly direct questions about dreams and how he could awaken himself, I was left with no answers and was no closer to finding an escape from my bad dreams.

My nightmares intensified over the passing weeks. I reluctantly found myself willing to meet again with Billy. Since my psychiatrist had little interest in my health and more interest in duping my parents out of their money, he hadn't found any process more suitable.

Billy sat stiffly in his chair. "Use a quarter," Billy said.

I blinked, not knowing if Billy spoke to me or the wall behind me, the latter the only thing Billy had looked at ever since he sat down. His eyes slowly shifted from the wall to me, like a slug oozing across a rock. He continued, "It's a technique I like to use."

"Excuse me?" I heard the unease in my raspy voice.

"The first step to escaping a nightmare is to recognize that you're having one."

"I'm afraid I'm not following—"

"Go to bed in pajamas with pockets. Find a quarter and mark it. Scratch it, bite it, paint it—doesn't matter, just mark it. Then, when you get into bed, put it in your pocket. First thing in the morning after you wake up, take the quarter out of your pocket and place it on your nightstand. Do this every night until—"

"Until I can train myself to check my pocket for that quarter. If I have it, then I'm dreaming. Correct?"

A smile oozed across Billy's face. "Correct."

I followed Billy's advice, figuring I had nothing to lose since my parents, my psychiatrist, my priest, and my teachers weren't able to help a whit.

I gilded an average quarter with gold paint. During the day, I trained myself to consciously reach into my pocket, assuring myself there was no quarter. As instructed, I slid the quarter in my pocket when I hopped into bed; I intended to remove it upon waking and then place it on my nightstand.

Staring at the ceiling, alone in the darkness, echoing thoughts of paranoia and stress clamored about my head. The soul-crushing quest for perfection at school brought on mental and emotional lashes from my parents, the omnipresent taskmasters of my life. "Work harder"; the sting of the whip. "Not good enough"; the resulting lesion.

My lips dry and my tongue tacky, I arose to fetch a glass of water. I began my downstairs trek light of foot, lest the slightest creak on the wooden floors waken my parents.

The banister had an intricate curl at both beginning and ending. I placed my hand on the banister, outlining the wooden curvature. Photographs of dead relatives blanketed the wall. I felt like I was being watched. I always hated them; those oily eyes seemed to follow me all the way down. One of the pictures blinked.

Dozens of embedded eyes glared with anger. Or hunger. The banister pulsed beneath my hand, the curl became a forked tongue that licked my arm. The stairs formed jagged teeth that ensnared my feet, ripping my flesh and crunching my bones. I screamed, but no noise escaped my mouth.

The quarter.

I reached inside my pocket and snatched the golden quarter.

I awoke with a start and sat up straight. Sweat coated my skin, and hair stuck to my face. And then I laughed, my golden quarter resting in my palm.

The next day I was excited to share my news with Billy, to tell him that his idea worked. As before, a faceless adult led Billy into the room and escorted him to his chair. My nerves tickled, waiting for the door to shut, to share my secret. Billy's lethargic gaze set toward nothing while I prattled on, exhorting every detail. Almost out of breath, I finished. "I did it. I escaped from my nightmare."

His sticky stare found my eyes. "Why be satisfied?"

A pang of disappointment touched me, upset that he did not share my joy. "Excuse me?"

"The nightmares aren't finished. They will return. Again. And again. All you did was learn how to abbreviate them. Why run from them when you can *control* them?"

A panicked confusion rose up within me, the inference being I had to spend more time in my nightmares. "What do you mean?" Just when I thought I understood the game, it seemed a new set of rules were about to be unveiled. Was there no surcease of suffering to be found?

"I mean," Billy said, his gaze unfocused, "that you can do more than simply make them stop for a little while. You can beat them. Make yourself more powerful. You know . . . affect the outcome. Tell me you haven't wanted to do something like that from the first time they happened?"

"Wait, wait, wait! Slow down a little, will you?" I protested. "This is all happening a little bit too fast for me to figure out. I thought I did control them. Last night. I made them go away."

"Sure you made them go away. But I just thought—"

"Thought about confusing me?"

An ember sparked behind Billy's eyes. "You got it all wrong. Look, you don't realize how far you can go with this. This is your chance to be like . . ." his Adam's apple bobbed as he swallowed hard, then he spat out the last words of his sentence, "an adult!"

"I'm not—"

"Or at least how adults should be." Billy's nostrils flared, and he pressed on hurriedly. "How to properly use power. How to be fair and serve justice. How they should treat you!"

He was getting worked up. His shoulders pumped like pistons while he spoke, his breathing ragged like an asthmatic. This kid had creeped me out a little bit before, and there was no sense of emotion to him. I figured I was the bigger of the two of us, and I could handle him if he tried anything. Now I wasn't so sure I could take him. Not in this state anyhow. And it downright scared me.

I needed to calm him down. Defuse the situation somehow. Most of all, I needed to keep my own composure. I had a hunch he was two seconds from hitting bully status. No one had checked on us during the last few sessions until it was time to leave, and I sure didn't want that to happen while I was stuck here alone with him for at least another hour.

Unsure what to do, I sat and stared at the quaking boy before me. Then he stood. The only times I had ever seen him ambulatory was when he was brought into the room, to this chair. I related the chair as a part of him. But as he loomed before me, he became ominous. I cowered as he stood over me, his wicked eyes glowing red.

Red?

I reached into my pocket and procured my quarter.

Laughing, Billy's towering body deflated to size. With a wave of his hand, the walls melted, giving way to a landscape shaped by mildewed concrete. Rectangular lumps of various sizes sprawled endlessly on all horizons. The clouds in the crimson sky looked like scabs upon blistered skin. Small droplets of flame rained from above. "Do you see now?" Billy asked.

My eyes tried to take in this somber world. "What . . . ? How . . . ?" was all I could say.

"Control," Billy replied. "I'm controlling this. Adults created the world we live in, giving us nightmares. To exist, we simply need to learn to control those nightmares."

"Whose nightmare is this? Mine or yours?"

Billy furrowed his brows. "Does it matter? We're in this together, and we need to work together to survive and thrive. Now you try."

Every night was a new lesson, a new experience. As with every skill learned, my first few attempts were unbalanced and awkward. I moved objects. Big whoop. But after gaining confidence through experience, I learned to *control* objects. Then *create* them. When the banisters in my nightmares turned to snakes, I learned the benefit of making them blind the eyes on the photographs on the wall. After the stairs turned to teeth, they no longer gnashed at me; they gnashed for me. Demons that once tormented me months ago now bowed to me. I matriculated through my daily routine, doing everything necessary to embrace my nightmares, forgoing human contact for that of monsters and trolls.

My change in behavior did not go unnoticed.

I sat in the principal's office as I had done so many times before. Due to my nightmares, I would fall asleep in class. Not participate. My grades suffered from lack of sleep. Like all the other adults in my life, he dismissed my nightmares as childish excuses for laziness. His singular solution had been, "Shake them off and go back to sleep."

Now that I was able to control them . . .

"So, I see your grades have improved," he said, his mirthless words flitting the loose hairs of his thick mustache. His stone eyes embedded in the crags of his face. "Congratulations."

His words lacked nicety, so I replied with trepidation. "Thank you, sir."

"No more nightmares, I assume?"

"No, sir."

"Humpf!" he snorted. His mustache hairs fluttered again. "Doubt you had any to begin with."

"Excuse me?" I asked, not knowing where he wanted this conversation to go.

"I've been a principal for nine years. A teacher for eighteen before that. I've heard every excuse in the book for laziness. Including bad dreams."

I leaned forward in my chair, agitated. "It wasn't an excuse, sir."

He slapped his meaty hand against the desktop. "Oh please! You may have fooled others, but not me."

My chest burned with anger. How dare he trivialize my anguish. How dare he assume to know me and my torments.

I jumped from my chair, fists clenched. "My parents sent me to a therapist to sweep my problem under the rug. And my therapist is useless. Useless!"

A deep grumble emanated from behind his mustache within his floppy jowls as he stood. His prodigious body seemed to take up the whole office. His fists planted on the desktop.

I checked my pocket.

I pulled out my quarter.

Resting in my hand was the permission needed to uncage my ire. I clenched my teeth with enough force to make my temples throb. I outstretched my hands. Under my control, the books on the shelves behind him extended, paper fingers unfurled then grabbed my principal by his shoulders.

Fear swept across his blubbering face, his mustache twitching. I ignored his screams as I commanded the desk to split in half, the jagged wood now teeth of a hungry mouth. It roared while its book-made arms pushed his head closer to the gaping maw. He screamed and squirmed as he was forced into the splinter-lined hole, well past his shoulders. My curled fingers interlocked. I commanded the desk to clamp shut. Popping wood and snapping bones were almost indistinguishable. Blood sprayed when his body burst like an over-ripe tomato. His hips and legs twitched on the floor, his torso having been swallowed.

Applause.

"Well done," Billy said, clapping as he walked from behind my principal's still spinning office chair. "How do you feel?"

Panting, sweat flowed down my forehead and cheeks. "Invigorated. Liberated."

"Now that you can conquer your demons while asleep, you have found that you can conquer them while awake."

True, I was now able to move effortlessly through adults' dreams. After my principal had woken from his induced daymare, he gave me no trouble, save for a stray glance now and again. When he did make eye contact with me, I held his gaze with the strength and confidence I'd never had. I gave him a look of predator to prey, knowing I could rend his fat body to shreds any and every time I lay down to slumber. I quit my services as altar boy and told my priest those very words. I strode from church leaving him aghast, relishing the horrors I supplied to him night after night.

I spoke to my therapist in full, uninterrupted, complete thoughts. During the day, I joyously shared my nightmarish details, his pencil never stopping and nary a glance to his watch.

And my parents were dismayed, uncertain about my relatively abrupt change in attitude. Though my grades had improved dramatically, they berated me about my standoffishness to my teachers and principal and asked why I quit being an altar boy. While awake, I offered them an apathetic ear and simple smile and apologetic words. While asleep, I sent them utter and pure wrath. And Billy had been with me through most of it.

"Are you ready?" he asked, sitting at the foot of my bed.

I jumped from under my covers, ready to start the night's festivities. "Absolutely!" Billy and I tiptoed to the stairs. The banister slithered into its serpentine form, its eager tongue flicking my cheek. The photos on the wall were now allies in my wickedness. The stairs rippled, then undulated. Their waves glided us to the bottom, and a wagging tongue turned into an escalator. He and I scoffed at how childish I was at one point in time, so afraid of what now gave me comfort. When we reached the bottom of the stairs, there in the living room sat my priest, my principal, my therapist, and my parents.

"Oh, this will be delicious," Billy said from behind me.

"Oh, it certainly will," I replied. "This scene is one of my favorites."

"Son? What are you doing awake?"

"Just curious as to why you're all in the living room this time of night." I could not keep my lips from twisting into a smile as I sauntered closer, keeping my hands behind my back.

My therapist chimed in. "We're worried about you. We believe you have some troubling issues and that you don't have a viable outlet for them."

"Oh, but I do. I have turned inward and developed my own outlet."

"My child," my priest started. "Do not turn inward when troubled, but turn to those who love you. Those in this room. God. Come back to the church and I will personally—"

He said the same thing he always said. At the same part of the nightmare, I could take no more of his pontification, his withered hands and wrinkled lips. "No!" I pulled my hands out from behind my back. Both arms were now gleaming steel, razor sharp, and tapered to points. The adults gasped, as they always did.

I rushed for the priest, slicing the Sign of the Cross through his face and torso. He fell to the floor with a wet, bloody splat. Next, I turned to my inept mother. She was unable to offer a modicum of resistance as my blades cut through her stomach. I felt as if I gave her mercy. Shocked, my father remained frozen on the couch. All my life he pushed me, exposing the flaws he found within me. Not this time. One flawless stroke sliced through his neck. My principal tried to run, but his thick legs could not effectively move such a shapeless mass. He fell and I pounced, carving layers off the pig.

Lastly, my therapist. He wasn't looking at his watch now. He had fallen during the commotion and backed away on his haunches into a corner. I strode toward him, lording over him, blood dripping from my bladed arms. With a meek voice, almost a helpless mew, he asked, "Why?"

"Because you're an adult! You adults make nightmares for children. Children like me and Billy."

I slid my hot blades gently through his ribs. His face crumbled with panic. Blood accompanied his coughed question. "Who's Billy?"

"Doesn't surprise me that you don't know who he is. We're all just numbers to you, aren't we? He's the one you paired me up with."

Every time I had delivered justice to him before, he looked at me with fear and regret. However, this time, his brows wrinkled with confusion as the light faded from his eyes. Incensed, I yelled, "You remember Billy! He's standing right over there!"

I looked up.
There was no Billy.
I dropped the knives and reached into my pocket.
There was no quarter.

THE DAY IN THE LIFE OF A NAVY HELICOPTER PILOT, 1989

by Michael L. Hawley

Captain Nash gazed at the officers seated around the war room table. The ship's medical corpsman, Petty Officer First Class Jared LaRue, unofficially known by the entire ship's company as "Doc," folded his hands and raised his head, attentive.

"Gentlemen, a US spy plane just crashed some forty miles away from us, just a mile off the Philippine coast, and we've been tasked to take control of the waters until the salvage ship arrives in four days. 'Unfriendlies' would love to get their hands on that plane. A Special Forces team recently arrived on the beach from Clark Air Base and has made contact with the local village chief." He paused for a moment, then continued. "Apparently, there are communist factions in the area, but the chief assures us he is no friend of theirs."

The ship's operations officer raised his hand. The captain acknowledged him.

"Sir, do you know if the pilots in the spy plane survived and, if not, are we tasked to recover the remains?"

The captain gave a slight nod. "They survived, and apparently they will be returning on scene to assist in salvage operations." He glanced over at the executive officer, the "XO." "Our mission for the next four days, other than to control these waters, is to win the hearts and minds of the local villagers by whatever means necessary." He turned back to LaRue. "Doc, you are to organize teams to go into the village and give medical assistance and any other kind of assistance you can think of." He paused. "Hell, if they want their buildings painted 'haze gray', then by all means, paint them to look like ships."

"Yes, sir," LaRue replied.

Captain Nash cleared his throat. "I want Petty Officer Reynolds on the team for Tuesday morning."

LaRue cringed. "Sir? Petty Officer Reynolds?" His strong accent held confusion.

"Reynolds just joined ship's company," the XO explained. "I'll send him to you, Doc."

The captain glanced over at the XO, nodded, then eyed the four aviators. "Commander Tanner, coordinate with LaRue and the XO and set up a flight schedule." He looked to the map in his beefy hands. "The village is situated in the middle of a jungle. Where will you drop them off?"

"Right on the beach, sir," Tanner replied. "It's the quickest and safest place."

Captain Nash nodded. "Flight quarters in thirty minutes. That is all." Once the captain left, the XO scanned the room. "We have our orders, gentlemen. Flight quarters in thirty minutes. Doc, set up a meet and greet, and bring gifts and hugs."

As everyone began to exit, Tanner addressed the other aviators. "Hanes and Walker, are you two all set? Do you remember how to land on a beach?"

Hanes shook his head. "Sir, don't ever underestimate my skills. Beach landings are my forte," he boasted. "Do a quick flyby to look for electric wires or other obstructions on the beach, keep the helo's nose into the wind, land softly to see if the wheels sink into the sand, and if not, drop the collective and settle in for a landing."

"And takeoff?" Tanner asked.

"Do a quick hover and take off away from the beach immediately," Hanes replied. "Don't sit and hover and let the sand blow up and block our vision. A whiteout is not a good thing."

Tanner grinned. "Good, because that's exactly what happened when President Carter ordered the rescue of the hostages in Iran with helicopters. The pilots hovered and crashed in whiteout."

Petty Officer LaRue approached the aviators. "Gentlemen. I guess you're my chauffeurs for the next few days."

"Walker and I are honored to take first shift, Doc," Hanes answered. "Maximum of four people per flight, so your meet and greet will be a small contingent."

"No problem," LaRue replied. "Later, we can take advantage of the utility boat and bring bigger numbers with supplies."

Peeler gave an inquisitive stare. "Interesting accent, Doc. You Cajun?"

LaRue grinned. "True dat, Sir, through and through. I'm from the Bayou in Southern Louisiana.

"Isn't there another Cajun onboard?" Peeler asked.

LaRue nodded. "Yes, Sir, Petty Officer Joe Castle." He frowned. "He's a dick, so don't think all Cajuns are like him. I'm gonna force him to come with us tomorrow and the next day. Maybe he'll get lost in the jungle or somethin'." He glanced over at Hanes. "I'll get the first contingent ready in a jiffy and see you in the hanger, Sir."

"See you there," Hanes agreed.

Thirty minutes later, Hanes and Walker were seated in the cockpit of the SH-2F Seasprite helicopter with the engines blasting and rotors turning. The helicopter was secured to the ship's flight deck by chains, fastened from the helicopter landing gear to deck hooks in the helo pad, pitching and rolling with the aft end of the ship. Petty Officer LaRue and three other sailors stood next to the wall decked out in helmets and safety gear ready to board the helo. "Ready for our passengers, Petty Officer Sanchez?" Hanes spoke over the helo's intercom to his air crewman who was standing just outside the fuselage door.

Sanchez pushed the intercom button on his helmet wire. "All set, Sir, I have their seats and harnesses ready."

Hanes radioed the helicopter control officer in the tower, located on the port side of the helo pad. "Tower, Easyrider 53, ready for takeoff."

"Easyrider 53, wait one," the helicopter control officer replied, then contacted the captain on the intercom radio. "Captain, HCO here. We have a thumbs up; request takeoff."

Sitting in the captain's chair on the bridge, staring straight ahead, Captain Nash could make out the coastline of the Philippines. He quickly eyed some gauges, then picked up the phone. "Good winds, pitch one, roll three, green deck."

"Green deck, aye," the helicopter control officer replied, then flipped a switch. The flashing red light located at the top of the hangar changed to flashing green. "Easyrider 53, pitch one, roll three, you are cleared for takeoff."

"53, Roger." Hanes gave the flight deck officer a thumbs up.

Once the chains were cleared away from the helicopter, the deck officer gave the signal for a takeoff.

"We're off," Hanes commented over the helo's intercom, then flew straight for the beach at 160 knots.

"Sir, I've connected Doc to the intercom," Sanchez commented. "He can now hear you."

"Doc," Hanes yelled, "once we land on the beach, I'm going to give Sanchez the okay for you to exit the helo. Special Forces should be greeting you. I'll wait for a thumbs up from you, and then we're departing the beach."

"Sounds great, Sir!" LaRue yelled.

"We'll be in the air for another three hours, so if you need us, call on your handheld radio," Hanes directed. "We'll hit the beach in minutes."

"Will do, Sir," LaRue replied.

LaRue had a clear view of the ocean surface rushing by just fifty feet below. Since the helo's side door was off, he was open to the elements. He glanced over at Sanchez and pushed his intercom button. "How cool is this!"

Sanchez grinned. "Just wait for Lieutenant Hanes' beach landing."

LaRue gazed out the six-foot-wide helo fuselage door. The Philippine coastline was just a few miles ahead.

Walker pushed the intercom button. "Landing site's at your 1230," he reported to Hanes.

"Roger, I've got a visual," Hanes replied, then pointed to his two o'clock position at some smoke emanating from a clearing in the jungle. "See the smoke billowing south? Looks like I'll keep the nose pointing north for landing." As they neared the beach, Hanes clicked the intercom button. "Eyes open for obstructions, everyone. I'm doing a flyby."

Walker turned around toward everyone in the back. "Watch for those huge fruit bats with the four-foot wingspans, too."

Once they reached the beach, LaRue spotted the Special Forces team on the ground watching them. They seemed to have cleared a large area on the beach.

After a quick hover, Hanes landed on the beach.

"Clean landing. It's all yours, Sanchez," Hanes reported.

"Roger," Sanchez replied, then eyed the passengers. "You're cleared to disembark. Give us a call when you're ready to be picked up." LaRue and his team quickly joined the Special Forces team. He gave the pilots a thumbs up. The helo lifted and left the beach just as fast as it had arrived.

"That pilot's a nut," the Special Forces team leader commented to LaRue. "My kind of pilot." He slapped LaRue on the back. "Follow me, gentlemen. We'll introduce each other en route to the village. The chief's waiting."

* * *

Three days later, in the village.

Petty Officer Castle wiped the sweat off his brow. A couple of monkeys screeched above in the jungle canopy. Castle turned to Lasher, the other petty officer teamed up with him on the shack's paint detail. "Where's that lowlife LaRue with our chow? I'm starving."

Lasher pointed with his paintbrush to an old Filipino lady roasting eggs over a fire. "Why don't you partake in the local cuisine?" He grinned. "I hear the balut is delicious!"

Castle cringed. "No thanks. What the hell is balut, anyway?"

"Hardboiled egg with chick embryo in it," Lasher explained. "You crack open the egg and eat everything; bones, beak, skull, and all."

"Figures they'd eat somethin' like that in this god-forsaken place," Castle complained, then stared at two young Filipino girls running and playing nearby. "Now, there's a dish I'd like to try."

Lasher glanced over at the girls, then shook his head. "You're a sick bastard, you know that, Castle."

"To each his own," Castle replied.

"Finally," said Lasher, dropping his brush into the paint can. "Here comes LaRue."

LaRue handed Castle and Lasher their boxed lunches and drinks.

Lasher raised his beer to LaRue. "Thanks, Doc."

"What took you so long, LaDick?" Castle blurted as he opened his box.

LaRue grinned. "Four more long hours until the utility boat comes and picks you up." He pointed to two SEAL team members speaking with the new guy, Petty Officer Reynolds, and three rough-looking dark-skinned locals carrying machetes. "Why not pick a fight with them, Castle!" He yelled loud enough for them to hear him. "No longer king of your castle, eh, Castle?" LaRue sauntered away, then stopped momentarily and pointed at the half-painted shack, grinning. "You missed a spot."

Castle glanced at the SEALs and company. They walked toward a path, and the two SEAL team members glared at Castle until they vanished in the green haze of jungle. Castle turned back to LaRue and gave him the finger, then spit on the ground. "See; they ran away just like you, bitch!" He sat on a makeshift seat next to a patch of three-foot-high weeds and began to eat his lunch, one of the MREs brought off the ship.

"Be careful, Castle," Lasher warned, nodding toward the weeds. "This place is filled with poisonous snakes and bugs."

Castle shook his head. "You forget; I'm from the Bayou. I sleep with gators." His eyes followed the two young girls as they ran into a shack just thirty feet ahead. He smirked wickedly. "Once I finish my lunch, maybe I'll have to take a short nap in that shack over there."

"We're supposed to steal the hearts and minds of these villagers," Lasher replied, "not their children. Don't you even care if you emotionally scar them?"

"Not my problem." Castle finished his sandwich and crumbled up his cardboard box. "Nothin' wrong with just takin' a peek in that shack." He glanced around. "This looks like a good place to ditch the trash." He shoved the box in the weeds. "Ouch!" He jerked his hand out and rubbed it. "What the hell?" he snarled. "Somethin' pricked my hand."

"You okay?" Lasher asked. Castle spun on his heels, then crashed to the ground on his back. Lasher rushed to him and shook his shoulder. The weeds waved and rustled. "Castle! Oh, shit!" Lasher turned, looking for help. LaRue was about twenty yards away, speaking to two other sailors and an old Filipino man. "Doc! I think Castle's been bitten by a snake!"

LaRue and the others rushed over. He kneeled over Castle. LaRue's mouth formed a thin line. He glanced up at one of the sailors. "Call the helo in. We have a medical emergency!" As the sailor rushed away, he turned to Lasher. "Go into our tent and grab my medical bag! Now!"

The old Filipino man searched the bushes with his machete. He gasped and raised his blade. It rang as he sliced through the air, then thunked on the ground where it struck. Reaching into the greenery, he pulled out a long, twisting, headless bright-green snake. "Pit viper."

Lasher came running with LaRue's medical bag. "Here it is."

LaRue searched through the bag, grabbed a sealed package containing a needle, and gave Castle a shot. "Damn. Pit viper venom attacks red blood cells instead of the nervous system, like other snake venom. I'm not sure if I have enough of this CroFab." He shook his head. "That helo has to come soon."

The old Filipino man touched LaRue's shoulder. "He needs Adelfa leaves and Kamatgui flowers, now, or he will die. A flavonoid found in our plants will help. We need to take him to our medicine woman immediately."

LaRue nodded and understood that the locals had been treating snakebites for generations. "Okay." He stood. "Where do we go?"

Minutes later, Castle was lying inside a tent on a table. Humidity hung in the air, and sweat blanketed LaRue. A gray-haired village medicine woman attended Castle. No more than four feet tall, she was shabbily-dressed in loose, dirt-covered pants and a torn khaki shirt, hair in an unkempt updo. He hoped her hands were clean as she rubbed a pasty substance on the wound and inside his cheeks. The woman then pulled an egg from her pocket and rolled it with her wrinkled hand along Castle's chest and neck. With her free hand raised to her shoulder level, she shook it while she chanted quietly in Tagalog.

The old Filipino man leaned into LaRue's ear. "She must call in the spirits to help. It is very serious."

LaRue nodded, convinced that it was not these so-called spirits that would save Castle, but the pasty substance she applied all over him, along with the generic anti-venom shot.

The tent flap parted, and a sun-weathered sailor shuffled up to LaRue. "ETA for the helo is thirty minutes, Doc. The plan is to land right here in the village and medivac him straight to Clark Air Base."

LaRue nodded.

The medicine woman stopped chanting. She grabbed the arm of the old Filipino man, fear in her eyes. She spoke hastily to him in Tagalog.

The old man raised his brows. He turned to LaRue. "In order to save him, our medicine woman had to remove a powerful blocking protection spell on this man; an old spell has been lingering from before his time."

LaRue sighed. Though he did not share their concern, and this spirit-thing was way out in left field, he also remembered his orders to give their beliefs respect. He rubbed the back of his neck, massaging the tension knot. "Okay, but does she think he'll live?"

The old man nodded. "Yes, but she says his soul is dark; Aswang no longer dormant."

LaRue had no idea what an "Aswang" was, but he had always known Castle to be maladjusted.

The sailor put his hands on his hips. "We need to prep him for flight, Doc. The helo will be here soon."

LaRue straightened his shoulders. "Thank you both," he said to the old man and the medicine woman. "You've been helpful, but I need to prepare him for his flight to the hospital."

The medicine woman frowned when LaRue stepped in her way. She made room for LaRue to prepare Castle for the flight to the base hospital. She then grasped LaRue's arm and spoke to him in heavily accented English. "Believe and beware." Seconds later, she released him, then rushed out of the shack.

"Ahhhhhhhhh!"

LaRue turned to see Castle screaming; his once limp body now writhed.

* * *

Walker read off a mandate list before landing. He then pushed his intercom button. "Landing site's at your 1200," he reported to Hanes.

Hanes turned the helicopter right and circled for a landing. "Gear's down, prep for landing."

Sanchez eyed the village as Hanes neared the beach landing site. His jaw dropped. "Wave off, Sir, wave off!"

Hanes immediately aborted the landing and flew away from land. "What's the matter, Sanchez?"

"Do a flyby over the village, Sir. Something is really wrong."

Hanes hovered over the village. He and Sanchez stared out the windows at mutilated bodies on the ground. "Oh my God," Sanchez said. "Nothing's moving. Blood is everywhere."

* * *

Years later, Smithsonian National Zoo.

Alan Blake presented his season pass to the ticket lady at the front entrance.

"Enjoy your day at the National Zoo," she said as she scanned and returned his pass.

He nodded. "Thank you." He walked straight to the nearby picnic pavilion. *Washington Post* reporter Dick Turner waved to him from one of the tables. Blake strode toward him.

Turner stood and shook Blake's hand. "Nice seeing you again, Dr. Blake." He handed over a folder. "Here's the file of my own investigation after the incident when I worked as a detective for the Naval Criminal Investigative Service." Both he and Blake sat. "I was very thorough, although nothing came of it." Blake thumbed through the file. "We certainly appreciate you reviewing this for us, Dr. Blake, knowing you as an authority in anthropology."

Blake smiled, then scanned the picnic area. "So, why did you ask to meet here? You could have easily given me this at your office."

Turner grinned. "Why, you don't like the zoo?"

"Course I do. I'm actually a zoo member. Though my wife and I rarely have time to visit, we like to contribute."

"Well," Turner began. "You see, my editor and I weren't being entirely forthcoming at our first meeting."

Blake eyed him over his glasses. "Is this a sensitive issue?"

Turner waved his hand. "No, no, it's just that my editor doesn't want you to think we take pseudoscience seriously."

Blake furrowed his brows. "What?" he asked in a rather high voice.

Turner glanced around to make sure they weren't being watched. "There actually was an eyewitness to the village attack in the Philippines back in 1989, and she works here."

"Oh?"

Turner nodded. "She's Filipino and lived in the village as a teenager at the time. She later met an American serviceman. They married, and she followed him here to DC." He paused and leaned forward. "Her testimony is right out of a horror novel with the killer being a ghoul-like monster. Contrary to my editor's opinion, I think you should listen to this Filipino and maybe get kernels of truth from her story."

Blake nodded and surveyed the area, wondering if she was close by. "Sounds good. Where is she?"

Turner pointed down the sidewalk past the Big Cats exhibit. "She'll be here on her lunch hour, which is in a few minutes." He pointed at the file. "As an expert on tribal culture, what is your professional opinion on what happened at this Filipino village?"

Blake pulled out photos of massacred villagers, stared at them, frowned, and shook his head. "What a tragedy. Absolutely no concern for the sanctity of human life." He flipped between the photos. "These seem to be efficient, opportunistic murders."

"What are you thinking?" Turner asked.

Blake popped his head up, then eyed the photos again. "There are no signs of organization within the chaos. Warring tribal groups have an agenda; a message of complete domination. In order to pacify any future threats, it's common for the victors to leave a calling card, such as scalping or a field of impaled bodies." He shook his head. "I don't see organization in this case. The carnage seems haphazard, like animalistic rage with one agenda—kill and kill quickly." Blake tapped the file. "I notice that the original NCIS investigation reported no definitive evidence of warring factions, even though that's their conclusion."

Turner raked his hands through his hair. "As you'll see, neither did I. Since I found nothing to conclusively contradict their findings, I was forced to officially support the earlier conclusion." He shook his head. "I even asked the eyewitness about this—the one you're about to meet—and she said their neighbors loved the servicemen. Even the local communist groups had a warm relationship with them. The villagers were afraid of the Negritos, the jungle people. She said they could be this ruthless but is convinced they weren't involved."

Blake nodded. "The Negritos possess ancient DNA and were the first wave of human beings out of Africa, populating Southeast Asia tens of thousands of years ago. The villagers likely came from the later Mongoloid Polynesian expansion. They're also known to have worked hand-in-hand with US Special Forces operating in the jungles."

Turner sighed. "Exactly. Now, the Navy knew of the Negritos' reputation, so they investigated this angle." He scratched his chin. "No physical evidence pointed to them, but they made the top of the 'warring group' list."

Blake read the file further. "I see they were particularly concerned that Petty Officer Castle's body was never found."

Turner spotted a middle-aged Filipino woman approaching them. He stood and quickly whispered to Blake. "Just wait until you hear the eyewitness account." Turner approached the woman and gently shook her hand. "Hi Malaya, thank you for meeting us on your lunch break." He faced Blake. "This is Dr. Blake, the man I spoke to you about. Dr. Blake, this is Malaya Santos."

"Pleasure to meet you, Mrs. Santos."

"Nice to meet you, too, Dr. Blake," Malaya replied in a Filipino accent.

All three sat down at the table. "We'll be brief, Malaya, so we don't take up all of your lunch," Turner said. "As I told you over the phone, we're reinvestigating the terrible massacre that took place in your village years ago, and Dr. Blake has offered to help. I felt it was necessary for him to hear your account of the events."

Malaya frowned slightly. "I understand."

"If it's too difficult to talk about," Blake responded, "we can stop at any time."

Malaya shrugged. "I'll be fine."

"Who did this?" Blake asked in a kindly tone.

Malaya stared at Blake. "It was the Aswang."

Blake glanced at Turner. "I see. As I recall, Aswang are Filipino monsters, which have been in their folklore for many generations. They are shapeshifters; human by day and creature by night. There are many versions of it." To Malaya, he said, "The villagers where Malaya was raised are convinced that the Aswang is something like a mixture between an animal and a ghoul."

Malaya raised her chin. "Yes, and the Curse of the Aswang is a family curse."

Blake rubbed his chin. To Turner, he said, "A family curse is an inherited curse; kind of like the Original Sin is said to be inherited by all mankind."

Blake turned back to Malaya. "Did you see this Aswang?"

Her eyes widened. "Yes, but I mostly heard it." She frowned again. "My father, mother, and I were eating dinner in our village home; a shack really. Our medicine woman came in and approached my father. She seemed terrified. She told him that the American she just treated for a deadly snake bite had the Curse of the Aswang."

Turner looked directly at Blake. "Petty Officer Castle."

"Our medicine woman," she continued, "said that he was likely unaware he was cursed. It was kept dormant by a very old and powerful protection spell. She said she had to break the protection spell in order to save his life, and she was afraid that she may have released the Aswang."

Turner frowned. "Sounds like the curse took hold immediately."

Malaya swallowed hard. "We heard everyone screaming outside. People were running by our front door. I saw something flash past, chasing them. It was huge and loping on all fours."

"Did you see what it looked like?" Blake asked.

Malaya shrugged her shoulders. "It was fast, so I didn't get a good look, but I could tell it wasn't human." She paused. "My father rushed to the door, then he ran back into the house, grabbed me, and threw me into a closet." She dropped her head. "Something busted through and into our home. It growled and smashed through the house for a few seconds, then left. By the time I heard the helicopter, no one was screaming anymore. I wouldn't leave my hiding spot until someone found me. When I left the closet, I saw my parents, dead."

Blake mashed his lips together. "Malaya, it is perfectly clear that you are very lucky to be alive."

Malaya gave a half-smile. "It sounds incredible, Dr. Blake, but that's what I saw . . . and heard."

Blake reached across the table and patted her hand. "Oh, I don't doubt you for a minute, Malaya."

Malaya, visibly shaken, stood. "I must get back to work soon, so I'd better grab lunch."

Turner stood with her. "Thank you again for sharing your story with Dr. Blake."

The men watched her dash away.

Turner turned to Blake. "So, what do you think?"

Blake took a deep breath. "Well, regardless of the truth, your editor will find it difficult for you to publish this. I can't go on record confirming the reality of the Aswang."

"Dr. Blake, Aswang or not, it sounds like a werewolf mutilated the village."

Blake's eyes widened. "You think this Petty Officer Castle mutilated these villagers . . . as a werewolf? He paused. "And is he back in the States?"

Turner gathered the file off the table. "They never found Castle's body. I think it's time to find out more. This is a whole new can-a-worms, and I fear we'll find out more than we can handle."

THE KINDLY DARK

by J. B. Toner

Originally appeared in Page & Spine, *May 2018.*

No bleakness is complete without a crow. A ruined church, a barren moor, a graveyard by a gray and empty sea—without the brooding shadow of a solitary rook, their desolation lacks its full potential. What old forgotten skull could molder properly without the croak and mutter of a murder overhead, the hop and flutter of black wings?

Mind you, we're a merry folk. We glory in the gloom, and this dark world has plenty to spare. But when Father McReady installed a new electric light above the rectory door, my favorite eaves were flooded with a bloodless yellow glare. It wouldn't do.

My name is Quick of Lurkwood Murder. We are wise and fast. I've seen sweet summers and bitter winters in the lands around Saint Bernadette's, and the honor of old age descends upon me now. Life's flight should fall in veiling shade, a crimson leaf on autumn's dusky breeze—not in the dry click of a motion detector. I was perched upon the steeple's topmost needle, thinking on these things, when Sharp came gliding by.

"Ho, Quick! What news from the west?"

I made no answer. The cold red sun declined among the mountains.

"You look troubled, Quick. What can I do?"

"Light," I said. "They've made a light beneath my favored rest."

He flapped a bit and cocked his head. "I see no light."

"Fly down and perch there, lad."

"In your rest?"

"It's all right."

He swooped down to the door, beat the air, and swooped up to my spot below the eaves. As he did, that ugly yellow light came on. He squawked indignantly and flew back to the chapel roof.

"Twenty thousand lightnings! There you rest most every night, and have done these many seasons past. It's man's meanness, sheer and clear!"

"Not so, I think. He's a kindly sort, the vicar."

Yes, we know your temperaments. We know your faces. And we can tell each other which of your folk have decent hearts and which of you are cruel. Only two creatures in all of life are cleverer than my people: you, and those oafish dolphins. But only we can fly. We, and the dead.

"Then why, Quick?"

"Like me, the man grows old. I saw him slip and nearly fall some mornings ago. The light is no doubt for his safety."

"The man's just a man! Pluck the eyes of his safety, pluck and gulp 'em both."

I shifted from foot to foot, considering. Of course a crow's life comes before a man's—but a crow's convenience? After all, the rectory was his home, too, in a way. But on the other hand, our life-flight is so much shorter. In a few more seasons, I'd be gone, and Father McReady could install a hundred lights.

Beyond the west, the blood-orb sank. As darkness rose, the buzzing bulb grew brighter down below. "How long does it burn?" Sharp asked.

"An hour. Every time it lights."

He said nothing.

After a pause, I concluded: "It must be destroyed."

* * *

Seagulls. Idiot birds. Their chattering woke me early. "Hey look, food! Guys, there's food here! Hey guys, look at the food!" Seven or eight of them in a dirty white ring around the jetsam of some satiated human's breakfast sandwich. I dropped to the earth right in their startled midst.

"Be off, or I'll stuff your holes with your own fat heads."

They scattered, screeching admonitions. "Look out, it's a crow! Hey, guys, look out for the crow!"

"Morons." It was a warm, bright day, and my mood was grim. I'd stayed up late examining that hateful light, and slept in a hollow pine. The bulb was protected by some manner of metal cage that surpassed my solving abilities. No rook likes to meet the limit of his wit.

The sandwich, however, broke my fast more pleasantly than I had expected. Better still, as I glanced up from snatching down the last morsel, I glimpsed a distant shadow moving through the orange-blue dawn and caught a faint scent of rain. My spirits kindled cautiously.

"Well. If wisdom fails, use speed." An age-old proverb of my kin. "It is time for the shine-star."

I went to the secret place, the ancient place. There, by the fallen stone, beneath the rotten root, the shine-star lay hidden. Many times had the leaves of Lurkwood turned since I took it from a dead woman's hand. It was my greatest treasure.

"Gather!" I cawed, rising above the trees. "I, Quick, summon the Murder to meet. Gather!"

The call went out, and swiftly spread. My wing-mates came floating through the wood as the welcome storm clouds began to congregate above us. It wasn't long before we had a quorum, nor long before Glint came hobbling up the branches to his venerable rest.

"Lurkwood Murder," he rasped. "By the power of the sacred Moon, I call this parliament to order. Who has summoned us together, and for what purpose? Speak!"

We were hatchlings together, Glint and I. Long ago. I was always faster, but he was always smarter. I did not challenge him for the leadership. He was the better choice, and I've never regretted standing down.

"The call was mine," I said. "I seek a boon from the council."

"What boon, friend Quick?"

"The old man of Saint Bernadette's has made a light beneath my favored perch. The slightest movement ignites it, and it burns away the hours of my slumber."

"It's true!" cried young Sharp, several branches below. "An affront to our brother, and to all our kind."

"What boon do you ask of the rookery?" Glint demanded.

"I ask this," I said.

And set forth my plan.

There was silence. The spirits of thunder were stirring overhead. A few of our brethren rustled in the trees, ruminating. At last, Glint replied: "You ask much, my old friend."

"I offer much."

I ducked my beak beneath my wing and brought forth the shine-star, and a murmur ran through the parliament. Solemnly, I trod the bending twigs to the perch of honor and laid the glimmering stone at Glint's feet.

"Much indeed," he said quietly. "Knock!"

"Here, sir." Knock was as big as a raven, our strongest fighter. An old scar marked his breast, and his left wing was white as bone.

"Will the raptors fly on such a day as this?"

A wry note entered Knock's voice. "Only the boldest and the dumbest."

"Perfect. Ready your team."

"Yes, sir."

As he spoke, the first globed raindrop tapped upon the leaves.

* * *

Hawks. Accursed birds. They care for nothing but the hunt, and few who fare the sky are deadlier hunters. Their eyes are needles of ice, their talons the grip of despair.

Four of us flew in the vanguard: myself and Knock, and his lieutenants, Sharp and Trunk, young and battle-eager. Behind us were half a dozen more tough rooks, flapping grimly as we climbed toward combat.

Knock gave me a sidelong glance as the rain grew heavier. "Quite a plan you've hatched here, Quick."

"My days are going down into the west, my friend. I want to live them out in solace."

"If things go ill, good carrion awaits us both in the shadow-fields of the Moon."

"Truly said."

"No fear," said Sharp. "We can handle those goblins."

"I can handle two!" said Trunk.

"Just keep to the plan, lads," Knock said harshly.

I pointed with my beak. "There."

A single bird, cruciform, sailed through the wet gray empyrean with never a twitch of those tireless wings. Ancestral dread coiled in my gut. But I am a crow of Lurkwood. Fear is for the foolish and the slow.

"You!" I cawed. "You trespass in our nesting grounds."

The bright, keen beak swung toward me. The merciless gaze regarded me. "And if I do?"

"Then Murder be upon you!"

No more talk, then. The raptor wheeled and dove, his terrible claws outstretched. We broke formation to the four winds, but his ire was fixed on me. At the crucial instant, I rolled to my back in midair and caught his plunging feet in my own, entangling us. His power and weight were far beyond mine, and we plummeted down toward the spinning treetops.

Knock sprang on the monster's back, shrieking like the gale, and his lieutenants attacked its mighty wings. Lightning blazed. I was upside-down, blinded by the driving rain and the pounding pinions of my foe, but I could sense the earth hurtling up to meet us.

Somehow Sharp and Trunk managed to turn the wings, steering our whole grappling quintet in the necessary direction. I clung tenaciously to the talons as it dragged me through the howling, weeping skies. We were parallel to the ground now, soaring toward the target.

Then the hawk made an impossible barrel roll, flinging my friends clear. Over the shattering thunder, I heard the deep cold voice: "Die now."

But six more of us pounced, weighting our enemy, forcing it downward, blocking its view. From the corner of my eye, I saw the steeple of Saint Bernadette's flash by. I heard Knock's frantic cry: "Now, Quick, now!"

And I ripped myself free just as the hawk smashed into Father McReady's light.

* * *

There were revels that day. We flew and spun and danced our corvine dances. We sang together and retold ageless tales of heroes past. The storm raged and the day waned, and at eventide I went home to my favorite eaves to slumber in the kindly dark.

The night was frosty cold. When I awoke and fluttered down to the windowsill to stretch my wings, I saw patches of ice on the walkway outside the vicar's door. I glanced up at his light: the little cage was dented in, the bulb and fixture cracked beyond repair. And then I glanced in through the window.

Father McReady was buttoning his coat. On the dresser by his bed, in a nest of blankets, was my injured enemy, the hawk. It stirred in its sleep, and one of its wings flapped crookedly—broken, evidently, in the impact. The old priest set a dish of water by its beak and left the room.

A hawk and a human—they were nothing to me. And yet, the one had fought with honor and the other showed kindness and mercy. Perhaps they deserved more respect than I had given.

As I thought these thoughts, the front door opened and the old man emerged, walking slowly in the predawn gloom. His vision was less keen than mine, and his agility as well; I saw him heading straight for an icy patch and knew that he would fall. I croaked a warning and flung myself through the air, landing on the ice just before his foot came down.

He gazed at me with a puzzled smile and said something in the strange liquid tongue of your people. Then, looking closer, he saw the ice. His smile grew, and he spoke again, and from his pocket he drew a muffin in a napkin. Breaking it in half, he set it on the pavement in front of me. I shuffled and gave a quiet caw of thanks, and he was on his way.

The next morning, we did the same. That evening, I moved a loose stone on which he would have turned his ankle, and he gave me meat. A few days later, the parish handyman removed the broken fixture of the light. And a few weeks after that, the hawk recovered and returned to the distant sky. Neither hawk nor light were seen again.

Since those days, a friendship has grown between myself and McReady—a greater friendship than I ever thought I could forge with one of your kind. And at every funeral Mass, I come and perch by his side. That is why you see me here today. I cannot vouch for certain that your soul will reach the Moon; but I will travel with you as far as I can. No dying is complete without a crow.

THE HANGIN' TREE

by Thomas M. Malafarina

Two old men sat quietly on a covered patio as the sun began its gradual descent into the western horizon. They each rocked slowly, whiskey sours in their hands as birds flew to and from bird feeders, to birdhouses and back again, gathering their final meals of the day.

John, a widower from down the street, took a loud sip of his drink. "You sure do have a lot of birdhouses back here, Bob."

"Yeah, I s'pose I do. Last time I counted I believe there were better than twenty of them."

"That's a good many houses. And did I see what, three feeders?"

"Actually, there's four. I got one near the back over there behind the shed."

"I believe that's a good many feeders as well, Bob. You surely must like birds."

"I s'pose I do. That's partially because of Sallie. We often would sit out here after dinner, talking and watching the birds till bedtime. We'd never get tired of it."

John hesitated for a moment of uncertainty. "I'm sure you miss her terribly."

Bob took a pull of his drink. "That I do, John. That I do."

"I can tell you from experience; it never gets any easier. It just gets different."

They both sat sniffing and grunting for some time, just watching the birds. Then Bob asked, "John, you and I have been friends for how long now, like thirty years?"

"Since the day you and Sallie moved in."

"We probably told each other so damn many stories we likely know more about each other than our wives ever knew about us."

"Yep."

"Well, since Sallie passed, I've been thinking a lot about my life, you know, stuff from back when I was a kid."

"Bob, sometimes it's good to reflect back, to recall past memories, especially the happy ones. When you get to be our age, old memories are often all we have. Personally speaking, I remember fifty years ago like it was yesterday, and I forget yesterday like it was fifty years ago."

"That's a good one."

"You say that every time I tell a joke."

"Only after every bad one. But lately, I've been thinking about something from way back when I was a kid. It was something I never told anyone, not even Sallie."

"Why not? You didn't rob no bank or murder somebody or anything like that, did you?"

Bob chuckled. "Hell no, at least so as I can remember."

"If you did, you can feel free to tell me. God knows I won't remember it tomorrow. For all I know you might have confessed to me yesterday. Hell, you're safer telling me than a priest."

"I haven't told you or anyone this because it's really strange. It always sorta made me feel a bit embarrassed and maybe a little guilty. Even though I was a kid at the time . . . well, I guess I never wanted people to know about it. And I think it has a direct correlation as to why I feel this need to help out birds."

"Now you've really got my attention, Bob. Do tell. Do tell."

"Remember what it was like being a kid back in the early sixties? You know, home for summer vacation and playing outside from early morning till late at night?"

"Yeah, Bob. I remember those days very well. But you didn't grow up around here did you?"

"Nope. I'm a transplant. We moved here because this was Sallie's home. I come from much more humble beginnings. I'm originally from a little coal region town called Ashton, about sixty miles north. Our town was blue-collar, a lower-income place that while I was growing up seemed to have kids everywhere. No matter where you went you were bound to find someone to hang out with. None of us had any money so we had to find our own ways to fill the long summer days after school let out.

"Well one summer back in like '65, me and a group of neighborhood kids were looking for something to do. It was that time of year when it was so hot the tar would blister on the road, probably late July or early August. By that time of summer we had played all the baseball, basketball, and touch football we could stand. We'd built treehouses and hung out telling ghost stories till they weren't scary anymore. Some of us were actually looking forward to school starting to end the boredom. It was a perfect time for restless boys to get into trouble."

John took a long sip from his drink. "Yeah, I know what you mean. We didn't have all the electronics and stuff kids have today."

Bob nodded, then continued. "Our neighborhood was at the outer edge of town surrounded by hills and small woods of scrub trees. On this one particular day, we were walking along a seldom-used road. One of the kids, I believe it was Charlie Janko, shouted, 'Hey, what's that up there?' I could see something large and white alongside the road ahead. As we got closer we saw it was some kind of large bird . . .

"What the heck is that?" Davie Gardner asked. Davie was the youngest member of our crew and always had questions about everything.

Ronny Wharton, an older kid with a natural tendency to ridicule, chimed in. "It's a bird, numbnuts. What did you think it was?" At the time we didn't know why Ronny was the way he was, but later we realized his home life was not a good one. He had an abusive mother and an alcoholic father.

Davie got flustered and began stammering as he always did when confronted by Ronny's comments. "I . . . I know it's a b-bird Ronny. I was w-wondering what kind of bird it is."

"It's a dead one, dickweed," Ronny chided. "Even a retard like you can see that."

"Actually, it's a goose," Jimmy Thompson said. Jimmy was something of a mystery to our neighborhood gang. He visited us from time to time from several blocks away. He lived in an area with few kids, so he was sort of adopted by us. As such, he had an unspoken honorary pass. A thin boy of average height and muscular for his age, Jimmy carried himself with a confidence that made him seem older. It also made you not want to screw with him. Even Ronny stopped his rude comments whenever Jimmy spoke.

I could never quite figure out what it was, exactly, but something seemed a bit off with Jimmy. He had a strange way of looking at you. Made your skin crawl, you know? Gave you the willies. There were lots of stories about Jimmy circulating around town. If even half of them were true, then I had no idea why Jimmy wasn't in jail. I'm not ashamed to say that boy scared me plenty. But after what happened that day, not to mention years later, I was smart to have been afraid.

Jimmy studied the area like a detective, as if seeing things the rest of us couldn't. "The goose must have tried to land and was hit by a car or something. Charlie Janko scratched his head. "It must have just happened this morning, 'cause I was up here yesterday and this thing wasn't here."

Jimmy found a long branch about two inches around. He poked the goose with it. The white feathered body shifted a bit, and its long neck flopped over, revealing its head and bill. Odd that there was no blood on its feathers.

"So what are we gonna do with it?" I asked.

That was too much of an opportunity for Ronny to pass up. "That's a retarded question if I ever heard one. What are we going to do with it? It's a dead stinking goose. Hows about we put lipstick on it and you can take it on a date to the movies, Bobby."

I was never one to put up with Ronny's nonsense, even though he could probably have kicked my butt. Whether a blessing or a curse, I was born with a smart mouth of my own. I knew Ronny was sweet on a girl in his class named Donna Williams. "That goose is probably more your type, Ronny. Come to think of it, she looks a lot like Donna Williams with her duck lips. But at least the goose can't say no when you ask her out."

The whole gang laughed hysterically at that jab. I knew I'd eventually pay for it, but at the time it was too good to pass up.

"Seriously, guys," said Charlie. "This is too cool. Must be something we can do with it."

Ronny seemed to have an epiphany, which in his case was never a good thing. His ideas were bound to end badly. His eyes glowed with mischief. "Charlie, you live the closest. Go get some string or twine from your house."

"Um, yeah. I think I know where some is. Why?"

"Don't worry about it. I'll tell you when you get back."

Charlie took off like a shot and Ronny said, "Jimmy, let me see that stick you were using."

Jimmy handed it over. Ronny tested it for strength and flexibility. "Yeah, this will work fine."

Jimmy's eyes glazed all creepy. "What are you thinking about, Ronny?" If Ronny having an idea was bad, having Jimmy involved could only make things worse.

Ronny grinned like a Cheshire cat. "I was thinking we could string it up by the neck from this pole and carry it around the neighborhood scaring any girls who are out playing."

My stomach lurched at the idea. By the look in both Ronny's and Jimmy's eyes, this *was* going to happen. I was going to have to be part of it or wind up ostracized by the gang. Pussyfied might be a better description. So I went along to get along, as they say.

Charlie returned with some heavy-duty twine. Ronny held the pole steady while Jimmy wrapped the string around both the pole and the goose's neck. My knees weakened at the sight, but I held on somehow. Since they were the tallest, Ronny lifted one end of the pole and Jimmy lifted the other, resting the pole on their shoulders. The goose dangled ridiculously from its neck between them, its feet inches from the ground.

Looking far happier than any sane person should, considering what we were about to do, Jimmy shouted, "Let's go!" Davie and I stayed as far toward the back of our twisted little parade as possible. If and when this turned into a disaster, I wanted to be able to distance myself quickly. Part of me realized this was really warped, but another part of me thought it was really awesome, if that makes any sense. I suddenly had visions of my Mom crying, wondering what was wrong with her son. I then thought of my Dad pulling his belt from his pants ready to strap me, yet I stayed with the pack.

Needless to say, a group of boys carrying a dead goose hanging from a pole was bound to attract attention. Soon our ragtag parade increased in size as other neighborhood boys joined us. This was also good for me because now I was one of many, which essentially allowed me to be invisible. Somebody started chanting, "Dead goose," in a low whisper, and soon all of us joined in. "Dead goose, dead goose."

We had managed to scare one small group of girls, although, by the looks on their faces, it was more likely that all we did was disgust them. The father of one of the girls, Janice Dawson, was home from work on vacation. She ran home to tell her old man what we were doing. Her dad was a big man, a former high school football star and still very athletic and muscular. When Mr. Dawson caught up with us and saw the goose and heard the chanting, he shouted, "What the hell is wrong with you boys? You sick, twisted, little bastards. I have a good mind to beat each of you to a pulp."

Had he chosen to give us all a whooping, not only could he have gotten away with that back then, but we'd still have to answer to our folks, who would pick up where his whooping left off. Davie and I dodged behind a nearby tree, doing our best to hide. "I don't know where you boys found that disgusting thing, but you have thirty seconds to turn around and dump that God-forsaken thing somewhere up in the hills. Do I make myself clear?"

A few voices rang out clearly in unison. "Yes, sir." Others remained quiet. Jimmy didn't say a word. He was glaring at Mr. Dawson like he wanted him hanging from the pole instead of the goose. Jimmy started to turn, and Ronny followed. Soon, we were all on our way out of town and back up the road to discover something that would become part of our lives for many summers—and would eventually lead to the end for Jimmy Thompson.

As we approached the area where we had found the goose, our numbers had diminished back to the original group of five: Charlie, Ronny, Davie, Jimmy, and me.

"So now what are we supposed to do with this stupid thing?" Ronny asked.

Jimmy replied in a strange, distant voice. "I know." Then he pointed toward a large tree in a clearing up ahead. It was growing from an outcropping of large, flat rocks high above the road. "We'll hang it from that tree."

As we marched toward the tree like pallbearers carrying a casket to a graveyard, that weird feeling crept back into my stomach. I should point out here that I never liked dealing with death and dead things. I still don't. And even though I was just an observer, my displeasure with all things non-living simply got worse.

When we got close to the tree, Ronny and Jimmy placed the goose on top of a flat section of rock, and Jimmy began looking around the ground.

Ronny asked, "What you looking for, Jimmy?"

"I need a . . . oh, there's one." Jimmy picked up a large rock with one side split to form a sharp, knife-like edge. "This goose is too heavy for that branch. We can bury the body but only hang the head."

Ronny's mouth fell open. He was rendered speechless. Jimmy acted completely casual, as if decapitating a goose was something he did every day. Jimmy grabbed the head, stretched out the neck, and began hacking at feathers and flesh, pulling the sharp edge across the thing's throat. Little Davie stared for a few horrified seconds before puking in the grass. I swallowed down my barf. I could tell Ronny wanted to say something about Davie, but he looked like he kept swallowing over and over, having trouble not tossing his cookies. Dragging a dead goose around the neighborhood was pretty warped, but this seemed to cross over into some new level of depravity.

I looked around for Charlie. He was hunched under an over-hanging tree branch, digging a hole in the soft dirt using a wide stick like a shovel. I decided to help him because anything was better than listening to Davie puke or watching our resident psycho hack a goose's neck. Within a few minutes, we had dug a nice-size hole. Ronny dragged the goose over by its feet, its headless neck flipping side to side. He tossed it into the hole and without being told to do so, and Charlie and I began covering it with dirt. Soon, the job was done. We were both drenched in sweat. Jimmy walked toward us with the upside-down goose head dangling from its twine noose.

I'll never forget the look in Jimmy's eyes. At my young age I'd say he looked crazy, but in retrospect—as an adult—I'd describe his look as manic euphoria. I think he loved decapitating the thing. He walked over to the branch, still smiling in that strange way, and tied the twine, the head dangling. The head spun slowly in the warm summer breeze as flies landed on the rotting skull. Jimmy gazed on with a longing stare as if he had found his life's calling.

This was a side of Jimmy I never wanted to see again. As things worked out, I never would.

* * * * * * *

From that day on, we referred to that tree as "The Hangin' Tree." We didn't go back to the tree for a few weeks after that momentous day. Jimmy stopped coming around the neighborhood as well. I'll never know if he ever went back to the tree on his own. After a while, Ronny, Davie, and I decided to check on the status of the goose. None of us knew what to expect, but we rightfully assumed it might be gross. At some time, the skull must have slipped from the noose and fallen to the ground, which only made it easier for nature's scavengers to make short work of the flesh. It was covered with ants and beetles. A skull and a few patches of featherless skin remained.

We should have known that the goose's body would have been dug out of the ground and likewise consumed. A number of feral dogs and cats roamed the hills. They probably smelled the corpse and dug up the remains. All around the area, remnants of feathers could be seen caught in the bases of various wild bushes. Then again, this was 1965, and we were just a bunch of naïve preteens with no prior experience dealing with dead stuff. The length of twine we had used to hang the goose lay on the ground nearby. I discreetly picked it up and tucked it into my pocket. I had no idea why I did this, but it seemed like it was something I should do. Later, I put it in a collectibles box I kept in my parents' cellar, where it remained for many years.

"So, what should we do with these bones?" I asked the gang.

Davie stammered, "I-I dddddon't know."

"Just throw the bones back in the hole and bury it," Ronny said. "Ain't no wild animals gonna care about it anymore now that the meat's all gone."

So that's what we did. And Ronny was right. After that, no creatures ever dug up the goose remains again. From that day on, any animal we happened to find dead was taken up to the hanging tree and buried at its base. Over the years—thanks to cars—there were plenty dead; rats, squirrels, birds, frogs, and even a snake. Occasionally, on particularly dark nights when the wind howled through the trees, I'd dream of a goose head dangling from a string with blowflies buzzing around it as maggots crawled from its empty eye sockets. But other than those few early hauntings, I eventually forgot about the hanging tree. The tree grew, and its branches thickened. No doubt the dead critters served as fertilizer. We grew older, too, and the hanging tree became a fading memory.

Until the year of my twenty-third birthday, when the legacy of what we did that day at the hanging tree became all too real, and the meaning of that long-ago strange look in Jimmy Thompson's eyes became apparent.

* * * * * *

As I mentioned, Jimmy never came around the neighborhood again. I'd occasionally see him around town or at school, where he might ignore me most days or on occasion acknowledge me with an insignificant nod, but he never spoke to any of us again. A few years later, I heard through the grapevine that Jimmy had gotten a girl pregnant. They both dropped out of high school and got married. The girl lost the baby, but neither of them went back to finish school. They ended up living in a trailer at the lower end of town, working dead-end minimum-wage jobs.

The year I turned twenty-three, Jimmy would have been twenty-five or so. I was home for the summer after graduating from college and had just sleepily stumbled down the stairs for breakfast. I picked up a copy of the *Ashton Daily News* and was blown away by the headline screaming up at me. It read, "Local murder, dismemberment and suicide horrify community."

Three pictures loomed under the headline. The first was a high school picture of Jimmy Thompson. The second was a picture of his wife, and the third, which was the most disturbing of all, was a picture of the hanging tree—our hanging tree. In the shot, an empty rope fashioned in a noose dangled from the same branch where we'd hanged the goose. Of course now the branch appeared much thicker and stronger.

I first read the story in shocked disbelief, and then read it two more times to get all the facts straight and make sense of something that defied sensibilities. Police were investigating, but no motive was available at that time. Whatever his reason, Jimmy had apparently lost his mind and taken his wife to the hanging tree, where he slit her throat and dismembered her on the very same huge rock that he had decapitated the goose on so long ago.

Our police chief was described as being overcome with emotion. He was quoted as saying, "It . . . it was beyond description . . . so much blood . . . so many pieces."

I can imagine Jimmy smiling the same strange smile he wore when he decapitated the goose. I envision that weird look in his eyes as he systematically butchered his wife on that rock.

The paper reported that after killing and chopping up his wife, Jimmy put a noose around his own neck, then tied it around the tree branch. The branch was too low for him to hang himself in the traditional fashion, so he stretched out his legs in a sitting position with the rope elevating him slightly, his butt several inches off the ground. This was not a quick, neck-breaking death. It would have been a slow, grueling self-strangulation. At any point during the process, Jimmy could have simply grabbed the rope and hauled himself up. For reasons known only to him, Jimmy wanted to die in a way almost as horrendous as the one dealt to his wife.

* * *

John's eyes widened, and astonishment was plastered on his face. "Holy crap, Bob! That was some story. I don't think I ever heard of anyone who went nuts and murdered someone, let alone chopped them to pieces."

"Yeah, well I tried not to make a habit of retelling it. When I take the time to think about it, it still freaks me out. It was a lot to absorb and it screwed with my head.

"I've spent the last fifty years keeping watch for anyone with Jimmy's same strange look. You'd be surprised how many times I've seen it. Many more than I care to mention. The sad truth is, John, there are a lot of crazy and dangerous people living, working, and functioning among us. Whenever I met up with anyone having what I called 'that Jimmy look,' I always steered clear of them. I often wondered if that's the reason I've managed to live this long."

John nodded. His whiskey glass was empty, and so he set it on the nearby table. "I think I know what you're talking about. I've seen that look too. I call it 'crazy eyes.'"

Then Bob reached into his pocket and pulled out his keys. They were secured around a woven length of twine. "I don't suppose you ever noticed my keychain before. I consider it something of a talisman. I made it back when I was about sixteen. I've carried it with me for almost fifty years. I use it to remind me to watch out for those people with that look."

John stared down at the chain, woven into a circle, and said with awe, "Is that the piece of twine from . . . ?"

"Yes," Bob said and tucked the keys back into his pocket. "I s'pose it is."

BURNING FOR YOU

by Will Falconer

I turned into the parking lot of my dilapidated apartment complex in Springfield after another forgettable day at the office. No need to describe where I worked or what I did for a living. It doesn't matter anymore. It never did. Picture the steel-and-glass façade of any publicly traded tech company. Inside, working stiffs shuffling papers, tapping keyboards, sipping lukewarm coffee or diet soda, fluorescent lights illuminating their anemic, vapid faces and isolating cookie-cutter cubicles (one of them mine). Just a typical workday. One more mind-numbing, demoralizing step closer to death.

I really miss those days.

I parked my leased car in its designated parking spot, turned off the engine, and had my usual depressing thought: Most of my friends own homes, and I'm still renting. But it was hard to save up for a down payment when I was buried in student debt.

Okay, full disclosure. I liked to party. Not cheap nowadays. The cost of beer alone could really add up. Have you been to a dispensary lately? I couldn't get out of there without dropping a Benjamin or two. Most nights I'd order takeout, have it delivered, which was pricey, but hey, gotta quell those munchies. And wining and dining the ladies. *Muy expensivo*; though I hadn't been doing a lot of that lately. I was spending most of my free time playing the latest new-release video game on my state-of-the-art gaming rig.

You play, you pay. Know what I mean?

I walked to a row of ugly, metal mailboxes attached to the front of my building and put the key in the lock below the #9 on my box. That was my apartment. Now you know in case you want to visit sometime. You know, do the whole dark tourist thing. I turned the key and pulled the little door open. The narrow compartment was stuffed full.

Every week at that moment I realized another uneventful seven days of my life had come and gone, never to return. Must be Tuesday. Junk-mail day.

When I say 'junk mail,' I'm not talking about spam or phishing emails or all that other cyber-junk bombarding our cell phones and laptops daily. I'm talking about that outdated, so-last-century means of communication commonly referred to as 'snail mail.'

Does anyone even use that anymore? I know someone who does. Not for business. For personal reasons. But I'm getting ahead of myself.

I reached into the mailbox and pulled out the flyers and business postcards and metered envelopes. They'd be in the recycling bin in a matter of minutes. It always seemed like such a waste. Not just environmentally, which is bad enough. I mean these ads—these concepts—had been thought up by people who probably think they're very clever—so clever, in fact, that they can influence us to buy anything they're selling, from processed food that will slowly kill whoever eats it to credit cards with interest rates north of twenty percent to a ceramic plate featuring a portrait of Ronald Reagan (the first in a collection). Things like that.

Ad layouts are created and printed out, circulars stuffed in envelopes (or not), all of it metered and dropped off at the post office. Then they're sorted, put into mail bags or boxes, loaded into those stubby mail trucks, and finally delivered to my door, so to speak. Seems like a lot of work for instant recycling, but we all know there are lots of gullible people out there who are eating unhealthful food and running up credit card debt—take it from me, they will regret it—and forking out an entire social security check or two for the complete Ronald Reagan collection.

Not me. (Sorry, Uncle Ronny.) Right in the recycling—after I've examined the junk for anything that might actually be important, like a bill or something. It's rare, but on two or three occasions my mailwoman (or is it mailperson?) has slipped something important into the Tuesday junk mail. Just to keep me on my toes, I guess. How thoughtful. So I always go through the junk—every piece of it—just to make sure. And on this particular Tuesday, there was something.

A plain, white, commercial-flap envelope addressed to me in stylish feminine—I assumed—handwriting using black ink. No return address. Inside my apartment, I tore it open, pulled out a single sheet of plain white paper that matched the envelope, unfolded it, and read the words written in black ink in the same delicate handwriting.

My dearest David,

I'm going to call you David because saying, "Hi, Dave" is just a shade too Kubrickesque, don't you think? I'm not as malevolent as HAL. Or maybe I am. We'll see. I'm only human, after all. Aren't all human beings malevolent at times especially under the right circumstances? What do you think, David? Search your heart. Feel free to put this letter down if you need a few moments to find it.

I hate myself when I'm sarcastic. And I'm tired of hating myself.

So back to the burning issue. Can I light a fire in that damned heart of yours? If not, I will have failed. I'm new to this. I don't know if I'll be successful. Please be patient, which is hard for you. As is controlling yourself (your temper and your libido, just to name two). I'm sure you're the first to admit that you have a problem with anger, and we both know from experience that anger spills over into your sexual relationships with women.

I'm sure you think I'm getting way too personal way too quickly, but I've wasted so much of my life acting coy, demure, submissive. Deferring my own happiness. Worrying about what men think. Trying to please them. Making them feel good about themselves no matter how shitty they made me feel. I'm done with that.

Let's be honest. You don't much like women, do you, David?

Now I'm sounding judgmental, not to mention cryptic. I don't mean to be. So I'll just play nice and stick to the facts from here on out.

I'm starting in Hartford, which is appropriate. A hart, as you know, is an adult male deer. You're definitely male, no doubt about that. I've seen the evidence. Adult? Depends on how you define adult. And deer? You're dear to me, but are you game? I like to think so. And a ford is a shallow place in a river that seems safe, but you can still drown. Don't worry, drowning is not something you have to worry about, being a fire sign, not a water sign. Although I'm sure you spend a great deal of time in the shallows of your own self-absorbed thoughts.

There I go again, being critical. Shame on me, right, David?

Hartford, my Hartford, will do nicely as a starting point. I'll perform the first rite in my li'l ol' apartment. I would have liked to have started in Amherst, where we met one dark night, no stars. You were my back door man, remember?

Nothing? Well, don't bother your pretty little head about it. Put it out of mind, and when you least expect it, my face will pop right into that hot little head of yours.

Speaking of hot, are you burning for me? You will be soon, I hope. For now, my dear hart, just know that my love for you is a flame.

All my dark love,

Lily

What. The. Hell. What kind of fatal-attraction, I-will-not-be-ignored bitch got ahold of my mailing address? What's her problem? My mind was racing, and I have to admit, so was my pulse.

Should I call the police? I looked again at the envelope. No return address. No full name. Just *Lily*. She lives in an apartment in Hartford, but what would the police do with that? Look up every Lily who lives in an apartment in Hartford and take handwriting samples? Maybe, or maybe they would just laugh after pretending to give a shit. A nice chuckle for them on their way to the drive-thru or the local law enforcement watering hole.

I tucked the creepy letter inside its matching envelope and tossed it into a drawer. Don't know why. Maybe as evidence? But of what? The whole thing just seemed so stupid.

I went out onto the balcony, sat down in my wobbly, frayed lawn chair, and rolled a joint. I quickly forgot about the whole thing.

Until the next letter.

My dearest David,

I've been thinking of you, my hart. Have you been thinking of me? Warmly, I hope. I realize my first letter must have threatened your staid little existence, my words muddying the clear waters of your safe, lazy shallowness.

There, I've gone and revealed my poetic nature to you, made myself vulnerable. But it's true, I am a sensitive soul, and easily bruised. Easily damaged. It's easy for men like you, isn't it, David? Do you even realize what you do to women?

Sadly, no, you don't. You won't. Not now and, I fear, not ever.

There I go, sounding judgmental again. You must hate me. Maybe you won't if I also reveal to you that I don't consider myself a victim, not any more than you do right now. I've made my choices, and I've lived with the consequences. Passively. For years. It's taken me that long to realize some things about myself and take action. If all this sounds confusing, please be patient. I hope to make everything painfully clear in these letters. And beyond.

I'll return to the facts.

I'm in Middlefield. When we met, you were playing the field with your frat-boy friends. Or is it frat boyfriends? I often find that misogynists are lambs in wolves' clothing. Sweet little lambs, take it as you will.

What do you think, David? Do you think, David?

More importantly, do you feel? I mean emotionally, of course, not the indiscriminate groping and ham-handed fondling and flaccid humping you and your fraternity bros subject women to. And that's just for starters as you and I well know. Remember that night out on the football field? Or was it a soccer field? You remember, don't you? If not, I'm going to do my damnedest to help you remember the night the entire course of my life was changed in the middle of that field. Middlefield. Perfect, don't you think?

I need you to understand. I'm not doing this just because I'm pissed off and want revenge. So don't think you're some kind of crucified martyr taking it up the ass for every victimized woman who ever did. No, this isn't about you. This is about me. What I'm doing now has given new meaning to my life. I'm proceeding as planned. I've performed the second rite here in Middlefield. Tomorrow, I'll move on to the next town.

I'm feeling ever closer to you, my flaming lamb. I'm coming for you. Do you feel it? The burning? Are you burning for me yet, David?

Always know that my love for you is an eternal flame that can never be extinguished.

All my dark love,

Lily

I grabbed a beer out of the fridge. Crazy bipolar bitch. That's all I could think when I finished reading her words. Like a broken record. Crazy bipolar bitch. That much was clear.

That and the fact that she might have been with me and some of my frat buddies in the middle of some field one night in college, and now she regrets what she did and feels like she's damaged in some way, at least in her mind. I honestly don't remember. That may seem like a crock of shit, but there was a lot of drunken partying and good-natured mayhem back in the day at ZooMass before they got all strict and PC and respectable. There were a few nights I was so shitfaced I blacked out. Maybe that was one of them. How does she expect me to remember shit I can't remember? I was just having a good time. She probably was, too, but now she feels guilty about it is all. So now I'm supposed to pay? How? For what?

I guzzled the last of my beer and helped myself to another. I read the first letter again, and then reread the second. Definitely disturbed. But I didn't want to go to the police. What if I *had* done something questionable to her in the past? You know, under the influence. We all have. Not that I would ever do anything bad to a girl. I wouldn't. Not on purpose, anyway. I'm a nice guy. Now some girl I don't even know is offended over something that happened years ago and she's gone all psycho on me and . . . It just really pissed me off. And what were these rites she was talking about? Weird. I had to calm down and think about this. I fired up the bong.

I felt better after a few hits, sitting on my balcony overlooking the parking lot, watching the other tenants come and go. I listened to some tunes on my phone and tried to chill, but I couldn't get the letters out of my mind. I tried to come up with a plan for how to deal with this psycho, but I couldn't concentrate. Her inky words flapped around in my head like a colony of rabid bats. *Sweet little lamb*. What the hell does she mean by that? What's this bitch's problem anyway? What is it with women nowadays? You touch their ass, they scream sexual harassment. Drama queens. It's screwed up, man.

I was getting myself all worked up obsessing about that alleged night in the field, trying to remember. It was a real buzzkill. I'm always super mellow when I'm high. It's all good, right? I had a few more hits and watched the smoke drift up into the pretty pink sky. Just another perfect sunset in paradise. I was looking forward to a cool, comfortable night, but even after darkness crept in and a light breeze began to blow, I felt hot. I was angry. Like they say, my blood was boilin'. Was I sweating?

I told myself to calm down, I was just having a panic attack. Or was it a heart attack? I won't give the bitch the satisfaction of dropping dead, that's for damn sure. I'm not even thirty. Can a man my age even have a heart attack? I was a little overweight. Just a few pounds. Not obese or anything. Probably just a panic attack. Too much stress, dude. Time to reload the bong.

I took a cool shower and tried to put the letters out of my mind. I ordered a pizza and played a video game for a while. Then I sparked a joint, lay down on the couch, and streamed a movie. Somewhere in the middle, I fell asleep. I don't remember. Must not have been very good.

Maybe that's why I can't remember this girl. She was an unmemorable lay.

After that second letter, I dreaded going to the mailbox. It was the anticipation more than anything. Imagining myself walking up to the box. Opening it with my little key. Staring at the mail standing on edge in that narrow metal slot. Reaching in. Pulling out the mail—quickly, so nothing could bite my fingers off. Then feeling silly and laughing at my foolishness between swigs of beer as I sorted through the junk and the bills up in my apartment. Hoping there was no letter. Then seeing one addressed by hand to me. Black ink on plain white envelope. Flowing, old-fashioned cursive. Weird symbols on the flap. What was that all about?

As anticipated, the third letter came a few days later. I didn't open it right away. I dropped it on the kitchen table, got a beer out of the fridge, sat down, and stared at the letter like I was half expecting it to come to life. It couldn't, of course, but it could have poison or chemicals or shit inside, like that one time somebody sent letters out with anthrax in them.

Damn, I was letting her get to me, letting her make me all paranoid. Those goddamn letters. Shit! I couldn't stay in the apartment, not with that letter sitting there unopened. Waiting. Forever, if necessary.

I was going to read it. It's not like I wasn't going to read the letter. I had to read it. I knew that. Just not right away. Maybe after a couple of beers. It would still be there on the table when I got back.

I walked to a sports bar on Cooley Street that served good late-night food and had my favorite beer on tap. I was on edge as I walked down the sidewalk, constantly on guard, looking down dark alleyways, giving a wide berth to shadowy doorways, peering into the darkness that pressed in on me from all sides. How had she signed her letters? *All my dark love.* How the hell do you see the darkness coming in the dark? Every sound, every shadow, every person was suspect. One good thing: At least I only had to keep an eye out for the ladies. Hell, I do that anyway.

I watched the Sox game while I wolfed down a cheeseburger with everything but onions—hey, you never know when a babe might walk in—cheesy fries, and a couple of beers. Maybe more. No hot babes. I shuffled home around eleven, took a long piss, and got a beer out of the fridge. One more couldn't hurt. I twisted off the cap and tossed it on the table.

Damn. The letter, lying there in the middle of the green Formica. Still. Plain. Innocent. An old soul from another era, a forgotten time. There it lay, a reminder.

Heartburn kicked in. Could have been the letter, but my money was on the burger and fries. Good thing I told them to hold the onions. I tried for a good long belch. Nothing. Was it getting worse?

I chugged half my beer. I wasn't going to let her get to me. I tore open the envelope, careful not to rip the letter inside.

Dearest David,

How are you? I worry about your health. Are you still in good health?

That's so silly of me. You can't write back to me, so how can you answer my impassioned inquiries? You can't talk back. You're not allowed. I'm doing all the talking this time. I've found my voice, and my words will be hobgoblins reverberating in that thoughtless little mind of yours for eternity. How does that sound? Sounds like poetic justice to me.

I promised myself not to be judgmental in this epistle. Well, I promise you, my lamb, from this moment forward I shall not be. And I will speak plainly, not cryptically as I have done in the past. What was it I wrote in my first letter?

I'll just stick to the facts from here on out.

I'm in Union. That name depresses me because it has one meaning for you and another quite different one for me, which demonstrates just how far apart we are mentally, psychologically, spiritually. Spiritual separation is most heartbreaking. All our problems—ours and humanity's—stem from our severance from spirit, don't you think? Oh, what do you know. To you, union *means the physical union of male and female. The old in-out-in-out, love.*

But to me, union *means a melding of two souls that have been conjoined through eons of lifetimes for the purpose of teaching each other how to love and be loved and how to love even more, and evermore, unconditionally, and these two souls, playing their different roles in each subsequent lifetime, one after the other, birth and death and birth, round and round the wheel turns, repeating the cycle, the same but different each time, and with each new life the living and the longing and the loving, on and on, detaching then together again, evolving, separate but as one until they meld with the eternal, achieve nirvana, regain paradise. No pressure there.*

Actually, David, the pressure's off. We're already in paradise. Well, we were until you men fucked it up. Gaia is our Great Mother, and like the goddess, every woman has the power to bring life and love and goodness into the world. And every man . . . ?

Every man for himself. Right, David?

Why do we women waste our time—our precious time—on your kind when you're so unkind? Like the rest of your sex, you, David, will never learn, what with your caveman brain and your nonexistent moral compass and

221

*your lack of anything resembling a conscience and your shrunken little . . .
What was that about promising not to be judgmental? Whoops!*

*But it's true. You'll never learn, not until it's too late. What was it
Oppenheimer said when they dropped the first atomic bomb? Have you forgotten? Look it up, genius. I'm sick of doing all the work.*

*In Union, I performed the third rite. I thought it went very well. What
do you sense? Do you have any? Perhaps you never did. I do wish you could
tell me how you feel when you finally do feel something. Then I could pretend
to care.*

*I seem to be losing interest. I don't know if I'm drained from performing
the rites, or if I don't care anymore about making it right between you and
me, or maybe it's just the ol' existential ennui creeping in. I wish you knew
me better. You had your chance. But it's not going to happen. Not now. Not
ever. I'm playing hard-to-get this time.*

Are you burning for me, my lamb?

Mon amour pour toi est une flamme.

All my dark love,

Lily

I didn't feel better after reading the letter. I hoped a few bong hits
would help. They didn't. I had a restless night and spent the next day in
bed. I wasn't sick, but I felt like shit. Couldn't work. Couldn't focus. And
the wicked heartburn.

It went on for days like this. Lying there, staring at the ceiling, wondering what she would say in the next letter. How far would she go?

I was almost relieved when the fourth letter came.

Dearest David,

*I imagine you must be feeling pretty bad right about now. After all, I
haven't been very nice, have I? I must seem like a total lunatic to you. It
hadn't occurred to me until quite recently that I could be coming across as a
little . . . Weird? Strange? Peculiar?*

Dangerous? Bipolar? Psychotic?

*I've spent an awful lot of time feeling bad, hurt, sick—hiding out from
the world, in bed under the covers, all day. Staring at the TV, seeing nothing
but all the shitty pictures in my head. And the support groups. Boy, are there*

a lot of fucked-up women out there. Brace yourself for some breaking news: We didn't fuck ourselves up. We had a little help. A little push. From men. So we women gather together to listen to each other, support each other, unfuck each other.

Misery loves company, as they say. I never lack a sympathetic ear. Sometimes there's a woman who says something that really helps me, like this woman I met a few weeks ago. She told me about spells. Magical rites. Witchcraft.

Unbelievable, right? But she showed me things that made me a true believer. She taught me a few spells, and I am in her debt because for the first time I feel empowered. I'm not just talking. I'm taking action, and that will set me free once and for all.

I'm tired of talking—and crying and agonizing and obsessing—reliving that night over and over in my mind. I can't do it anymore. I've made a decision that's taken me years to make. After all this is over, I will not waste one more second of my life on you. The rest of my life is mine, all mine.

My witchy plan of revenge against one of the men (guess which one?) who deceived and violated and debased and humiliated me will soon be complete. I'll dish it out cold, you'll take the heat, and your pathetic, meaningless life in this world will burn and turn to ash and blow away in the wind.

I felt good about the fourth rite in Colebrook, which means "cool stream." You'll wish you could bathe in a cool stream when the burning starts, but you'll never find relief. For eternity you'll envision that flowing stream. You'll hear its soothing sound and imagine how it would feel to step into the cool, healing water, but you will never bathe in it. You can never stop the burning. Never ever.

Are you burning for me yet, my lamb? You will be. Soon.

I'm already on my way to Hardwick to perform the fifth and final rite. That's when you'll really start to feel the burn. Tomorrow night, so mark your calendar.

I know how you become when you don't get your daily dose of instant gratification, so here's a preview of coming attractions. You'll become conscious of a flicker, a warm feeling in the center of your heart as if Old Nick himself had lit the spark. This wildfire will spread quickly to the farthest extremities of your physical body, which will be consumed by the flames. You've heard of spontaneous combustion? The fire will burn itself out in seconds, but to you the agony will seem to last for years.

The immolation of your physical being will be nothing compared with the burning of your soul. Once your earthly body has been consumed by the fire, your soul will suffer the wrathful flames of damnation for eternity. You will burn but never to ashes. The conflagration consuming your soul can never be extinguished, not by anyone save God himself.

Good luck with that.

The reckoning is coming, dearest David. Don't think that because I don't write I must be mad at you. I'm just done with you is all. The amount of time I've wasted feeling like shit. Ashamed, afraid someone might find out. Blaming myself, wondering what I could have done differently to stop it. Listening to the same sob story over and over in support groups, hearing my own plaintive, pathetic words—the same sickening words—repeated over and over in one therapist's office after another.

Enough!

So this is goodbye, David. The last letter. Tomorrow, the final rite in Hardwick. (Do you think of yourself when you hear that name, my lamb, or maybe some other strapping, lusty young lad at the office?) Then it's back to Hartford for me. Home sweet home. By that time you'll be in your new abode. A few words of warning about that.

Lasciate ogne speranza, voi ch'intrate.

Hope will become your enemy—when you're burning. For me.

For eternity.

My love is and will always be a flame.

All my dark love,

Lily

Holy shit, this was some weird-ass bullshit. I had to call the police. I didn't care what I might have done back in the day—this girl was a freak!

I picked up my cell phone, then set it down and fired up the bong instead, popped open another beer, and spent the rest of that sleepless night wondering who might have put her up to this. Maybe somebody at the office. I do work with a lot of assholes. I wouldn't put it past them.

The next morning I called in sick. I wasn't sick, of course. Not really. But I was too freaked out to concentrate. I spent most of the day playing video games. I tried to eat, but it didn't agree with me. Like that last letter. Upsetting.

When it got dark, I fired up the bong. Self-medication. I distracted myself with some funny online videos, but my mood didn't improve. The darker it got, the more her words consumed me. What she'd said in the letter about this fifth rite in Hardwick and about me burning and suffering for eternity and abandoning hope (I Googled the quote).

Where was Hardwick, anyway? And the other towns. Maybe I could find them on a map. It was better than sitting around doing nothing. Waiting. Worrying. Obsessing.

I remembered I had a big old road atlas (is there any other kind) that belonged to my dad. I'm not sentimental. I'd kept it for practical reasons. The GPS goes out, I'll still know where I'm going. I found it on the shelf in the coat closet. I set it on the kitchen table and opened it up to Massachusetts. I got out the letters and made note of the towns she had mentioned, the ones where she performed the rites.

Hartford was easy. Big city down in Connecticut. The other four were harder to find, but I finally did. Two in Connecticut, two in Massachusetts. I noticed something interesting.

They were all about the same distance from where I lived. I drew arcs from one town to the next, joining them in a circle. Sure enough, Springfield was right in the center. But why five? Five dots on a map. Five points . . .

A star.

In the kitchen, I rummaged in the junk drawer for a ruler. I connected the towns with lines. Almost a perfect star. And not just any random star.

An inverted pentagram. With my home right in the middle. This wannabe witch had created a giant magic circle with me, her sacrificial lamb, her burnt offering, in the middle.

In that moment of realization I felt a spark. Tiny flames flickered in the center of my chest. The flames spread quickly as if my insides were stuffed with straw being rapidly consumed by fire. I unbuttoned my shirt and looked down at my chest. Under my skin and rib cage, tiny flames licked glowing orange embers. I was burning up from the inside out.

My love is a flame, she'd said.

In one of her letters, Lily had written, *When you least expect it, my face will pop into that hot little head of yours.* She was right. It did.

I saw her—tight jeans, small breasts, overbite. Not exactly a homely face, just . . . Nothing special. Plain. A five at best. Images flashed and flickered in my mind, and I remembered what I, what we—a few fraternity brothers and I—did to her that stormy night in the field under the overcast umbrella of darkness. Her startled, panicked face looking up at me from the grass. Her fear. Her pleading for us to stop, to let her go. To shut her up I turned her over and pressed her face into the wet grass and mud while my buddies pulled down her jeans. She squirmed at first, then gave in and lay still. I went first. Then I helped hold her down while the others took turns. Not everybody. Some of the guys left. None of us did anything to stop it. She said, "No!" over and over, but none of us listened. Her muddy face, full of pain and confusion and terror at first, eventually drained of all emotion. Traumatic shock. By the time we'd finished, she was a floppy, half-naked rag doll with matted hair. I remember now. What we did to her, what I did. Was that even me?

Yeah, it was. I remember. I see her. Lily.

The flames spread into my lungs, my stomach, my kidneys, my arms and legs, my groin. I heard myself scream.

Blackened and blistered inside and out, I heard her melancholy voice. "You'll never learn. Not until it's too late." She was right. I see that now. I *feel* that now. It was a hard lesson, burned into every particle of my being.

I wanted a second chance. I wanted to be forgiven, but that wasn't going to happen.

The vengeful fire consumed my flesh and bones in a matter of minutes. They would find gritty ashes with pulverized bone and teeth on scorched tiles of the kitchen floor. They could not explain how my body had burned without an apparent cause and without an accelerant. They knew only one thing for certain: My body was gone from this world. Ashes to ashes.

But my spirit—my soul—lives on in infinite darkness and pain and hopelessness. I sense I can move through some type of pitch-black space—whether it is physical or not I do not know—but I never arrive anywhere; I never touch anything. Or anyone. I am truly and completely alone, lost, eternally burning in unilluminating flames, feeling nothing but blistering, excruciating torment.

Lily said, "Misery loves company," but not even the Devil is with me here, wherever "here" may be. I continually pray, pleading with God to pull me out of this dark fiery pit or at the very least put me out of my misery, but God is silent. God has forsaken me. So has Lily, but her bitter words echo within me incessantly.

Do you feel it? The burning? Are you burning for me, David?

Yes, Lily, I am. I feel every soul-searing flicker of your dark love. I can't bear your pitch-black fire for even one more moment, but I must endure it. I will burn for you.

For eternity.

AN OCCURRENCE AT OWL CREEK BRIDGE

by Ambrose Bierce

CHAPTER I

A man stood upon a railroad bridge in northern Alabama, looking down into the swift water twenty feet below. The man's hands were behind his back, the wrists bound with a cord. A rope closely encircled his neck. It was attached to a stout cross-timber above his head and the slack fell to the level of his knees. Some loose boards laid upon the ties supporting the rails of the railway supplied a footing for him and his executioners—two private soldiers of the Federal army, directed by a sergeant who in civil life may have been a deputy sheriff. At a short remove upon the same temporary platform was an officer in the uniform of his rank, armed. He was a captain. A sentinel at each end of the bridge stood with his rifle in the position known as "support," that is to say, vertical in front of the left shoulder, the hammer resting on the forearm thrown straight across the chest—a formal and unnatural position, enforcing an erect carriage of the body. It did not appear to be the duty of these two men to know what was occurring at the center of the bridge; they merely blockaded the two ends of the foot planking that traversed it.

Beyond one of the sentinels nobody was in sight; the railroad ran straight away into a forest for a hundred yards, then, curving, was lost to view. Doubtless there was an outpost farther along. The other bank of the stream was open ground—a gentle slope topped with a stockade of vertical tree trunks, loopholed for rifles, with a single embrasure through which protruded the muzzle of a brass cannon commanding the bridge. Midway up the slope between the bridge and fort were the spectators—a single company of infantry in line, at "parade rest," the butts of their rifles on the ground, the barrels inclining slightly backward against the right shoulder, the hands crossed upon the stock. A lieutenant stood at the right of the line, the point of his sword upon the ground, his left hand resting upon his right. Excepting the group of four at the center of the bridge, not a man moved. The company faced the bridge, staring stonily, motionless. The sentinels, facing the banks of the stream, might have been statues to adorn the bridge. The captain stood with folded arms, silent, observing the work of his subordinates, but making no sign. Death is a dignitary who when he comes announced is to be received with formal manifestations of respect, even by those most familiar with him. In the code of military etiquette silence and fixity are forms of deference.

The man who was engaged in being hanged was apparently about thirty-five years of age. He was a civilian, if one might judge from his habit, which was that of a planter. His features were good—a straight nose, firm mouth, broad forehead, from which his long, dark hair was combed straight back, falling behind his ears to the collar of his well fitting frock coat. He wore a moustache and pointed beard, but no whiskers; his eyes were large and dark gray, and had a kindly expression which one would hardly have expected in one whose neck was in the hemp. Evidently this was no vulgar assassin. The liberal military code makes provision for hanging many kinds of persons, and gentlemen are not excluded.

The preparations being complete, the two private soldiers stepped aside and each drew away the plank upon which he had been standing. The sergeant turned to the captain, saluted and placed himself immediately behind that officer, who in turn moved apart one pace. These movements left the condemned man and the sergeant standing on the two ends of the same plank, which spanned three of the cross-ties of the bridge. The end upon which the civilian stood almost, but not quite, reached a fourth. This plank had been held in place by the weight of the captain; it was now held by that of the sergeant. At a signal from the former the latter would step aside, the plank would tilt and the condemned man go down between two ties. The arrangement commended itself to his judgement as simple and effective. His face had not been covered nor his eyes bandaged. He looked a moment at his "unsteadfast footing," then let his gaze wander to the swirling water of the stream racing madly beneath his feet. A piece of dancing driftwood caught his attention and his eyes followed it down the current. How slowly it appeared to move! What a sluggish stream!

He closed his eyes in order to fix his last thoughts upon his wife and children. The water, touched to gold by the early sun, the brooding mists under the banks at some distance down the stream, the fort, the soldiers, the piece of drift—all had distracted him. And now he became conscious of a new disturbance. Striking through the thought of his dear ones was sound which he could neither ignore nor understand, a sharp, distinct, metallic percussion like the stroke of a blacksmith's hammer upon the anvil; it had the same ringing quality. He wondered what it was, and whether immeasurably distant or near by—it seemed both. Its recurrence was regular, but as slow as the tolling of a death knell. He awaited each new stroke with impatience and—he knew not why—apprehension. The intervals of silence grew progressively longer; the delays became maddening. With their greater infrequency the sounds increased in strength and sharpness. They hurt his ear like the thrust of a knife; he feared he would shriek. What he heard was the ticking of his watch.

He unclosed his eyes and saw again the water below him. "If I could free my hands," he thought, "I might throw off the noose and spring into the stream. By diving I could evade the bullets and, swimming vigorously, reach the bank, take to the woods and get away home. My home, thank God, is as yet outside their lines; my wife and little ones are still beyond the invader's farthest advance."

As these thoughts, which have here to be set down in words, were flashed into the doomed man's brain rather than evolved from it the captain nodded to the sergeant. The sergeant stepped aside.

CHAPTER II

Peyton Fahrquhar was a well to do planter, of an old and highly respected Alabama family. Being a slave owner and like other slave owners a politician, he was naturally an original secessionist and ardently devoted to the Southern cause. Circumstances of an imperious nature, which it is unnecessary to relate here, had prevented him from taking service with that gallant army which had fought the disastrous campaigns ending with the fall of Corinth, and he chafed under the inglorious restraint, longing for the release of his energies, the larger life of the soldier, the opportunity for distinction. That opportunity, he felt, would come, as it comes to all in wartime. Meanwhile he did what he could. No service was too humble for him to perform in the aid of the South, no adventure too perilous for him to undertake if consistent with the character of a civilian who was at heart a soldier, and who in good faith and without too much qualification assented to at least a part of the frankly villainous dictum that all is fair in love and war.

One evening while Fahrquhar and his wife were sitting on a rustic bench near the entrance to his grounds, a gray-clad soldier rode up to the gate and asked for a drink of water. Mrs. Fahrquhar was only too happy to serve him with her own white hands. While she was fetching the water her husband approached the dusty horseman and inquired eagerly for news from the front.

"The Yanks are repairing the railroads," said the man, "and are getting ready for another advance. They have reached the Owl Creek bridge, put it in order and built a stockade on the north bank. The commandant has issued an order, which is posted everywhere, declaring that any civilian caught interfering with the railroad, its bridges, tunnels, or trains will be summarily hanged. I saw the order."

"How far is it to the Owl Creek bridge?" Fahrquhar asked.

"About thirty miles."

"Is there no force on this side of the creek?"

"Only a picket post half a mile out, on the railroad, and a single sentinel at this end of the bridge."

"Suppose a man—a civilian and student of hanging—should elude the picket post and perhaps get the better of the sentinel," said Fahrquhar, smiling, "what could he accomplish?"

The soldier reflected. "I was there a month ago," he replied. "I observed that the flood of last winter had lodged a great quantity of driftwood against the wooden pier at this end of the bridge. It is now dry and would burn like tinder."

The lady had now brought the water, which the soldier drank. He thanked her ceremoniously, bowed to her husband and rode away. An hour later, after nightfall, he repassed the plantation, going northward in the direction from which he had come. He was a Federal scout.

CHAPTER III

As Peyton Farquhar fell straight downward through the bridge he lost consciousness and was as one already dead. From this state he was awakened—ages later, it seemed to him—by the pain of a sharp pressure upon his throat, followed by a sense of suffocation. Keen, poignant agonies seemed to shoot from his neck downward through every fiber of his body and limbs. These pains appeared to flash along well defined lines of ramification and to beat with an inconceivably rapid periodicity. They seemed like streams of pulsating fire heating him to an intolerable temperature. As to his head, he was conscious of nothing but a feeling of fullness—of congestion. These sensations were unaccompanied by thought. The intellectual part of his nature was already effaced; he had power only to feel, and feeling was torment. He was conscious of motion. Encompassed in a luminous cloud, of which he was now merely the fiery heart, without material substance, he swung through unthinkable arcs of oscillation, like a vast pendulum. Then all at once, with terrible suddenness, the light about him shot upward with the noise of a loud splash; a frightful roaring was in his ears, and all was cold and dark. The power of thought was restored; he knew that the rope had broken and he had fallen into the stream. There was no additional strangulation; the noose about his neck was already suffocating him and kept the water from his lungs. To die of hanging at the bottom of a river!—the idea seemed to him ludicrous. He opened his eyes in the darkness and saw above him a gleam of light, but how distant, how inaccessible! He was still sinking, for the light became fainter and fainter until it was a mere glimmer. Then it began to grow and brighten, and he knew that he was rising toward the surface—knew it with reluctance, for he was now very comfortable. "To be hanged and drowned," he thought, "that is not so bad; but I do not wish to be shot. No; I will not be shot; that is not fair."

He was not conscious of an effort, but a sharp pain in his wrist apprised him that he was trying to free his hands. He gave the struggle his attention, as an idler might observe the feat of a juggler, without interest in the outcome. What splendid effort!—what magnificent, what superhuman strength! Ah, that was a fine endeavor! Bravo! The cord fell away; his arms parted and floated upward, the hands dimly seen on each side in the growing light. He watched them with a new interest as first one and then the other pounced upon the noose at his neck. They tore it away and thrust it fiercely aside, its undulations resembling those of a water snake. "Put it back, put it back!" He thought he shouted these words to his hands, for the undoing of the noose had been succeeded by the direst pang that he had yet experienced. His neck ached horribly; his brain was on fire, his heart, which had been fluttering faintly, gave a great leap, trying to force itself out at his mouth. His whole body was racked and wrenched with an insupportable anguish! But his disobedient hands gave no heed to the command. They beat the water vigorously with quick, downward strokes, forcing him to the surface. He felt his head emerge; his eyes were blinded by the sunlight; his chest expanded convulsively, and with a supreme and crowning agony his lungs engulfed a great draught of air, which instantly he expelled in a shriek!

He was now in full possession of his physical senses. They were, indeed, preternaturally keen and alert. Something in the awful disturbance of his organic system had so exalted and refined them that they made record of things never before perceived. He felt the ripples upon his face and heard their separate sounds as they struck. He looked at the forest on the bank of the stream, saw the individual trees, the leaves and the veining of each leaf—he saw the very insects upon them: the locusts, the brilliant bodied flies, the gray spiders stretching their webs from twig to twig. He noted the prismatic colors in all the dewdrops upon a million blades of grass. The humming of the gnats that danced above the eddies of the stream, the beating of the dragon flies' wings, the strokes of the water spiders' legs, like oars which had lifted their boat—all these made audible music. A fish slid along beneath his eyes and he heard the rush of its body parting the water.

He had come to the surface facing down the stream; in a moment the visible world seemed to wheel slowly round, himself the pivotal point, and he saw the bridge, the fort, the soldiers upon the bridge, the captain, the sergeant, the two privates, his executioners. They were in silhouette against the blue sky. They shouted and gesticulated, pointing at him. The captain had drawn his pistol, but did not fire; the others were unarmed. Their movements were grotesque and horrible, their forms gigantic.

Suddenly he heard a sharp report and something struck the water smartly within a few inches of his head, spattering his face with spray. He heard a second report, and saw one of the sentinels with his rifle at his shoulder, a light cloud of blue smoke rising from the muzzle. The man in the water saw the eye of the man on the bridge gazing into his own through the sights of the rifle. He observed that it was a gray eye and remembered having read that gray eyes were keenest, and that all famous marksmen had them. Nevertheless, this one had missed.

A counter-swirl had caught Farquhar and turned him half round; he was again looking at the forest on the bank opposite the fort. The sound of a clear, high voice in a monotonous singsong now rang out behind him and came across the water with a distinctness that pierced and subdued all other sounds, even the beating of the ripples in his ears. Although no soldier, he had frequented camps enough to know the dread significance of that deliberate, drawling, aspirated chant; the lieutenant on shore was taking a part in the morning's work. How coldly and pitilessly—with what an even, calm intonation, presaging, and enforcing tranquility in the men—with what accurately measured interval fell those cruel words:

"Company! . . . Attention! . . . Shoulder arms! . . . Ready! . . . Aim! . . . Fire!"

Farquhar dived—dived as deeply as he could. The water roared in his ears like the voice of Niagara, yet he heard the dull thunder of the volley and, rising again toward the surface, met shining bits of metal, singularly flattened, oscillating slowly downward. Some of them touched him on the face and hands, then fell away, continuing their descent. One lodged between his collar and neck; it was uncomfortably warm and he snatched it out.

As he rose to the surface, gasping for breath, he saw that he had been a long time under water; he was perceptibly farther downstream—nearer to safety. The soldiers had almost finished reloading; the metal ramrods flashed all at once in the sunshine as they were drawn from the barrels, turned in the air, and thrust into their sockets. The two sentinels fired again, independently and ineffectually.

The hunted man saw all this over his shoulder; he was now swimming vigorously with the current. His brain was as energetic as his arms and legs; he thought with the rapidity of lightning:

"The officer," he reasoned, "will not make that martinet's error a second time. It is as easy to dodge a volley as a single shot. He has probably already given the command to fire at will. God help me, I cannot dodge them all!"

An appalling splash within two yards of him was followed by a loud, rushing sound, DIMINUENDO, which seemed to travel back through the air to the fort and died in an explosion which stirred the very river to its deeps! A rising sheet of water curved over him, fell down upon him, blinded him, strangled him! The cannon had taken an hand in the game. As he shook his head free from the commotion of the smitten water he heard the deflected shot humming through the air ahead, and in an instant it was cracking and smashing the branches in the forest beyond.

"They will not do that again," he thought; "the next time they will use a charge of grape. I must keep my eye upon the gun; the smoke will apprise me—the report arrives too late; it lags behind the missile. That is a good gun."

Suddenly he felt himself whirled round and round—spinning like a top. The water, the banks, the forests, the now distant bridge, fort and men, all were commingled and blurred. Objects were represented by their colors only; circular horizontal streaks of color—that was all he saw. He had been caught in a vortex and was being whirled on with a velocity of advance and gyration that made him giddy and sick. In few moments he was flung upon the gravel at the foot of the left bank of the stream—the southern bank—and behind a projecting point which concealed him from his enemies. The sudden arrest of his motion, the abrasion of one of his hands on the gravel, restored him, and he wept with delight. He dug his fingers into the sand, threw it over himself in handfuls and audibly blessed it. It looked like diamonds, rubies, emeralds; he could think of nothing beautiful which it did not resemble. The trees upon the bank were giant garden plants; he noted a definite order in their arrangement, inhaled the fragrance of their blooms. A strange roseate light shone through the spaces among their trunks and the wind made in their branches the music of AEolian harps. He had not wish to perfect his escape—he was content to remain in that enchanting spot until retaken.

A whiz and a rattle of grapeshot among the branches high above his head roused him from his dream. The baffled cannoneer had fired him a random farewell. He sprang to his feet, rushed up the sloping bank, and plunged into the forest.

All that day he traveled, laying his course by the rounding sun. The forest seemed interminable; nowhere did he discover a break in it, not even a woodman's road. He had not known that he lived in so wild a region. There was something uncanny in the revelation.

By nightfall he was fatigued, footsore, famished. The thought of his wife and children urged him on. At last he found a road which led him in what he knew to be the right direction. It was as wide and straight as a city street, yet it seemed untraveled. No fields bordered it, no dwelling anywhere. Not so much as the barking of a dog suggested human habitation. The black bodies of the trees formed a straight wall on both sides, terminating on the horizon in a point, like a diagram in a lesson in perspective. Overhead, as he looked up through this rift in the wood, shone great golden stars looking unfamiliar and grouped in strange constellations. He was sure they were arranged in some order which had a secret and malign significance. The wood on either side was full of singular noises, among which—once, twice, and again—he distinctly heard whispers in an unknown tongue.

His neck was in pain and lifting his hand to it found it horribly swollen. He knew that it had a circle of black where the rope had bruised it. His eyes felt congested; he could no longer close them. His tongue was swollen with thirst; he relieved its fever by thrusting it forward from between his teeth into the cold air. How softly the turf had carpeted the untraveled avenue—he could no longer feel the roadway beneath his feet!

Doubtless, despite his suffering, he had fallen asleep while walking, for now he sees another scene—perhaps he has merely recovered from a delirium. He stands at the gate of his own home. All is as he left it, and all bright and beautiful in the morning sunshine. He must have traveled the entire night. As he pushes open the gate and passes up the wide white walk, he sees a flutter of female garments; his wife, looking fresh and cool and sweet, steps down from the veranda to meet him. At the bottom of the steps she stands waiting, with a smile of ineffable joy, an attitude of matchless grace and dignity. Ah, how beautiful she is! He springs forwards with extended arms. As he is about to clasp her he feels a stunning blow upon the back of the neck; a blinding white light blazes all about him with a sound like the shock of a cannon—then all is darkness and silence!

Peyton Farquhar was dead; his body, with a broken neck, swung gently from side to side beneath the timbers of the Owl Creek bridge.

BIOGRAPHIES
(IN ALPHABETICAL ORDER)

AMBROSE BIERCE

Ambrose Gwinnett Bierce was born June 24, 1842, in Meigs County, Ohio, and it is assumed he died somewhere around 1914. He was a soldier and writer of many different genres. He was married and had three children. Bierce was best known as a short story writer and Civil War veteran. Bierce was ranked alongside Edgar Allan Poe and H. P. Lovecraft for his horror writing. In December 1913, Bierce traveled to Mexico, to experience the Mexican Revolution. He disappeared, and was never seen again.

WILL FALCONER

Will Falconer attended film school at Los Angeles Valley College and graduated from the University of Massachusetts, Amherst, with a BA in English and a MEd. He has been a professional musician and a teacher and has also worked in video and motion picture production. Born and raised in Western New York, he now lives with his family in Southern California.

MICHAEL L. HAWLEY

Michael L. Hawley holds a Master's degree in science (invertebrate paleontology) and secondary science education at State University of New York, College of Buffalo, and a Bachelor's degree in geology and geophysics at Michigan State University. He has lectured at the Jack the Ripper Conference (2017) in Liverpool, England, on American quack doctor, Francis Tumblety. He was on an episode of the series Legend Hunter (2019, Icon Films) on the Travel Channel, hosted by Pat Spain; the subject of the episode the identity of Jack the Ripper in light of these damning discoveries. Hawley's book, *Jack the Ripper Suspect Dr. Francis Tumblety* (2018), incorporates these discoveries and paints the most up-to-date and complete picture of this American narcissist. Mike also lectured at the Jack the Ripper Conference (2016) in Baltimore, Maryland, on his previous book, *The Ripper's Haunts* (Sunbury Press, 2016). Hawley has published over a dozen research articles in journals dedicated to the Whitechapel murders/Jack the Ripper mystery and has published online articles for numerous websites. He's been interviewed on nearly a dozen international, national, and local podcasts/radio shows, such as *Beyond Reality Radio* and is a co-host on NBC Radio House of Mystery. Hawley is also the author of The Watchmaker Revelations, a mystery/thriller fiction trilogy: *The Ripper's Hellbroth* (2017), *Jack's Lantern* (2019), and "Curse of the Bayou Beast" (exp. 2020). Additionally, he authored *Searching for Truth with a Broken Flashlight* (2010). Mike is a commander and naval aviator in the US Navy (retired) and is currently enjoying a career in secondary science education. He resides with his wife and six children in Greater Buffalo, New York.

CATHERINE JORDAN

Catherine Jordan is a published novelist who edits and writes in multiple genres. She has been featured in a variety of publications and anthologies including the upcoming *New Scary Stories to Tell in the Dark*, edited by Jonathan Maberry. Catherine is the review coordinator for Horrortree.com. She was privileged to serve as a judge for the Bram Stoker Award and the ITW Young Adult Award. Ms. Jordan also facilitates writing courses and critique groups. Catherine lives in Pennsylvania with her husband and five children.

Her books are available at sunburypress.com, Amazon.com, and through her website, catherinejordan.com. Like Catherine on Facebook.com/CatherineJordanBooks. Follow on Twitter @CatherineBooks.

JOHN KACHUBA

John B. Kachuba is the award-winning author of eleven books and numerous articles, short stories, and poems. *Shapeshifters: A History* is his most recent nonfiction book; *Dark Entry* his most recent novel. Kachuba also has written five books about ghosts and the paranormal. John is a frequent speaker at conferences, universities, and libraries and on podcasts, radio, and TV, speaking about metaphysical and paranormal topics. He teaches creative writing at Ohio University and the Gotham Writers Workshop, and is a member of the Historical Novel Society, the Horror Writer's Association, and the American Library Association's Authors for Libraries. For more information, see www.johnkachuba.com.

BRIAN KOSCIENSKI AND CHRIS PISANO

Brian Koscienski & Chris Pisano skulk the realms of South-central Pennsylvania. Brian developed a love of writing from countless hours of reading comic books and losing himself in the worlds and adventures found within their colorful pages. In tenth grade, Chris was discouraged by his English teacher from reading H. P. Lovecraft; and being a naturally disobedient youth, he has been a fan ever since. They have logged many hours writing novels, stories, articles, comic books, reviews, and the occasional ridiculous haiku. To find out where they may be skulking next, visit them at www.novelguys.com. If you happen to see them at one of the various conventions they participate in, feel free to stop by their table and say, "Hi." They're harmless!

H. P. LOVECRAFT

Howard Phillips Lovecraft was born in Providence, Rhode Island, on August 20, 1890, and died on March 15, 1937. After being essentially unknown during his lifetime, he achieved posthumous fame through his works of horror fiction. He died of cancer, penniless, at the age of forty-six, however, he is now considered one of the most significant twentieth-century authors of horror and weird fiction.

THOMAS M. MALAFARINA

Thomas M. Malafarina (www.ThomasMMalafarina.com) of Berks County, Pennsylvania, is an author of horror fiction. He was born on July 23, 1955, in the blue-collar coal region town of Ashland, Pennsylvania.

To date he has published seven horror novels: *What Waits Beneath*, *Burner, From The Dark, Circle Of Blood, Dead Kill Book 1: The Ridge of Death, Dead Kill Book 2: The Ridge Of Change,* and *Dead Kill Book 3: The Ridge Of War*. He has published six collections of horror short stories; *Thirteen Deadly Endings, Ghost Shadows, Undead Living,* and most recently *Malaformed Realities Vol. 1, Vol. 2,* and *Vol. 3*. He has also published a book of often-strange single-panel cartoons called *Yes I Smelled It Too; Cartoons For The Slightly Off Center*. All of his books are published through Hellbender Books, an imprint of Sunbury Press (www.Sunburypress.com).

In addition, many of Thomas' stories have appeared in anthologies and e-magazines. Some have been produced and presented for internet podcasts and radio plays as well. Thomas is best known for the twists and surprises in his stories as well as his descriptive, often gory passages. Thomas is an artist, musician, singer, and songwriter. He lives in Western Berks County, Pennsylvania along with his wife, JoAnne.

TRAVIS LEIBERT

Travis Liebert is a twenty-year-old Kentucky native and student at the University of Louisville. He is a lover of horror, fantasy, science fiction, and poetry. His books are available on Amazon, and you can find him on Instagram at @travisliebert.

EDGAR ALLAN POE

Edgar Allan Poe was born in Boston on January 19, 1809, and died October 7, 1849. He was best known for his macabre poetry and short stories. He has been credited for being the creator of the detective fiction genre. At the age of two, Edgar Poe was orphaned and was taken in by

John and Frances Allan of Richmond, Virginia. He later added Allan to his name.

On October 3, 1849, Poe was found wandering the streets of Baltimore in a delirious state. He died on Sunday, October 7, 1849, never having been coherent long enough to explain his condition. All medical records and his death certificate were lost.

KYLE ALEXANDER ROMINES

Kyle Alexander Romines is a teller of tales from the hills of Kentucky. He enjoys good reads, thunderstorms, and anything edible. His writing interests include fantasy, science fiction, horror, and western.

Kyle's debut horror novel, *The Keeper of the Crows*, appeared on the Preliminary Ballot of the 2015 Bram Stoker Awards in the category of Superior Achievement in a First Novel. He obtained his MD from the University of Louisville School of Medicine.

You can contact Kyle at thekylealexander@hotmail.com. You can also subscribe to his author newsletter to receive email updates and FREE electronic copies of his "Warden of Fál" prequel short, *The Path of Vengeance*, AND his horror/science fiction novella, *The Chrononaut*, at http://eepurl.com/bsvhYP.

J. B. TONER

J. B. Toner studied Literature at Thomas More College and holds a black belt in Ohana Kilohana Kenpo-Jujitsu. He has held many occupations, from altar boy to homeless person, but has always aspired to be a writer. His first novel, *Whisper Music*, was released by Hellbender Books in 2019. Toner currently lives in Massachusetts and just had his first daughter, Ms. Sonya Magdalena Rose.

Made in the USA
Monee, IL
29 July 2020